PAUL JENNINGS'
SPOOKIEST STORIES

ALSO BY PAUL JENNINGS

Unreal!
Unbelievable!
Quirky Tails
Uncanny!
Unbearable!
Unmentionable!
Undone!
Uncovered!
Unseen!

Tongue-Tied!

Paul Jennings' Funniest Stories
Paul Jennings' Weirdest Stories

The Cabbage Patch series
(illustrated by Craig Smith)

The Gizmo series
(illustrated by Keith McEwan)

The *Singenpoo* series
(illustrated by Keith McEwan)

Wicked! (series) and *Deadly!* (series)
(with Morris Gleitzman)

Duck for Cover
Freeze a Crowd
Spooner or Later
Spit it Out
(with Terry Denton and Ted Greenwood)

Round the Twist
Sucked In . . .
(illustrated by Terry Denton)

For adults

The Reading Bug
. . . and how you can help your child to catch it.

For beginners

The *Rascal* series

Novel

How Hedley Hopkins Did a Dare . . .

More information about Paul and his books can be found at
www.pauljennings.com.au and **www.puffin.com.au**

PAUL JENNINGS'
SPOOKIEST STORIES

VIKING
an imprint of
PENGUIN BOOKS

VIKING

Published by the Penguin Group
Penguin Group (Australia)
250 Camberwell Road, Camberwell, Victoria 3124, Australia
(a division of Pearson Australia Group Pty Ltd)
Penguin Group (USA) Inc.
375 Hudson Street, New York, New York 10014, USA
Penguin Group (Canada)
90 Eglinton Avenue East, Suite 700, Toronto, Canada ON M4P 2Y3
(a division of Pearson Penguin Canada Inc.)
Penguin Books Ltd
80 Strand, London WC2R 0RL England
Penguin Ireland
25 St Stephen's Green, Dublin 2, Ireland
(a division of Penguin Books Ltd)
Penguin Books India Pvt Ltd
11 Community Centre, Panchsheel Park, New Delhi – 110 017, India
Penguin Group (NZ)
67 Apollo Drive, Rosedale, North Shore 0632, New Zealand
(a division of Pearson New Zealand Ltd)
Penguin Books (South Africa) (Pty) Ltd
24 Sturdee Avenue, Rosebank, Johannesburg 2196, South Africa

Penguin Books Ltd, Registered Offices: 80 Strand, London, WC2R 0RL, England

This collection published by Penguin Group (Australia), a division of Pearson Australia
Group Pty Ltd 2007

10 9 8 7 6 5 4 3 2 1

Individual stories copyright © Lockley Lodge Pty Ltd
Without a Shirt, *Skeleton on the Dunny* and *Lighthouse Blues* from *Unreal!*, 1985
Inside Out and *Birdscrap* from *Unbelievable!*, 1987
A Dozen Bloomin' Roses, *Spooks Incorporated*, *The Copy*, *Sneeze 'n Coffin* and *Stuffed* from
Quirky Tails!, 1987
Know All and *A Good Tip for Ghosts* from *Uncanny!*, 1988
Grandad's Gifts from *Unbearable!*, 1990
Batty from *Undone!*, 1993
The Velvet Throne from *Unmentionable!*, 1994
Listen Ear from *Uncovered!*, 1995
Shadows and *Seeshell* from *Unseen!*, 1998
Mobile from *The Paul Jennings Superdiary 2002*, 2001
Naked Ghost, first published by Addison Wesley Longman Australia Pty Limited, 1991

The moral right of the author has been asserted.

Cover and text design by Adam Laszczuk © Penguin Group (Australia)
Cover illustration by Bob Lea
Typeset by Midland Typesetters, Australia
Printed and bound in Australia by McPherson's Printing Group, Maryborough, Victoria

National Library of Australia
Cataloguing-in-Publication data:

Jennings, Paul, 1943–
Paul jennings' spookiest stories.

ISBN 978 0 67002 891 7 (pbk)

I. Title

A823.3

puffin.com.au

Contents

Without a shirt

Mr Bush looked at the class. 'Brian Bell,' he said. 'You can be the first one to give your History talk.'

My heart sank. I felt sick inside. I didn't want to do it; I hated talking in front of the class. 'Yes, Mr Bush without a shirt,' I said. Sue Featherstone (daughter of the mayor) giggled. Slowly I walked out to the front of the class. I felt like death warmed up. My mouth was dry. 'I am going to talk about my great great grandfather,' I said. 'He was a sailor. He brought supplies to Warrnambool in his boat without a shirt.'

Thirty pairs of eyes were looking at me. Sue Featherstone was grinning. 'Why didn't he wear a shirt?' she asked. She knew the answer. She knew all right. She just wanted to hear me say it.

'His name was Byron. People called him Old Ben Byron without a shirt.'

'Why did they call him Old Ben Byron without a shirt?' Sue asked with a smirk. 'That's a funny name.'

'Don't tease him,' said Mr Bush. 'He is doing his best.'

She was a mean girl, that Sue Featherstone. Real mean. She knew I couldn't help saying 'without a shirt'. After

I had finished saying something I always said 'without a shirt'. All my life I had done it – I just couldn't help it. Don't ask me why. I don't know why; I just couldn't stop myself. I had been to dozens of doctors. None of them knew what caused it and none of them could cure me. I hated doing it. Everyone laughed. They thought I was a bit weird.

I looked at Sue Featherstone. 'Don't be mean,' I said. 'Stop stirring. You know I can't stop saying "without a shirt" without a shirt.'

The whole grade cracked up. A lot of the kids tried not to laugh, but they just couldn't stop. They thought it was very funny. I went red in the face. I wished I was dead – and I wished that Sue Featherstone was dead too. She was the worst one in the form. She was always picking on me.

'Okay, Brian,' said Mr Bush. 'You can do your talk on Wednesday. You might be feeling a bit better by then.'

I went and sat down. Mr Bush felt sorry for me. They all felt sorry for me. Everyone except Sue Featherstone, that is. She never thought about anyone except herself.

2

I walked home from school with Shovel. Shovel is my dog. He is called Shovel because he loves to dig holes. Nothing can stop him digging holes. He digs up old rubbish and brings it home and leaves it on the doorstep.

Once the man next door went fishing. He had a sack

of mussels which he used for bait. When he got home he left them in the boot of his car and forgot about them. Two weeks later he found them – or I should say they found him. What a stink. Boy, were they on the nose! He had to bury them in his backyard. The next day Shovel dug them up and brought them home for me. He was always giving me presents like that. I didn't have the heart to punish him; he meant well. I just patted him on the head and said, 'Good boy without a shirt.'

Shovel was a great dog – terrific in fact. I am the first to admit that he didn't look much. He only had one eye, and half of one ear was gone. And he was always scratching. That wasn't his fault. It was the fleas. I just couldn't get rid of the fleas. I bought flea collars but they didn't work. I think that was because Shovel loved to roll in cow manure so much.

Apart from those few little things you wouldn't find a better dog than Shovel. He was always friendly and loved to jump up on you and give you a lick on the face. Mum and I would never give him up. He was all that we had left to remember Dad by. Shovel used to belong to Dad once. But Dad was killed in a car accident. So now there was just me, Shovel and Mum.

When I reached home I locked Shovel in the backyard. It didn't look much like a backyard, more like a battle field with bomb holes all over it. Shovel had dug holes everywhere. It was no good filling them in; he would just dig them out again. I went into the kitchen to get a drink. I could hear Mum talking to someone in the lounge. It was Mrs Featherstone (wife of the mayor). She owned our house. We rented it from her. She was tall and skinny and had blue hair. She always wore a long string of pearls (real) and spoke in a posh voice.

'Mrs Bell,' she was saying, 'I'm afraid you will have to find another place to live. It just won't do. That dog has dug holes everywhere. The backyard looks like the surface of the moon. Either you get rid of the dog or you leave this house.'

'We couldn't do that,' said Mum. 'Brian loves that dog. And it used to belong to his father. No, we couldn't give Shovel away.'

Just then Shovel appeared at the window. He had something in his mouth. 'There is the dreadful creature now,' said Mrs Featherstone. 'And what's that in its mouth?'

I rushed into the room. 'Don't worry,' I said. 'It's only Tibbles without a shirt.'

'Tibbles?' squeaked Mrs Featherstone. 'What is Tibbles?'

'Our cat,' I told her. 'It died six months ago and I buried it at the bottom of the yard without a shirt.'

Mrs Featherstone screamed and then she fainted. I don't know what all the fuss was about. It was only a dead cat. I know that Tibbles didn't look quite the same as when she was alive, but was that any reason to go and faint?

Anyhow, that is why we got kicked out of our house. And that is why we had to go and live in the cemetery.

3

When I say that we had to live in a cemetery I don't mean that we lived in a grave or anything like that. No, we lived in a house in the middle of the cemetery. It was a big, dark old house. Once the caretaker lived there, but he was gone now and no one else wanted to live in it. That's why the rent was cheap. It was all that we could afford. Mum was on the pension and we didn't have much money.

'You'll be happy here,' said the estate agent to Mum. 'It's very quiet. And it's the cheapest house in town.'

'I don't think that anyone can be happy in a graveyard,' said Mum. 'But it will have to do for now. It's all we can afford.'

The agent walked off to his car. He was smiling about something. Then he looked at Shovel. 'I hope your dog doesn't dig holes,' he said. 'It's not a good idea for dogs that live in cemeteries to dig holes.' He thought he had said something really funny. He was still laughing as he drove out of the gate.

'Big joke without a shirt,' I called out after him.

The next day we moved in. I had a little room at the top of the house. I looked out over the graves. I could see the sea close by. The cemetery was next to the beach – we just had to walk over the sand dunes and there we were at Lady Bay Beach.

I went up to my room and started to work on my talk for school. I decided to write the whole thing. That way I could make sure that I didn't have any 'without a shirt's in it. I didn't want to give Sue Featherstone the chance to laugh at me again. The only trouble was that the last time I tried this it didn't work. I still said the 'without a shirts' anyway. Still, it was worth a try – it might work this time. This is what I wrote.

OLD BEN BYRON

Old Ben Byron was my great great grandfather. He was the captain of a sailing ship. He sailed in with all sorts of goods for the town. He was one of the early settlers. This town is only, here because of men like Ben Byron.

One day a man fell overboard. My great great grandfather jumped over to help him. The man was saved. But Old Ben Byron was swept away. He drowned. His body was never found.

I know this might seem a bit short for a talk at school. It is. But something happened that stopped me writing any more.

Shovel had been gone for some time; I was starting to worry about him. I hoped he wasn't scratching around near any of the graves. I looked out the window and saw him coming. I ran downstairs and let him in.

He ran straight up to my room and dropped something on the floor. It was a bone.

4

I picked up the bone and looked at it. It was very small and pointed – just one little white bone. I could tell it was old. I knew I had seen a bone like that somewhere before, but I just couldn't think where. A funny feeling started to come over me. I felt lonely and lost, all alone. I felt as if I was dead and under the sea, rolling over and over.

My hand started to shake and I dropped the bone. I stared down at the bone on the floor. I was in bare feet and the bone had fallen right next to my little toe. Then I knew what sort of bone it was – it was a bone from someone's toe. It was a human toe bone.

'Oh no,' I said to Shovel. 'What have you done? Where have you been digging? You bad dog. You have dug up a grave. Now we are in trouble. Big trouble. If anyone finds out we will be thrown out of this house. We will have nowhere to live without a shirt.'

I put on my shoes and ran outside. The strange feeling left me as soon as I closed the bedroom door. I only felt sad when I was near the bone. Outside it was cold and windy. I could hear the high seas crashing on the other side of the sand dunes. 'Show me where you got it,' I yelled at Shovel. 'Show me which grave it was without a shirt.' Shovel didn't seem to listen; he ran off over the sand dunes to the beach and left me on my own. I looked at all the graves. There were thousands and thousands of them. It was a very old cemetery and most of the graves were overgrown.

I started walking from one grave to the other trying to find signs of digging. I searched all afternoon. But I found nothing. I couldn't find the place where Shovel had dug up the bone.

In the end I walked sadly back to the house. I didn't know what to do with the bone. If anyone found it, there would be a terrible fuss. We would be forced to leave the cemetery and would have nowhere to live.

When I reached the house Shovel was waiting for me. He was wagging his tail. He looked pleased with himself. He was covered in sand, and in his mouth he had another tiny bone. 'The beach,' I shouted. 'You found it at the beach without a shirt.' I snatched the bone from Shovel. As soon as I touched the bone the same sad feeling came over me. I felt lost and alone. I wanted something but I didn't know what it was.

It was another toe bone. I carried it up to my room and put it next to the other one. The feeling of sadness grew less. 'That's strange without a shirt,' I said to Shovel. I picked up the second bone and put it outside the door. The feeling came back. It was very strong. I opened the door and put the two bones together again. I didn't feel quite so sad. 'These bones are not happy unless they are together,' I said. 'They want to be together without a shirt.'

5

I decided to have a serious talk to Shovel. I took his head between my hands. 'Listen,' I said. 'You have to show me where you found these bones. I will have to fill in the hole. You can't go digging up dead bodies all over the place. You just can't without a shirt.' Shovel looked at me with that big brown eye. I had the feeling that Shovel knew more about this than I did. He ran over to the door and started scratching at it. 'Okay,' I told him. 'I'll come with you. But first I will hide these bones without a shirt.' I put the two toe bones in a drawer with my socks. They still felt sad. So did I. As soon as I closed the drawer the feeling went.

We headed off to the beach. It was blowing a gale. The sand blew into my eyes and ears. I didn't know what to expect – maybe a big hole that Shovel had dug, with a skeleton in the bottom. Maybe a body washed up on the beach.

We climbed over the sand dunes and down to the shore. There was no one else on the beach. It was too cold. 'Well,' I said to Shovel, 'show me where you got the bones without a shirt.' He ran off into the sand dunes to a small hole. It was only as deep as my hand. There was no grave, just this small hole. I dug around with my hand but there were no other bones. 'That's good,' I told Shovel. 'There is no grave, and there is no body. Just two toe bones. Tomorrow I will bury them and that will be the end of it without a shirt.'

Shovel didn't listen. He ran off to the other end of the beach. It was a long way but I decided to follow him. When I reached him he was digging another hole. He found two more toe bones. I picked them up and straightaway the sad, sad feeling came over me. 'They want to be with the others,' I said. 'See if you can find any more without a shirt.'

Shovel ran from one end of the beach to the other. He dug about thirty holes. In each hole he found one or two bones; some of them were quite big. I found an old plastic bag on the beach and put the bones in it. By the time it was dark the bag was full of unhappy bones. I felt like crying and I didn't know why. Even Shovel was sad. His tail was drooping. There wasn't one wag left in it.

I started to walk up the sand dunes towards home. Shovel didn't want to go; he started digging one more hole. It was a deep hole. He disappeared right inside it. At last he came out with something in his mouth, but it wasn't a bone. It was a shoe – a very old shoe. It wasn't anything like the shoes that you buy in the shops. It had a gold buckle on the top. I couldn't see it properly in the dark. I wanted to take it home and have a good look at it.

'Come on, Shovel,' I said. 'Let's go home. Mum will be wondering where we are without a shirt.' I picked up the bag and we walked slowly back to the house.

6

I put the two toe bones in the bag with the rest of them. Then I put the bag in my cupboard and shut the door. I felt much happier when the bones were locked away. They were unhappy and they made me unhappy. I knew what the trouble was: they wanted to be with all the other bones. I guessed that they were all buried in different places along the beach.

I looked at the shoe; it was all twisted and old. It had been buried in the sand dunes for a long time. I wondered whose it was. Then I noticed something – two initials were carved into the bottom. I could just read them. They were 'B.B.'

'Ben Byron,' I shouted. 'The bones belong to my great great grandfather without a shirt.'

I suddenly thought of something – Ben Byron's shoe had reminded me. Tomorrow was Wednesday; I had to give my history talk at school. I groaned. I knew that I wouldn't be able to sleep worrying about it. And the more I worried the more nervous I would get. The more nervous I got the worse I would feel. The last time I gave a talk at school I got one out of ten. One out of ten. You couldn't get much lower than that.

Then I had an idea – I would take along the shoe. I would tell everyone I had found Ben Byron's shoe. That would make it interesting. I might even get three out of ten for my talk if I had the shoe. I put the shoe in my sock drawer and took the bag of bones out of the cupboard. I wanted to have a closer look at them.

I tipped the bones out into a pile on the floor. There were three long bones and a lot of small ones. The sad, lonely feeling came over me once more. I sat down on the bed and looked at the pile of sad bones. Then something happened that gave me a shock. The hair stood up on the back of my neck. I couldn't believe what I was seeing – the bones were moving. They were slowly moving around the floor. The bones were creeping around each other like a pile of snakes.

The bones sorted themselves out. They all fitted together. They formed themselves into a foot and a leg. All the bones were in the right order. I had the skeleton of Ben Byron's leg.

The leg didn't move. It just lay there on the floor. I sat on the bed looking at it for a long time. I can tell you I was scared – very scared. But I couldn't just leave the leg there; Mum might come in and see it. Anyway, it was creepy having the skeleton of someone's leg lying on your bedroom floor. In the end I jumped up and swept all of the bones back into the bag and threw it into the corner of the room. Then I climbed into bed and put my head under the blanket. I tried to pretend that the bones weren't there.

7

The next day I had to give my talk at school. It went worse than I thought. It was terrible. I stood in front of the class for ages without saying anything; I was so scared that my knees were knocking. The words just wouldn't come out. 'What's up,' said Sue Featherstone. 'Haven't you got any shirts today?' A big laugh went up.

I managed to read the whole thing through to the end. I tried not to say anything else. I could feel it building up inside me – it was like a bomb waiting to go off. I kept my mouth closed tight but the words were trying to get out. My cheeks blew out and my face went red. 'Look at him,' laughed Sue Featherstone. 'He's trying not to say it.'

It was no good. The words exploded out. 'Without a shirt.'

I was embarrassed. I didn't know what to do. I grabbed the shoe. 'This is Ben Byron's shoe,' I said. 'It was washed ashore without a shirt.'

'It is not,' said Sue Featherstone. 'It's an old shoe that you found at the tip.'

Everything was going wrong. I would probably get nought out of ten for this talk. Then something happened that changed everything. A feeling of sadness swept over me. Everyone in the room felt it – they all felt sad. Then someone screamed. It was the leg – it was standing there at the door. It hopped across the room. My hands were shaking so much that I dropped the shoe. The leg hopped across the platform and into the shoe. It wanted the shoe.

Sue Featherstone looked at the skeleton leg and

started shouting out, 'Get rid of it. Get rid of the horrible thing.'

The leg started hopping towards her. It hopped right up onto her desk. She screamed and screamed. Then she ran for the door. Everyone else had the same idea – they all ran for the door at the same time. There was a lot of yelling and pushing. They were all trying to get out of the door at once. They were scared out of their wits.

The leg bones chased the whole class across the playground and down the street. I have never heard so much yelling and screaming in all my life.

I was left alone in the classroom with Mr Bush. He just sat there shaking his head. After a while he said, 'I don't know how you did it, Brian. But it was a good trick. I give you ten out of ten for that talk. Ten out of ten.'

'Thanks, Mr Bush without a shirt,' I said.

8

When I got home from school the leg was waiting for me. It was just standing there in the corner of my room; it didn't move at all. But it was so sad and it made me sad. I felt as if I were a skeleton myself. I felt as if my bones were being washed away by the waves, as if they were being scattered along a long, sandy beach. I knew that this was what had happened to Ben Byron. His bones had been washed up and scattered along Lady Bay Beach.

I looked at Shovel. 'We have to find the rest of the bones,' I said. 'This leg will never have peace until all the bones are together again. We have to find the rest of the bones and we have to find them now without a shirt.'

I took a spade and a sack and walked towards the beach. Shovel came with me and so did the leg. It hopped slowly behind us making a plopping sound as it came. It still had the shoe on. It was lucky that there was no one on the beach – they wouldn't have believed their eyes if they had seen a boy, a dog and a skeleton leg walking along the beach. I could hardly believe it myself.

I didn't know where to start looking. But the leg did. It hopped across the beach and stood still where it wanted us to dig. We spent all afternoon following the leg around and digging holes. In every hole we found some bones. I went as fast as I could; I wanted to get rid of the sad feeling. Tears were running down my face because I was so unhappy. Every time I found some more bones I put them in the sack. The bones were glad to be together; I could tell that. But they were still sad. They would not be happy until I found the last one.

After a long time I found the last bone. It was the skull. It was in a hole with an old shirt – a very old shirt. I had never seen one like it before. I put the skull and the shirt in the sack. Then I held open the top. The leg hopped into the sack with the other bones.

9

The feeling of sadness went as soon as the leg joined the other bones. The bones were happy, I was happy and so was Shovel.

'Now,' I said to Shovel. 'We have a job to do. We have to bury all the bones in the same hole without a shirt.'

I carried the bag of happy bones to a lonely place in the sand dunes, and Shovel and I started to dig a hole. We worked at it for hours and hours. At last it was deep enough. I took the bag of bones and tipped them into the grave. They fell into a pile at the bottom; then they started to move. They slithered around at the bottom of the hole. I should have felt scared but I didn't. I knew what was happening. The bones were joining up into a skeleton. After a while it was finished. The skeleton was whole. It lay still at the bottom of the grave looking up at me. It didn't look as if it was at peace. There was something else – it wanted something else. I looked in the sack. The shirt was still there.

I threw the shirt into the hole. 'Don't worry,' I said, 'I won't bury you without a shirt.'

The bones started to move for the last time. The skeleton moved onto its side with the shirt under its head. It was in a sleeping position. It was very happy.

GGHHHHH! NO!

Music seemed to come up out of the grave – silent music. I could hear it inside my head.

We filled in the grave and smoothed down the sand. I decided to say a few words; after all, it was a sort of a funeral. I looked out to sea. I could feel tears in my eyes. This is what I said: 'Here lie the bones of Ben Byron. At peace at last. Beside this beautiful bay.'

Shovel looked up at me. He seemed to be smiling.

'Hey,' I yelled, 'I didn't mention a shirt. I didn't say it.'

And I never did again.

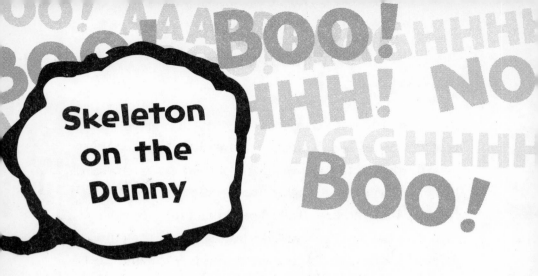

Skeleton on the Dunny

All right. So you want to hear the story of the ghost on the dunny. Everybody wants to know about it, so I am going to tell it for the last time. I will put it on this tape recording.

Someone else can write it down. My spelling is not too good. And anyway, I haven't got the time for a lot of writing.

I am giving you a warning: this is not a polite story. If your feelings get hurt it will be your own fault. I call a spade a spade. And I call a dunny a dunny.

If you live in Australia, you know what a dunny is. It is a toilet. A lavatory. Other names for it are throne, loo, WC, jerry, and thunderbox. I have heard it called other things, but I won't mention them here. I am not a rude person; I just get to the point.

Some dunnies are outside. An outside dunny is usually at the bottom of the garden, a long way from the house. If it rains you get wet. If it is night time you have to get a torch and go there in the dark. When you have finished you have to pull a chain to make it flush. There are no buttons or anything flash like that.

2

Anyway, I must get back to the story. It all started when I was fourteen years old. My parents died in a car accident and I went to live with my Aunty Flo. She lived in the country, at Timboon.

I was pretty broken up – miserable, in fact. One minute I was as happy as Larry, with a mother and a father, living in a big house in the city. The next minute I was with Aunty Flo in the bush.

Aunty Flo was nice. It wasn't her fault; I just felt low because of what happened. That sort of thing is very hard to take.

My new home was very old. It was a big wooden house with a verandah all around it. It had a tin roof; you could hear the rain falling on it at night.

Inside the house it was very dark. Gloomy. Every doorway had wooden beads hanging down on strings. There were old photos all over the walls, pictures of glum men staring down at you. In the hall was a tall clock, a grandfather clock. It ticked loudly. The house was so quiet that you could hear the ticking in every room. For some reason you always felt like whispering. It was like a library.

School had finished; it was the holidays. There wasn't much to do. I didn't know anybody in the town, so most days I went hunting rabbits. Or snakes.

Aunty Flo was very good to me. She liked me. 'Bob,' she would say, 'you need fattening up.' She made jam tarts and little cakes with icing, and set them up on the table with neat napkins. She was a very good cook, and very old. She didn't know much about boys. She let me go wherever I liked. She only had one rule. 'Be home for tea on time.'

I liked Aunty Flo. But I didn't like her outside dunny.

3

One day Aunty Flo took me aside. She was waving a bit of paper and she looked very serious. 'It is very sad about your parents, Bob,' she said. 'I am worried about your future. If I die there will be no one to look after you.'

She was a good-hearted old girl. A tear ran down her face. 'Anyway,' she said, 'I have made some plans. This is my will. It tells what will happen to my things if I die. I have left everything to you. If I die you will get the lot: the house and my money.'

I didn't know what to say. I looked at my shoes. She kept talking with tears in her eyes. 'The only thing you won't get is a painting I used to have. You can't have it because it is gone. Stolen. It was in my family for a long time. It was worth a lot of money – very valuable. It was a painting of this house. I wanted you to have it.'

I pretended not to notice her tears. 'Who stole it, Aunty?' I asked.

'I don't know,' she answered. 'I went away to England for two years. A man called Old Ned lived in the house and looked after everything for me. But when I came back he was dead, and the painting was gone.'

I asked Aunty Flo how Ned died. 'I don't know,' she said. 'I found him on the toilet at the bottom of the garden. He had been there for a year. There wasn't much left of him – just a skeleton, sitting on the toilet.'

4

Well, that was nice. That was very nice. Now I had to go and sit in an outside dunny where someone had died.

I didn't like going to that loo at the best of times. You had to walk down a long path, overgrown with weeds. Trees stuck out and scratched your face. When you got inside it was very dark – there was no light globe. There were cobwebs. And no toilet paper, just a nail on the wall with newspaper hanging on it. It wasn't even worth reading the paper. It was only *The Age*. Very boring.

Those cobwebs had me worried too. There could be spiders – redback spiders. Redbacks are poisonous. I knew that song about redbacks on the toilet seat. It wasn't funny when your pants were down, I can tell you that.

Redbacks, cobwebs, stories about skeletons and no one around. I didn't like sitting there with the door closed, especially at night. At night it was creepy.

One day I was in the dunny paying a visit. There

wasn't much to do. I started counting holes in the wall. A lot of knots had fallen out of the wood. They were little round holes that let in a bit of light. I had counted up to hole number twenty when I saw something that made my hair stand on end.

An eye was looking at me. Staring at me through the hole.

It was not just any old eye. I could see right through it. I could see the trees on the other side of it. It was not a human eye.

I pulled up my pants fast. No one has ever pulled up their pants that fast before. I ran up that path and back to the house like greased lightning.

I told Aunty Flo about it, but she didn't believe me. 'Rubbish,' she said. 'There is nothing down there. It's just your imagination.'

5

You can imagine how I felt. Very nice. Very nice indeed, I don't think. I was not going down there again. No way. Just think how you would feel at the bottom of the garden, in the dark, sitting on a dunny where someone had died. Not only died, but turned into a skeleton. Then there were cobwebs, redback spiders and eyes. Eyes looking at you through holes in the walls.

I made up my mind. I wasn't going down there again. Ever.

I didn't go there for a week. Then I started feeling

GGHHHHH! NO!

a bit crook. I felt terrible. 'You're not looking well,' said Aunty Flo. 'You've not been regular, have you, dear? You'd better have some medicine.'

The medicine fixed me up all right. I got the runs. I spent most of the day sitting down there. But what I was really worried about were the nights.

Sure enough it happened: I had to go to the loo in the night. I took a torch and went slowly down the dark path. The trees were rustling and something seemed to be moaning. I told myself that it was a bird. I hoped that it was a bird. It had to be a bird.

At last I reached the dunny. I went inside, shut the door, and locked it. I had no sooner sat down than something terrible happened. The torch slowly went out. The batteries were flat – as flat as a tack.

I think I should tell you what happens to me when I get scared. My teeth start to chatter. They go clickety click. Very loudly.

So there I was, sitting in the dark with my teeth chattering. I tried to stop it, but I couldn't. You must have been able to hear the noise a mile away.

I started to think about creepy things. Eyes. Bats. Vampires. Murderers. I was scared to death. I wanted to get out of there. My teeth were chattering louder and louder.

Then the moon came out. Moonbeams shone through the space on top of the door. I felt a bit better – but only for a second. I looked up and my heart froze.

A face was looking at me. An old man's face. He had a beard and was wearing an old hat. He just stood there staring at me over the top of the door. And even worse, much worse, the moon was shining right through him. I could see through him. He didn't block out the moonlight at all.

6

I couldn't get out. The old man was on the other side of the door. I was trapped. I started screaming out, 'Aunty Flo, Aunty Flo. Help! Help! A ghost!'

The face looked startled. Then it disappeared. I didn't waste any time – I kicked open the door and ran out. But fell flat on my face. I had forgotten to pull my pants up.

When I finally pulled up my pants the ghost had gone. I tore up the path screaming out for Aunty Flo.

Aunty Flo didn't believe me. She knew I was scared. But she didn't believe there was a ghost. 'Nonsense,' she said, 'there are no such things as ghosts. I have been going down there for sixty years, and I have never seen one.'

I tried to make the best of it. I smiled. A weak smile, but a smile. Aunty Flo did not smile back. She was staring at me. Her mouth was hanging open. 'Bob,' she shouted. 'Bob. One of your teeth is missing. One of your beautiful teeth.'

I put my hand up to my mouth. Sure enough a front

tooth was gone – broken clean off. I knew what had happened. My teeth had chattered so hard that the tooth had broken. That ghost had done it, now. I was starting to get mad with that ghost.

Aunty Flo was upset. 'You must have done it when you fell over,' she said. She put some new batteries in the torch. Then we went to look for the tooth. There was no sign of it. There was no sign of the ghost either.

The next day we went to the dentist. He had bad news for me. 'You'll have to have a plate,' he said. 'The tooth is gone and the piece that is left is split.'

'What's a plate?' I asked.

'Like false teeth,' he told me. 'But you will only have one tooth that is false. And you will have to look after it. They cost a lot of money, so don't lose it. Clean it every night and put it in water when you go to bed. And don't break it by biting string or hard objects.'

The plate cost two hundred dollars. Can you believe that? Two hundred dollars. Aunty Flo had to pay up. It was a lot of money. She made sure I looked after that tooth. I had to clean it every night and every morning. She checked on it when I was in bed. Every night she looked at the tooth in the glass of water. If the plate wasn't clean she made me do it again. She wouldn't let me take it out of my mouth in the day. She thought I might lose it.

That ghost had caused a lot of trouble. I had lost a tooth. And Aunty Flo had wasted two hundred dollars.

7

I didn't see the ghost again for about a month. I stayed away from the bottom of the garden at night time. I only went in the day. He didn't come in the day any more. All the same, I made my visits very short.

I did a lot of thinking about that ghost. Who was he? Why was he hanging around a dunny? I asked Aunty Flo about Old Ned who had died down there. 'Aunty Flo,' I said one day, 'you know that old man who lived here when you lost your painting? What did he look like?'

She looked sadly at the place where her lost painting used to hang. And then she said, 'He always wore an old hat. And he had a beard. A long grey beard.'

I knew at once that the ghost was Old Ned. I felt a bit sorry for him. Fancy having your skeleton sitting on a dunny for a year.

All the same, I wished he would go away. I didn't want to see him again. But of course I did.

One night I just had to go. You know what I mean. I got my torch out and I went out into the dark, down to the bottom of the garden. I was scared – really scared. My teeth began to chatter again. They were really clacking. I was worried about my plate. With all the clacking it might break. I took it out and held it in my hand. There I sat, tooth in hand, and my real teeth chattering enough to wake the dead. I left the dunny door open. If Old Ned showed up I wanted to get away quickly. I didn't want to be trapped.

I did the job that I went for. Then I pulled up my pants. I reached up and pulled the chain. As I did so I could feel someone watching me. My hands started to shake. Badly. The plate slipped out of my hand and into the dunny. In a flash it was gone, flushed down the loo.

When I turned around I saw Old Ned standing there. I could see right through him – through his hat, through his beard, through his hands and his face.

He looked very sad – very sad indeed. I didn't run. I didn't feel quite so frightened now that I could see him properly. He was trying to say something. His mouth was moving, but no sound came out. And he was pointing. Pointing to the roof of the dunny. I looked up, but there was nothing to see. Just a rusty old roof.

'What do you want?' I heard myself say. 'Why are you hanging around this loo all the time?'

He couldn't hear me. He just kept pointing at the roof of the dunny. Then he started to fade. He just started to fade away in front of my eyes. Then he was gone – vanished.

I walked slowly up the path. I wasn't scared any more; not of the ghost. He looked harmless. But I was scared of something else. I was scared of what Aunty Flo was going to say when she found that my plate had gone.

8

The next morning I jumped out of bed early. I wrote a note for Aunty Flo. It said:

27

Aunty Flo
Gone for a ride on my bike.
I will be back for tea.

Bob.

I set out to look for my tooth. I wanted to find it before Aunty Flo knew that it was gone.

I knew where the sewerage farm was. It was twenty miles away to the north. My tooth had gone north.

It was a long way. The road was very dusty and hot. The paddocks were brown. All the cows were sitting under trees in the shade. There was no shade for me, but I kept riding.

By lunchtime I could tell that I was getting close to the sewerage farm. I could smell it. It was a bad smell – a terrible smell. As I rode closer the smell got worse.

At last I reached the farm. It had a high wire fence around it. Inside were a lot of brown ponds. In the middle of all the ponds was a hut. Inside the hut I could see a man. He was writing at a desk.

That man had the worst job in the world. He was sitting down working in the middle of a terrible stink – a shocking stink. But he didn't seem to mind. I held my nose with one hand and knocked on the open door.

'Come in,' he said. 'What can I do for you?'

He was a little bald man with glasses. He looked friendly. He didn't seem to care that I was holding my nose. 'Excuse me,' I said. 'Have you seen a plate? Has a plate come through the sewer?' It was hard to talk with my hand holding my nose. It sounded as if I had a cold.

'A plate?' he said. 'No. A plate could not fit through the pipes. It would be too big.'

'Not that sort of plate,' I told him. 'Not a dinner plate. A mouth plate. A plate with a tooth on it. A false tooth.'

'Ah,' he said, and smiled. 'Why didn't you say. False teeth. Yes, we have false teeth.'

He went over to the wall. There were a lot of baskets there. They all had labels. One said 'pens and pencils'. Another said 'watches'. He brought over a basket and dumped it in front of me. It was full of false teeth.

They were all dirty. They were brown. The man gave me a pair of tongs. I started to sort through them slowly. I felt a bit sick. I felt like throwing up. At last I found a plate with only one tooth on it. My precious plate! It looked yucky. It was brown and slimy. And it stank. I thought of where it had been. And where I found it.

I didn't know if I could ever put it in my mouth again. I wrapped it up in my handkerchief and rode slowly home.

When I reached home I went up to the bathroom. I scrubbed the plate. I scrubbed it and scrubbed it. It got a lot cleaner but it was still the wrong colour. The tooth was not white enough. Next I boiled it in water, but it was still a bit grey. That was as clean as I could get it.

I put it on the table and looked at it. I looked at it for

a long time. Then I picked it up and closed my eyes. I shoved it in my mouth very quickly.

9

Old Ned had a lot to answer for. He had caused a lot of trouble. But all the same I felt sorry for him. It couldn't be fun hanging around a toilet. I wondered why he was there, and why he looked so sad. I decided that I would go and see him to have a talk. I wasn't scared of him any more.

I waited until Aunty Flo had gone to bed. Then I took out my torch and set out for the dunny. It was very windy and wild. Clouds were blowing across the moon. The trees were all shaking. Leaves blew into my face. It seemed a long way to the bottom of the garden.

When I reached the dunny it was empty. There was no sign of Old Ned. It was cold out in the wind, so I went inside and sat down.

I waited for a long time. The wind started to get stronger. It blew the door shut with a bang. The moon went behind a cloud. It was very dark.

The dunny started to shake. The wind was screaming and howling. Then the walls started to lean over. The wind was blowing the dunny over with me in it. There was a loud crash and the whole thing collapsed. It fell right over on its side. Everything went black.

When I woke up the wind had stopped. My head hurt. But I was all right. No broken bones. Someone was bending over me. It was Old Ned.

He was just the same as before. I could see right through him. But he was smiling. He looked happy. He was pointing at the roof of the dunny. It was all smashed up. I went over and had a look.

Under a piece of tin was a picture frame. It was Aunty Flo's missing painting, the stolen painting.

I picked up the painting and put it under my arm. Aunty Flo would be glad to get it back. Very glad.

I started to say thanks to Ned. But something was happening. He started to float up into the air. He was going straight up. He looked happy. Happy to be leaving the earth.

He floated up towards the moon. He grew smaller and smaller. At last I couldn't see him any more. He was gone. I knew he wouldn't be coming back.

10

Aunty Flo was very pleased to get her painting back. She was so happy that she cried. She hung it on the wall in its old spot. She kept looking at it all the time.

I didn't tell her about Old Ned. She wouldn't believe it anyway. But I think I know what happened.

Old Ned stole the painting. He hid it in the dunny roof. When he died he was in Limbo. He was not in this world because he was dead. He could not go to the next world because he had done something bad.

So he had to hang around the outside loo, hoping

that Aunty Flo would find her painting. Now that she had got it back he was free to go. When he floated off into the air he was going to a happier place. Wherever that is.

Aunty Flo put in a new toilet. An inside one. It was all shiny and clean. A push-button job. No cobwebs, spiders or ghosts.

Well, that is just about the end of the story. Except for one thing.

One day I was looking at Aunty Flo's lost painting. It was a painting of her house in the old days, when it had just been built. It had no trees around it. Out the back you could see the outside dunny with the door open.

I looked very closely at that dunny in the picture. Someone was in it! Sitting down. I went and got a magnifying glass and looked again.

It was Old Ned, with his hat and his long beard. He looked happy. He had a smile on his face, and one eye closed.

He was winking at me.

Lighthouse Blues

Someone was playing music in the middle of the night. It sounded like a saxophone, or maybe a clarinet. I could only hear it when the wind dropped. But there was no mistake about it.

I shivered even though I was snug in bed. I wasn't cold. I was scared. Stan and I were the only people on the island, and he was in bed in the next room. I could hear him snoring. So who was playing the music?

It was cold outside and a storm was brewing. I could hear the sea pounding against the cliffs. I got out of bed and looked out of the window. All I could see were the black clouds racing across the moon, and the light from the lighthouse stabbing into the night. The music seemed to be coming from the lighthouse.

I thought about waking Stan up, but I decided not to. He was the lighthouse keeper. He was a nice old boy but I didn't want him to think I was scared. I was hoping to get a job as a lighthouse keeper myself one day. This was my first night on the island and I wanted to make a good impression.

I climbed back into bed and tried to get to sleep.

I tried not to listen to the music. It was soft and far away, but it crept into my brain. It was like a soft voice calling to me. It was saying something; it was speaking without words. I knew I had heard the tune before, but I couldn't think what it was. It was a slow and haunting tune. Then it came to me. I remembered. It was called 'Stranger On The Shore'.

Somehow I knew that the music was meant for me. I was the stranger. I had just arrived on the island. The supply boat had dropped me on the shore that very day. But who was playing the music? And why did it make me feel so sad?

I listened more carefully. It was a clarinet. It was definitely a clarinet. And man, I will tell you this: whoever was blowing it knew how to play. It was the saddest and most beautiful music I have ever heard.

Then the music changed. There was something different about it. Finally I realised what it was – another instrument had joined in. It was a saxophone. They were both playing 'Stranger On The Shore'. It was so sad that I felt like crying, but I didn't know why.

After a long time I fell asleep with the music still sounding in my ears.

2

The next morning at breakfast I asked Stan if he had heard anything. 'No, Anton,' he said. 'I didn't hear anything. I never do. But I know there is something there. Visitors to the island always hear it. Most people can't stand it. They get scared and leave. You are the third helper that I have had here this year. The other two left because of the music. They said it kept them awake at night. But the real reason was because they were scared – scared out of their wits.'

He looked straight at me when he said this. He was wondering if I was going to run off too. He glared at me with his one eye. He had a patch over the other one. He looked like a fierce pirate, but he was really a friendly bloke. He loved that island more than anything in the world.

'Well, who could be playing the music?' I asked him. 'And why can't you hear it?'

He looked at me for a long time. He looked straight into my eyes, as if he was trying to see what I was thinking. Then he said, 'The last boy went up to the lighthouse one Friday night. The music always plays on Friday night. He took a torch and went off to see who was playing. He was gone for two hours. When he came back he wouldn't say anything about it. He just said that he was leaving. He wouldn't speak to me. He wouldn't answer any questions at all. He just sat and looked at the wall. A week later the supply boat came and he left.'

'He must have seen something terrible,' I said. 'Don't you have any idea who could be playing?'

'Put on your coat, boy,' Stan said, 'and come with me. I'll show you something.'

A strong wind was blowing. It was coming from the south west. Stan took me along a track which ran along the top of the rocky cliffs. There were no trees; the wind was too strong for trees to grow on the island. At last we came to a small fence in the shape of a square. Inside were two graves. The headstones faced out to sea. It was a lonely, windswept spot, high on the cliff.

We opened a small gate and went inside the cemetery. I looked at the headstones. The first one was engraved like this:

CAPTAIN RICKARD

1895–1950

LIGHTHOUSE KEEPER FROM

1915–1950

R.I.P.

The second gravestone was not much different, but it had another name on it. It said:

ALAN RICKARD

1915–1960

LIGHTHOUSE KEEPER FROM

1950–1960

R.I.P.

Stan pointed to the grave of Captain Rickard. 'He was my grandfather,' he said. 'And Alan Rickard was my father.'

Both gravestones had a small drawing in the corner.

The one of Captain Rickard had a clarinet. Alan Rickard's grave had a saxophone.

'All the lighthouse keepers have been musical,' said Stan. 'The Captain played the clarinet. And my father played the saxophone. I play the violin. Do you play anything, boy?'

'Yes,' I replied. 'I play the flute.'

3

Stan and I walked slowly back to the house. The wind was blowing strongly. It flattened the grass and made my hair whip into my eyes. Stan had to shout so that I could hear.

'I can't play the violin any more,' he told me. 'My fingers won't work properly. I have arthritis. The violin is in the music room at the top of the lighthouse. My grandfather and father used to play up there when they were alive. It was something to do when they were on duty. I don't go in there any more; I can't bear to look at my violin.'

Stan's eye was wet. Perhaps the wind was doing it. Or was he crying?

We walked back to the house without speaking. I didn't know what to think. Did the two graves have anything to do with that sad music? The dead captain had played the clarinet. And his son had played the saxophone. But they were dead, and dead men play no tunes. Or that's what I thought.

One day I decided that I would go up to the top of the lighthouse. I might find some clues. But I was not going to go in the night time. Nor was I going to go on a Friday.

The next day was Thursday. I told Stan I was going for a walk to look around the island, but I went to the lighthouse. I had been there before. Stan had taken me up on the first day. I had been in and seen the huge light that went around and around at night. But I had not been in the music room, and I had not been up there on my own.

I pushed open the door at the bottom and went in. It was gloomy inside. There were small windows in the wall and they let in a little bit of light. The stairs went around and around. Stan had told me that there were twenty turns altogether. I went slowly up the stairs. It was as quiet as a grave. About half way up I looked over the side of the stairs. It was a long way down; I felt giddy. I sat down on a step and listened. Nothing. Not a sound. I was sure that I was alone.

At last I reached the top. There were two doors. One led into the light; the other was the door of the music room. I tried the handle. It was stiff, but it opened, and I stepped inside. The room looked like a cabin in a ship. It had bunks against one wall and maps all over another. There was a desk with a globe of the world on it. Instead of a window there was a small, round porthole. Pointing out of the porthole was a telescope. There was a music stand and a small table. On the table was a clarinet, a saxophone and a violin.

I went and looked at the musical instruments. They were covered in dust; they had not been played for a long time. The violin had a spider's web inside it. I picked up the clarinet and blew it. A terrible noise came out of it – it sounded like a bullfrog choking.

These instruments could not have been playing on Friday night.

They had not been played for years. I had not got any closer to solving the mystery, but I knew that the music had been coming from that room. I could feel it in my bones.

I decided to leave. There was something creepy about the room. I felt as if someone was watching me.

4

Over the next few months I was kept very busy on the island. I had to measure the rainfall and record the weather. I had to man the radio and listen for ships that were in trouble. And every night at five o'clock I had to climb the stairs of the lighthouse and start up the light. I didn't go into the music room, and I didn't say any more to Stan about the music.

But every Friday at about midnight the music would start. It was always sad, haunting music. I could never sleep while it was playing. It seemed to be calling me. The names of the tunes always seemed to have a special meaning – a meaning just meant for me.

It was upsetting. I wasn't scared any more, but I couldn't sleep on Friday nights. I just lay there waiting for the music to start. And then I lay awake waiting for it to stop. I couldn't stop thinking about it. I wondered who was playing and why.

In the end I decided to go and see. I made my plans carefully. I decided not to tell Stan. I put fresh batteries in the torch and found an old baseball bat. The baseball bat was in case there was any trouble. The next Friday I waited until Stan was in bed asleep; then I stepped out of the house and into the dark night.

It was cold and windy. The moon was hidden behind black clouds. Spray was blowing up from the sea and the waves were crashing and sucking beneath the cliffs. In the distance I could hear music. It was coming from the lighthouse. I walked slowly, fighting against the wind. At last I reached the lighthouse door.

It was dark inside. There was no light in the stairwell. But music was floating down from above. I had heard the tune before. It was 'Stay Away From Me Baby'. I knew it was meant for me. But who was up there? And why didn't they like strangers on the island? I was scared – I didn't want to go up. But I forced myself. My knees were knocking together as I climbed the dark stairs.

I went around and around. I was glad that I had my torch – it was creepy in there. The music echoed.

It seemed to be laughing at me. 'You won't get rid of me,' I said aloud. 'You won't scare me off like the others.' I tried to sound tough, but I didn't feel tough. I wanted to turn round and run back to the house. I forced my legs to take me all the way to the top.

There was light coming under the music-room door. The music was very loud. It was definitely coming from the music room. Suddenly the tune changed. Now they were playing 'The Green Door'. I thought of some of the words. They were: 'What's behind the green door?' The door of the music room was green, and I wanted to know what was behind it. But I was too scared to go in. Whatever was in there knew where I was. Then the door started to open on its own. It just slowly opened.

I couldn't believe what I saw. I started shaking all over. The hair on the back of my neck stood up. I wanted to turn around and run, but I couldn't. My legs wouldn't do what I wanted them to. The clarinet was playing itself. And the saxophone was doing the same thing, They were both floating in mid-air. Someone or something was playing them, but they were invisible.

I was really scared. My knees were knocking together. I decided to get out of there. Then I thought about the other two boys who had left the island. I wasn't going to be scared off like them – no fear! No ghosts were going to chase me away. I took a step forward into the room.

As soon as I entered the room the music stopped. The clarinet and the saxophone floated through the air and landed on the table. Everything was quiet. I went over to the table and picked up the clarinet. It was covered in cobwebs; it looked as if it had not been played in years. I picked it up and blew in it. A cloud of dust came out of the end.

5

Something had been blowing those musical instruments only moments before, and now they were covered in dust. Ghosts. It had to be ghosts. The ghosts of Captain Rickard and Alan Rickard. Stan's father and grandfather. But why were they so unhappy? And why did they want to scare away everyone who came to the island?

I decided to talk to them. I was still scared. I had never met any ghosts before. But it was worth a try. 'Listen, guys,' I said. 'What's the matter? What are you trying to scare me away for? I won't hurt you, or the island. I won't even touch anything in this room. Come out and show yourselves.'

Nothing happened. The room was empty and quiet; I could hear myself breathing. Then I started to feel cold all over. I started to shiver. They were in the room with me but they wouldn't answer. I felt as if cold, cold hands were touching me. Cold hands from the grave. I let out a scream and ran for my life. I tore down the stairs and ran out into the dark night.

As I ran back to the house the music started up again. They were playing 'See You Later Alligator'. I knew they were laughing at me. They thought they had scared me off, but they were wrong. I was scared all right, but I wasn't leaving. No way.

I got back to the house and went into the kitchen. Stan was sitting at the table with his head in his hands. He looked up at me as I came in. I could see that he had been crying; he had been rubbing his one eye and his cheek was wet.

'I've just had a radio message,' he said. 'They are going to pull down the lighthouse.'

'Who is?'

'The people in charge. The government. They have been talking about it for years, but I didn't think they would really do it. They are going to put in a lighthouse that doesn't need a keeper. An automatic one. It will just be a tall tower with a light on the top.'

My mouth fell open. Stan would be out of a job and so would I. We would have to leave the island. 'They just can't do it,' I said. 'They just can't.'

'Yes, they can,' said Stan. 'They are coming next Friday. We are supposed to help them knock down the lighthouse.' He looked very old. He didn't know what to do. He just sat there shaking his head and staring into the fire. After a while he spoke again. 'My father died here. And my grandfather. I wanted to spend my last days here too. Now I will have to go and live on the mainland. They will probably put me in an old folks' home.'

Suddenly I had an idea. 'Wait a minute. Don't give up yet, Stan. We're not the only ones on this island, you know. We can get some help. We can put up a fight to save the lighthouse.'

Stan looked up at me sadly. He didn't know what I was talking about.

6

I thought I knew why the music was playing. The two ghosts lived in the lighthouse. They didn't want it to be knocked down. So they played spooky music every time a stranger came to the island – they tried to scare them off. They didn't care about Stan. He was their grandson and he loved the island. They knew he wouldn't hurt the lighthouse. That's why he never heard the music.

But playing music on Friday nights wouldn't work, not against the wreckers. They would come in the daytime. And it would only take one day to knock down the lighthouse. Then it would be gone forever. It would be too late to do anything then.

I had to talk to the ghosts. I had to tell them that I was friendly, that I didn't want the lighthouse to be knocked down, and that I needed their help to save it.

I ran out of the house and up to the music room. It was as quiet as death. The saxophone and clarinet lay on the table. I didn't waste any time. 'Listen, guys,' I said. 'I know you are here. And I know you can hear me. I want you to show yourselves. I'm your friend;

I want to help you. I don't want the lighthouse to be knocked down. I want to save it. But I need your help.'

Nothing happened, There was dead silence. I felt a bit silly. Maybe I was talking to myself. Maybe there weren't any ghosts. Had I dreamed it all? Was I going mad? Then I looked at the clarinet and saxophone. I knew I had heard them playing. I started to get angry.

'You stupid ghosts,' I shouted. 'Don't you know that this place is going to be knocked down? The wreckers are coming on Friday. We have to stop them. Stan and I need your help. Playing music on Friday nights won't stop them. We have to think of something else.'

Silence. If the ghosts were there they weren't saying anything. 'Okay,' I yelled. 'Have it your own way. Let them knock down the lighthouse. Let them throw poor old Stan out of a job. You won't have any home. You will just be blown around by the wind.'

When I said this I noticed something happen. Some drops of water were slowly dribbling through the air. They looked like raindrops running down a piece of glass. But there was no glass there. There were two lots of them trickling downwards. At first I felt frightened, but then I realised what they were. They were tears – tears running down invisible faces. The ghosts were crying.

7

I knew I had won. The ghosts were on my side; they didn't want the lighthouse to be knocked down. But they still weren't saying anything. Then I realised why. They couldn't talk. Ghosts can't talk.

'Look,' I said, 'this is no good. I can't see you and I can't hear you. I want you to pick up the musical instruments if you are going to help.'

Very slowly the clarinet and the saxophone started to rise in the air. As they did so, the dust and cobwebs fell off. They were sparkling like new. Then they started to play. I recognised the tune straight away. It was 'We Shall Not Be Moved'.

'That's the spirit,' I said. 'Now you will have to come outside. We need you to scare the wreckers off. You will have to come outside to do that. In the daytime. In broad daylight.'

The music stopped. The clarinet and the saxophone started waggling from side to side. The ghosts didn't want to go outside. 'It's no good doing that,' I said. 'You will have to come outside. You will have to scare the wreckers off before they get to the lighthouse. They might blow it up with dynamite from the outside. A bit of music at midnight won't do the trick. Come on. Come with me now, before they get here. You can practise going out in the daytime.'

I walked out of the room and started going down the stairs. Halfway down I looked over my shoulder to see if they were coming. They were. The saxophone and the clarinet were slowly floating down the staircase. They were bobbing up and down as they went. I couldn't see the ghosts. 'Hang on to those musical instruments,' I told them. 'It's the only way I know where you are.'

When we got to the bottom I looked outside. The wind was blowing a little bit. It was not very strong, only a breeze. I stepped outside and turned around. 'Come on, you two,' I said. 'There is nothing out here to hurt you.'

I was wrong about that, but I didn't know it at the time. They started waggling again. They didn't want to come out. I waved my arms at them. 'Don't you want to save the lighthouse?'

The clarinet and the saxophone slowly floated outside. Then something terrible happened – they started to blow off in the wind. The wind was blowing the ghosts away. They were drifting off towards the edge of the cliff. I ran over to the clarinet and tried to grab it. My fingers went right through it; it wasn't solid. When the ghosts touched the musical instruments they changed. They became ghostly. I tried to grab the saxophone, but the same thing happened. There was nothing I could do to help.

They drifted closer and closer to the edge. Then both instruments fell to the ground. They started to slowly move along the ground in little jumps. I knew what was happening. The ghosts were crawling. They were trying to crawl back to the lighthouse by hanging on to the grass. The wind started to blow more strongly. I was worried that they might blow out to sea. 'Come on,' I shouted. 'You can do it. Keep going. Keep going.'

And they did keep going. All I could see was a saxophone and a clarinet making small hops across the ground. It took a long time, but at last they got back to the lighthouse. They went inside. I tried to go after them but the door slammed in my face. I opened the door and was just in time to see the instruments floating quickly up the stairs.

When I got to the music room everything was quiet. The instruments were on the table, covered in cobwebs. And the ghosts were nowhere to be seen. 'Come on, guys,' I said. 'I'm sorry. I didn't know the wind would blow you away. Come back. We will think of something else.'

But there was no answer. They were mad at me. And I didn't blame them. After all, I had nearly got them killed, if you know what I mean.

8

I told Stan about what had happened. He believed me. I didn't think he would; I could hardly believe it myself. 'Yes,' he said. 'I knew something was up there. I thought that it might be Captain Rickard and my dear old dad. But I didn't really know. I have never heard them myself.'

'What are we going to do?' I asked him. 'How are we going to stop the wreckers? The ghosts won't help us now. They are mad at me.'

Stan shook his head sadly. 'I don't see what they could

do anyway,' he said. 'If they can't come outside they won't be much use to us. We'll just have to try and stop the wreckers on our own.'

I went up to the music room every day that week. I begged and I pleaded. But nothing happened; the room was empty and cold. There was no sign of the ghosts. I didn't know whether they could hear me or not.

At last Friday came. A ship arrived at first light. It unloaded five men and a bulldozer. There was also a tall crane with a huge steel ball on the end. I knew what that was for – it was to knock the lighthouse down. The men set up camp down by the beach.

Stan and I watched them from the house. 'I'm going down to see them,' said Stan. 'You wait here. I don't want you losing your temper. Let me handle it. I'll ask them to go away. I'll tell them that we are not going to help.'

'That won't do any good,' I said. 'They won't take any notice. It's no good talking. We will have to sit down in front of the bulldozer or something like that.'

'First I will try talking,' said Stan. 'It's worth a try.'

I watched him walk down to the beach. He was bent over and he walked slowly. His white beard was flapping in the wind. A strong south westerly was blowing. I saw him talking to the men – he was pointing to the lighthouse and shaking his head. One of the men started waving his fists at Stan. I could see that they were shouting at each other. Stan turned around and came back to the house.

'It's no use,' he said as he came in the door. 'They won't listen. They said they have a job to do. They have given us until lunchtime to get all our things out of the lighthouse. Then they are going to knock it down. The only thing I want is my violin,' he said. 'Not that I can play it any more – not with these old hands. Go and get it for me, will you, boy?'

I went up to the music room and picked up the old violin. I decided to leave the clarinet and the saxophone. They belonged to the ghosts. I decided to talk to them once more. 'Listen, ghosts,' I said. 'I'm really sorry that you were blown away in the wind. It's windy today so I know you can't go outside. But you must be able to do something. We need your help. Stan is too old. He can't do much to stop the wreckers. They are going to knock the lighthouse down this afternoon.' I waited a long time. But there was no answer. In the end I turned around and walked away. Stan and I were on our own.

9

After lunch the bulldozer and the crane started up towards the lighthouse. There was a very narrow part where the track went close to the edge of the cliff. The bulldozer and the crane would have to go past there. Stan and I sat down on the track. We held hands and waited. 'I hope they don't run over us,' I said to Stan.

'They won't,' he replied, but he didn't sound too sure.

It didn't take long for the bulldozer to reach us.

Its big steel blade stopped just in front of our faces. The driver got down. 'Get out of the way,' he said, 'or I'll squash you flat.'

'No,' said Stan. 'We're not moving.' His voice was shaking.

I looked up at the driver. He was an ugly-looking brute, and he was big. Very big. He picked Stan up with one hand and threw him out of the way. Stan landed on the ground with a thump. He didn't move. He looked as if he was hurt.

'Leave him alone,' I screamed. 'He is an old man. Leave him alone.'

The driver gave an ugly grin. 'Now it's your turn,' he said. He picked me up the same way. I kicked and struggled but it was no good. He threw me out of the way. Three other men came and held me down. The bulldozer and the crane moved up towards the lighthouse. The crane stopped right in front of the light-house door. The big steel ball started to swing backwards and forwards through the air.

Then I noticed something. The wind had stopped blowing. It was very still. I listened carefully. Yes, I could hear music. The door of the lighthouse opened and out came the clarinet and the saxophone. They were playing 'When The Saints Go Marching In.'

The driver of the crane couldn't believe what he was seeing. His eyes nearly popped out of his head. A saxophone and a clarinet were floating through the air and playing a tune. He jumped off the crane and ran down the track. He was screaming his head off.

The saxophone floated up above the seat of the crane. The crane started moving backwards towards the sea. One of the ghosts had put it into reverse gear. It rumbled slowly towards the cliff. The ghost was still sitting on it. I could see the saxophone – it was still over the driver's seat. Then the crane started to tumble over the cliff. At the last minute the ghost jumped clear. The saxophone came floating back.

The driver of the bulldozer let out a roar. He put the blade up and drove towards the lighthouse. Stan jumped up and pulled one of the levers. The bulldozer turned and headed towards the cliff. Stan and the driver were both struggling over the controls. The bulldozer got closer and closer to the edge. The driver suddenly jumped off. Stan tried to jump off too, but his leg was stuck. The bulldozer tipped over the edge and fell. Down, down, down it went. And Stan went with it. It tumbled over and over. And then it crashed on the rocks beneath.

The ghosts started playing louder and louder. It wasn't a tune, it was a loud roaring noise. It was angry and sad at the same time. Then both instruments fell to the ground. I didn't know where the ghosts were. Then I saw the driver rise up into the air. The ghosts were lifting him up. They suddenly dropped him. He fell onto his head. He let out a scream and started running down the track. The other men followed him. They were scared to death.

I went and looked over the edge of the cliff. The two ghosts picked up their instruments and stood next to me. I couldn't see them. I could just see the saxophone and the clarinet floating in the air. I knew that Stan was dead. No one would have lived through that crash.

The ghosts started playing a sad, sad tune. I knew the first lines. They were: 'We'll meet again. Don't know where, don't know when. But I know we'll meet again some sunny day.'

I looked at the grey sea. The wind was blowing the spray high into the air.

The wind.

'Quick,' I yelled. 'Back to the lighthouse. The wind is getting up.' But I was too late. A sudden gust of wind blew both ghosts over the edge and out to sea. I watched as the clarinet and the saxophone drifted away, getting smaller and smaller. They looked like two tiny leaves blowing along in a storm. In the end I couldn't see them any more; they were gone.

10

Well, that is just about the end of the story. Stan was buried in the tiny cemetery next to the other two graves. The wreckers left and didn't come back. Their union said that the men would not work on the island. They said it was too dangerous.

I was made lighthouse keeper. I have been here for a year now. I love the island; I hope I can always stay here. But it gets very lonely. I often wish that Stan was still alive.

Last night something happened. Something good. It was Friday. I was just closing my eyes when I thought I heard music. It was coming from the lighthouse. I jumped out of bed and ran as fast as I could. I stopped when I reached the music-room door. It was a saxophone and a clarinet. But something was different. I pushed open the door a tiny bit and peeped in. The clarinet and the saxophone were floating in the air as usual. But there was another instrument as well. It was a violin. It looked as if it was playing itself. But I knew that Stan was playing it. There were three ghosts now.

I smiled to myself and closed the door. As I walked back down the stairs I hummed a tune to myself. I knew the song well. It was 'Happy Days Are Here Again'.

GGHHHHH! NO!

'What did you get?' asked my sister Mary, looking at the video cassette in my hand.

'*Chainsaw Murder*,' I answered.

'You ratbag,' she screamed. 'You promised you would get something nice. You know I can't stand those horrible shows. I'm not watching some terrible movie about people getting cut up with chainsaws. And it was my turn. It was my turn to choose. You said you would get a love story if I let you choose.'

'It is a love story,' I told her. 'It's about a bloke who cuts up the girl he loves with a ch—'

'Don't give me that,' she butted in. 'It's another of those bloodthirsty, spooky, scary, horror shows. You know I can't watch them. You know I can't sleep for weeks after I see one of them.' Her voice was getting louder and louder and fake tears started rolling down her face. She was hoping that Mum would hear her and come and tell me off.

'It's no use yelling,' I said. 'Mum and Dad are out. They won't be back until two o'clock in the morning. They've gone out to the movies.'

'I'll get you for this,' she said in a real mean voice. 'You just wait.' She went out of the room and slammed the door behind her. What a sister. Mary was the biggest sook I had ever met. If the slightest scary thing came on the screen she would close her eyes and cover up her ears. She just couldn't take it. Not like me. I wasn't scared of anything. The creepier the show, the better I liked it. I wouldn't even have been scared if I met a real ghost. Things like that just make me laugh.

I put the cassette into the video player and sat down to enjoy the show. It was even better than I expected. It started off looking through a window at a bloke starting up a chainsaw. Suddenly the window was spattered in blood and you couldn't see through it. The whole movie was filled with dead bodies, skeletons coming up out of graves, ghosts with no heads and people getting cut up with chainsaws. It was great. I had never had such a good laugh in all my life.

After about an hour, I started to feel hungry. I went over to the pantry and made myself a peanut butter, Vegemite, banana and pickle sandwich. I wanted to put on a bit of mustard but I couldn't find any. While I was searching around for it I heard Mary come into the room. 'Changed your mind?' I asked without looking up. 'What's the matter? Are you scared up there all on your own in the bedroom?'

Then I heard a terrible sound. Mary had pushed the EJECT button on the video player. As quick as a flash she whipped out the cassette and ran out of the room with it. The little monster had nicked it. The terrible deed was done in a second. She was quicker than the villain in *Graveyard Robber* (a really good video about a freak who stole corpses). I ran up the stairs after her but I was too late. Mary slammed her bedroom door and locked it.

I banged on the door with my fists. 'Give that tape back, you creep. It's just up to the good bit where the maggots come out of the grave.'

'No way,' she said through the locked door. 'I'm not giving it back. I can hear all the screaming and groaning and creepy music from up here and I'm scared. I'll give you the video back if you go and change it for *Love Story*.'

'*Love Story*!' I shouted. 'Never. I'm not watching that mush.'

'I'm scared, Gordon,' she said. 'Please take it back.' How pathetic. She sounded just like the helpless woman in *I Married A Cannibal Chief*, a ripper movie with lots of gory bits about a bloke with a big appetite.

Mary was scared because Mum and Dad were out. That give me an idea.

'Give that tape back,' I said. 'Or I'm going out and leaving you here on your own.' There was no reply. She was being really stubborn so I turned round and walked down the stairs. I was mad at her because I really wanted to see the rest of that movie.

Just as I reached the front door she appeared at the top of the stairs. 'Come back, Gordon. I'll be frightened here all on my own.' I kept going. She had left it too late and it was time for her to be taught a lesson.

2

As I walked down the dark street I laughed to myself. Mary was really wet. She was scared of her own shadow. She would really be packing death alone in the house. I had a good laugh and then I started to wonder why she got so scared. I mean, I wasn't scared of anything. I had even watched *The Eyes Of The Creeping Dead* without one shiver. And yet Mary, my own flesh and blood, was exactly the opposite.

I started to think about all the horror movies I had ever seen. There wasn't one that had spooked me. Why, even if one of them had come true I wouldn't have worried. I was so used to seeing creepy things that a real ghost wouldn't have scared me. I would just tell it to buzz off without a second thought.

I walked past the 'All Night Video Shop' and down a dark lane. The moon was in and it was hard to see where I was going. Mary would have been terrified, but not me. I almost hoped that something creepy would happen. I walked on and on through the night into a new neighbourhood. The houses started to thin out until at last I was on a country track which wound its way amongst the trees.

After a short while I came to something I had not

expected to find out there in the bush. A letterbox. It was old and battered and stood at the edge of the narrow track leading off into the dark trees. I decided to follow the track and see where it went.

The track led to an old tumble-down house. I could see it quite clearly because the moon had come out. Its tin roof was rusty and falling in. Blackberry bushes grew on the verandah and all of the windows were broken. The front door was hanging off its hinges so there was nothing to stop me entering. I made my way into the front room. There in one corner was an old wooden bed. It had no mattress but it was a bed all the same. I was feeling tired so I staggered over to it and lay down. I wasn't scared. Not a bit. I decided that I would stay in this old shack and not go home until just before Mum and Dad got back. That would teach Mary a lesson.

I closed my eyes and lay there pretending I was the hero out of *Dark House Of Death*. I was a ghost hunter. I was invincible. Nothing could hurt me. At least that was how I was feeling at the time. That's why I hardly batted an eyelid when the candle came floating over.

3

Yes, a candle. A lighted candle. It just floated across the room and hovered next to the bed. I did nothing. I simply gazed at it with detachment. It came closer until it was only a few centimetres from my face. I took a deep breath and blew it out. I thought I heard a gasp.

Then the whole thing disappeared.

I turned over on my side and pretended to be asleep (a trick I had seen in a movie called *Blood In The Attic*). After a short while I heard a soft clinking sound coming from the next room. I ignored it. It grew into a rattling and then a clanking but still I took no notice. Then it became so loud it shook the floor and hurt my ears. 'Quiet,' I yelled. 'Can't a boy get a bit of sleep in here.' The terrible din stopped at once.

I knew something else was going to happen and I wasn't wrong. A moment later a green mist floated through the window and formed itself into a dim, ghostly haze that wafted to and fro across the room. 'You shouldn't smoke in here,' I said. 'You might set the place on fire.' The mist twirled itself around into a spiral and left the room through a knothole. This was great. This was good. It was just like what happened in *Spectre Of The Lost Lagoon*.

What happened next was a bit more creepy. I'm not denying that, but I decided I was handling the situation the right way. Whatever or whoever it was wanted me to go screaming off into the night. I decided to keep playing it cool. A huge pair of lips appeared and started to open and shut, showing nasty, yellow teeth. Next, a pair of bloodshot eyes appeared, floating just above the lips. From out of the mouth came an enormous forked tongue, dripping with saliva. The tongue licked its lips and then wormed its way over to me.

'Halitosis,' I managed to say. It obviously didn't know what halitosis was because it remained there, hovering in front of my face like a snake about to strike. 'Bad breath,' I translated. 'You've got bad breath. Just like the giant pig in *Razorback*.' I thought I heard another small sob just before the whole lot vanished. I wondered if I had hurt its feelings.

The next apparition consisted of a human skull with staring, empty eye sockets. 'Old hat,' I said. 'You'll have to do better than that.' Blood started to drip out of one eye. 'Still not good enough,' I told it. 'I saw that one in a movie called *Rotting Skull*.'

The other bones appeared and the whole skeleton began to dance up and down the room, twisting and turning as if to a wild beat. 'Not very cool,' I remarked a little unkindly. 'That went out years ago. Can't you do rap dancing?'

That last remark was too cutting. The spook just couldn't take it.

The skeleton sat down on a rickety chair and chang-ed into a small ghost. It was the figure of a punk rocker. He was completely transparent and dressed in a leather jacket which was covered in studs. He also wore tight jeans and had a safety pin through his nose. He had a closely shaved head with a pink mohawk hairdo.

4

He looked at me and then hung his head in his hands

and shed a few tears. 'It ain't no use,' he wailed. 'I can't even put the frighteners onto a school boy. I'm doomed. I'm a failure.'

'If you will kindly go away and be quiet, I'll leave at one o'clock,' I told him. 'All I want is a bit of peace.'

He shook his head. 'You can't go. I need you for me exam. If I pass you can clear out – if yer still alive that is. But if I fail me exam, you will have to go into suspended animation until the next one.'

'When is that?' I asked.

'Same time next year.'

'No thanks,' I replied. 'I have to get back to look after my little sister. She's at home alone and she gets scared. As a matter of fact I think I'll leave now.' I tried to stand up but I couldn't. It was just as if unseen hands were holding me down.

'See,' he said. 'I aren't lettin' you go anywhere. You stay here wiv me. If I pass me exam you can go. If not – cold storage for you until next year.' The safety pin in his nose waggled around furiously as he spoke.

I could move my mouth but nothing else. 'I have to go,' I told him. 'I can't stay here for a year. I've made a booking for a video called *Jack The Ripper* for tomorrow night.'

'Yer better help me pass then,' he said.

'What do you have to do?'

'The Senior Spook is comin'. I have to scare a victim, namely you. If it's scary enough, he passes me. If it's not, he fails me. But it don't look good. You don't scare easy. You just sit there givin' mouthfuls o' cheek no matter what I do. I must say it looks bad fer bof ov us. If I don't give you a good fright I won't pass me exam and if I don't pass me exam we'll bof have to stay here until the same time next year.'

'I'll fake it,' I yelled. 'I'll pretend I'm scared. Then you'll pass your exam and I can go.'

He shook his head sadly. 'No good. The Senior Spook is very experienced. That's how he got to the top. He can pick up vibes. He'll know if you're not really scared.'

'Let me loose,' I requested. 'I will help you think of something. You could try something out of *Terror At Midnight*.'

'Yer won't nick orf, will ya?' he said looking at me suspiciously.

'I promise.'

The unseen hands released me and I started to pace around the room. I thought of Mary. She would be frightened for sure, but there was no way that this little punk ghost would be able to scare me.

'Have you seen the movie *Night Freak*?' I said. 'That had some good ideas in it.'

'No, I missed that one,' he said. 'Now quick, sit on the bed. Here comes the Boss. Our exam is about to begin.'

***

5

I sat down where I was told and the Senior Spook floated through the wall. He was dressed in a pin-striped suit, white shirt and black tie. He carried a black leather briefcase in his left hand and wore a pair of gold-rimmed glasses. I could see right through him. He took no notice of me at all and not much more of the punk spook. He sat down on a chair, opened his case and took out a biro and a notebook. Then he looked at his watch and said to the punk, 'You have ten minutes. Proceed.'

I could tell that the punk was nervous. He really wanted to pass this exam, and to do that he had to give me a good fright. But I wasn't scared. Not a bit. All those years of watching horror videos made this seem like child's play. I was worried though because I didn't want to be put into cold storage until the same time next year when the punk could have his next exam in spooking. I tried to feel scared but I just couldn't.

The punk produced a tennis ball from nowhere and placed it on the table. Then he sprinkled some pink powder on it and said, 'Inside out, ker-proffle.' The tennis ball started to squirm on the table. A small split appeared and it turned inside out. Very impressive but not very spooky. My pulse didn't increase a jot. I could just see myself frozen for a year waiting for the punk to have his next chance. I groaned inside. My punk friend was going to have to do better than this. He had no imagination at all.

Next he produced a small sausage. He sprinkled some of the pink powder on it and again said, 'Inside out, ker-proffle.' The sausage split along its side as if it was on a hot barbecue. Then it turned inside out with all the meat hanging out and the skin on the inside. The senior spook wrote something in his notebook.

This wasn't good enough. It just wasn't good enough. It was more like conjuring tricks than horror. I wasn't the least bit scared. My heart sank.

The punk then produced a watermelon from no-where. Once again he sprinkled on the pink powder. 'Inside out, ker-proffle,' he said. The watermelon turned inside out with all of the fruit and the pips hanging off it. Once again the big shot wrote something in his notebook.

The punk looked at me. Then, without warning he threw some pink powder all over me and said, 'Inside out, ker—'

'Stop,' screamed the Senior Spook. Then he fainted dead away. He must have hit the floor a fraction before I did. Being a ghost he didn't hurt himself when he went down. I must have hit my head on the table just after I fainted. I didn't wake up for about half an hour.

When I woke up I looked around but the house was deserted. I couldn't find a sign of either of them except for something written in the dust on a mirror. It said, 'I got an A plus.'

I don't know how I managed to find my way back.

I was so scared that my knees knocked. I jumped at every sound.

When I reached home I went to bed because Mary was watching a really creepy movie.

It was called *The Great Muppet Caper*.

BirdScrap

The twins sat on the beach throwing bits of their lunch to the seagulls.

'I don't like telling a lie to Grandma,' said Tracy. 'It wouldn't be fair. She has looked after us since Mum and Dad died. We would be in a children's home if it wasn't for her.'

Gemma sighed. 'We won't be hurting Grandma. We will be doing her a favour. If we find Dad's rubies we can sell them for a lot of money. Then we can fix up Seagull Shack and give Grandma a bit of cash as well.'

'Why don't you wait until we are eighteen? Dad's will says that we will own Seagull Shack then. We can even go and live there if you want to,' replied Tracy.

Gemma started to get cross. 'I've told you a million times. We won't be eighteen for another three years. The last person who hiked in to Seagull Shack said that it was falling to pieces. If we wait that long the place will be blown off the cliff or wrecked by vandals. Then we'll never find the rubies. They are inside that shack. I'm sure Dad hid them inside before he died.'

Tracy threw another crust to the seagulls. 'Well, what

are you going to tell Grandma, then?'

'We tell her that we are staying at Surfside One camping ground for the night. Then we set out for Seagull Shack by hiking along the cliffs. If we leave in the morning we can get there in the afternoon. We spend the night searching the house for the rubies. If we find them, Grandma will have a bit of money in the bank and we can send in some builders by boat to fix up Seagull Shack.'

'Listen,' said Tracy to her sister. 'What makes you think we are going to find the rubies? The place was searched and searched after Dad died and neither of them was found.'

'Yes, but it wasn't searched by us. We know every corner of that shack. And we knew Dad. We know how his mind worked. We can search in places no one else would think of. I think I know where they are anyway. I have an idea. I think Dad hid them in the stuffed seagull. I had a dream about it.'

'Hey, did you see that?' yelled Tracy without warning. 'Where did that crust go?'

'What crust?'

'I threw a crust to the seagulls and it vanished.'

'Rubbish,' said Gemma. 'One of the birds got it. Bread doesn't just vanish.'

Tracy threw another scrap of bread into the air. It started to fall to the ground and then stopped as if caught by an invisible hand. It rose high above their heads, turned and headed off into the distance. All the other gulls flapped after it, squawking and quarrelling as they went.

'Wow,' shrieked Gemma. 'How did you do that?'

'I didn't,' said Tracy slowly. 'Something flew off with it. Something we couldn't see. Something invisible. Perhaps a bird.'

Gemma started to laugh. 'A ghost gull maybe?'

'That's not as funny as you think,' said Tracy. 'It's a sign. Something or Someone wants us to go to Seagull Shack.'

'Maybe you've got it wrong,' replied Gemma. 'Maybe something doesn't want us to go to Seagull Shack.'

The wind suddenly changed to the south west and both girls shivered.

2

Two days later Tracy and Gemma struggled along the deserted and desolate clifftops. They were weighed down with hiking packs and water bottles. Far below them the Southern Ocean swelled and sucked at the rocky cliff. Overhead the blue sky was broken only by a tiny white seagull which circled slowly in the salt air.

'How far to go?' moaned Gemma. 'My feet are killing me. We've been walking for hours.'

'It's not far now,' said Tracy. 'Just around the next headland. We should be able to see the old brown roof any moment . . . Hey, what was that?' She felt her hair and pulled out some sticky, white goo. Then she looked up at the seagull circling above. 'You rotten fink,' she yelled at it. 'Look at this. That seagull has hit me with bird droppings.'

Gemma lay down on the grassy slope and started to laugh. 'Imagine that,' she gasped. 'There are miles and miles of cliff top with no one around and that bird has to drop its dung right on your head.' Her laughter stopped abruptly as something splotted into her eye. 'Aaaaagh, it's hit me in the eye. The stupid bird is bombing us.'

They looked up and saw that there were now four or five birds circling above. One of them swooped down and released its load. Another white splodge hit Tracy's head. The other birds followed one after the other, each dropping its foul load onto one of the girls' hair. They put their hands on top of their heads and started to run. More and more birds gathered, circling, wheeling and diving above the fleeing figures. Bird droppings rained down like weighted snow.

The girls stumbled on. There was no shelter on the exposed, wind-swept cliffs – there was no escape from the guano blizzard which engulfed them.

Tracy stumbled and fell. Tears cut a trail through the white mess on her face. 'Come on,' cried Gemma. 'Keep going – we must find cover.' She dragged her sister to her feet and both girls groped their way through the white storm being released from above by the squealing, swirling gulls.

Finally, exhausted and blinded, the twins collapsed into each other's arms. They huddled together and tried to protect themselves from the pelting muck by holding their packs over their heads. Gemma began to cough. The white excrement filled her ears, eyes and nostrils. She had to fight for every breath.

And then, as quickly as it had begun, the attack ended. The whole flock sped out to sea and disappeared over the horizon.

The girls sat there panting and sobbing. Each was covered in a dripping, white layer of bird dung. Finally Gemma gasped. 'I can't believe this. Look at us. Covered in bird droppings. Did that really happen? Where have they gone?' She looked anxiously out to sea.

'They've probably run out of ammo,' said Tracy. 'We had better get to the shack as quick as we can before they come back.'

3

An hour later the two girls struggled up to the shack. It sat high above the sea, perched dangerously on the edge of a cliff which fell straight to the surging ocean beneath. Its battered tin roof and peeling, wooden walls stood defiantly against the might of the ocean winds.

Both girls felt tears springing to their eyes. 'It reminds me of Dad and all those fishing holidays we had here with him,' said Tracy. They stood there on the old porch for a moment, looking and remembering.

'This won't do,' said Gemma as she unlocked the door and pushed it open. 'Let's get cleaned up and start looking for those two rubies.'

Inside was much as they remembered it. There were only two rooms: a kitchen with an old table and three chairs, and fishing rods and nets littered around; and a bedroom with three mattresses on the floor. The kitchen also contained a sink and an old sideboard with a huge, stuffed seagull standing on it. It had only one leg and a black patch on each wing. It stared out of one of the mist-covered windows at the sky and the waves beyond.

'It almost looks alive,' shivered Tracy. 'Why did Dad shoot it anyway? He didn't believe in killing birds.'

'It was wounded,' answered Gemma. 'So he put it out of its misery. Then he stuffed it and mounted it because it was so big. He said it was the biggest gull he had ever seen.'

'Well,' said Tracy, 'I'm glad you're the one who is going to look inside it for the rubies, because I'm not going to touch it. I don't like it.'

'First,' said Gemma, 'we clean off all this muck. Then we start searching for the rubies.' The two girls cleaned themselves with tank water from the tap in the sink. Then they sat down at the table and looked at the stuffed seagull. Gemma cut a small slit in its belly and carefully pulled out the stuffing. A silence fell over the hut and the cliff top. Not even the waves could be heard.

The air seemed to be filled with silent sobbing.

'The rubies aren't there,' said Gemma at last. She put the stuffing back in the dead bird and placed it on its stand. 'I'm glad that's over,' she went on. 'I didn't like the feel of it. It gave me bad vibes.'

As the lonely darkness settled on the shack, the girls continued their hunt for the rubies. They lit a candle and searched on into the night without success. At last, too tired to go on, Tracy unrolled her sleeping bag and prepared for bed. She walked over to the window to pull across the curtain but froze before reaching it. A piercing scream filled the shack. 'Look,' she shrieked. 'Look.'

Both girls stared in terror at the huge seagull sitting outside on the windowsill. It gazed in at them, blinking every now and then with fiery, red eyes. 'I can see into it,' whispered Gemma. 'I can see its gizzards. It's transparent.'

The lonely bird stared, pleaded with them silently and then crouched on its single leg and flapped off into the moonlight.

Before either girl could speak, a soft pitter-patter began on the tin roof. Soon it grew louder until the shack was filled with a tremendous drumming. 'What a storm,' yelled Gemma.

'It's not a storm,' Tracy shouted back. 'It's the birds. The seagulls have returned. They are bombing the house.' She stared in horror at the ghostly flock that filled the darkness with ghastly white rain.

All through the night the drumming on the roof continued. Towards the dawn it grew softer but never for a moment did it stop. Finally the girls fell asleep, unable to keep their weary eyes open any longer.

4

At 10 a.m. Tracy awoke in the darkness and pressed on the light in her digital watch. 'Wake up,' she yelled. 'It's getting late.'

'It can't be,' replied Gemma. 'It's still dark.'

The shack was as silent as a tomb. Gemma lit a candle and went over to the window. 'Can't see a thing,' she said.

Tracy pulled open the front door and shrieked as a wave of bird droppings gushed into the room. It oozed into the kitchen in a foul stream. 'Quick,' she yelled. 'Help me shut the door or we'll be drowned in the stuff.'

Staggering, grunting and groaning, they managed to shut the door and stop the stinking flow. 'The whole house is buried,' said Gemma. 'And so are we. Buried alive in bird droppings.'

'And no one knows we are here,' added Tracy.

They sat and stared miserably at the flickering candle. All the windows were blacked out by the pile of dung that covered the house.

'There is no way out,' moaned Gemma.

'Unless . . .' murmured Tracy 'they haven't covered the chimney.' She ran over to the fireplace and looked up. 'I can see the sky,' she exclaimed. 'We can get up the chimney.'

It took a lot of scrambling and shoving but at last the two girls sat perched on the top of the stone chimney. They stared in disbelief at the house, which was covered in a mountain of white bird droppings. The chimney was the only evidence that underneath the oozing pile was a building.

'Look,' said Gemma with outstretched hand. 'The transparent gull.' It sat, alone on the bleak cliff, staring, staring at the shaking twins. 'It wants something,' she said quietly.

'And I know what it is,' said Tracy. 'Wait here.' She eased herself back down the chimney and much later emerged carrying the stuffed seagull.

'Look closely at that ghost gull,' panted Tracy. 'It's only got one leg. And it has black patches on its wings. And look how big it is. It's this bird.' She held up the stuffed seagull. 'It's the ghost of this stuffed seagull. It wants its body back. It doesn't like it being stuffed and left in a house. It wants it returned to nature.'

'Okay,' Gemma yelled at the staring gull. 'You can have it. We don't want it. But first we have to get down from here.' The two girls slid, swam, and skidded their way to the bottom of the sticky mess. Then, like smelly, white spirits, the sisters walked to the edge of the cliff with the stuffed bird. The ghost seagull sat watching and waiting.

Tracy pulled the stuffed seagull from the stand and threw it over the cliff into the air that it had once loved and lived in. Its wings opened in the breeze and it circled slowly, like a glider, and after many turns crashed on a rock in the surging swell beneath.

The ghost gull lifted slowly into the air and followed it down until it came to rest on top of the still, stuffed corpse.

'Look,' whispered Tracy in horror. 'The ghost gull is pecking at the stuffed one. It's pecking its head.'

A wave washed across the rock and the stuffed seagull vanished into the foam. The ghost gull flapped into the breeze and then flew above the girls' heads. 'It's bombing us,' shouted Gemma as she put her hands over her head.

Two small shapes plopped onto the ground beside them.

'It's the eyes of the stuffed seagull,' said Tracy in a hoarse voice.

'No it's not,' replied Gemma. 'It's Dad's rubies.'

They sat there, stunned, saying nothing and staring at the red gems that lay at their feet.

Tracy looked up. 'Thank you, ghost gull,' she shouted.

But the bird had gone and her words fell into the empty sea below.

See, this kid was hanging around outside the flower shop and Jenny (the shop assistant) thought he was a trouble maker. She reckoned he might be going to nick something. That's why she called for me. I have a black belt in judo and if I do say so myself I am quite good in a fight.

Not that I'm tough. No, generally I am as quiet as a lamb. I'm not big either. In fact a lot of people think I am about fourteen years old and they are amazed when I tell them I am really seventeen. I got the job at the flower shop because of my strength. They needed someone strong who could lump all the boxes around and lift heavy flower pots for Jenny. At first they didn't want me on account of my size but when they saw what I could do they changed their minds and gave me the job.

Anyway, to get back to the story. This kid (who looked about my age) really was acting strangely. He would peer into the shop looking at the flowers for sale. When anyone looked at him he sloped off down the street. About five minutes later, back he would come.

This happened about twenty times. I should add that I thought I had seen him hanging around before. Perhaps on the train.

'Don't worry,' I said to Jenny. 'I'll fix this weirdo up in no time at all.' I walked out of the door and approached the boy who was acting so strangely. Straightaway he turned around and started to walk off.

'Come back here,' I ordered in my sternest voice. 'I want to talk to you.' He turned around and went red in the face. I could see that he was nervous. His knees were wobbling like jelly and he just stood there with his mouth dangling open.

'What are you hanging around here for?' I asked. I started to feel sorry for him, he looked so nervous, and I had a feeling that maybe he was a bit sweet on Jenny. I have to admit that she is the spunkiest girl in all of Melbourne and he wouldn't have been the first one who fancied her.

He seemed to have trouble talking. It was as if he was being strangled by invisible hands but finally he managed to gasp out the word 'flowers'.

I grabbed his arm firmly and led him in to the shop counter. 'Here,' I said, giving a wink to Jenny. 'This gentleman wants flowers.'

Jenny turned on her fatal smile and said in her sweetest voice, 'What sort of flowers, sir?'

I grinned to myself. She always called the shy ones 'sir'. It made them feel better when they were embarrassed about buying flowers. The poor kid went even redder and looked around wildly. He obviously didn't know a kangaroo paw from a carnation. 'Roses,' he blurted out, pointing to our most expensive line.

I should tell you here what I found out later, at the funeral. This poor boy had twenty-six dollars in his pocket. Twenty of it was the change from his grandmother's pension cheque and six of it was his own. His grandmother needed this money badly to buy her week's groceries. Jenny looked at the roses. 'A good choice,' she said. 'They're beautiful, aren't they? How many would you like?'

Once again he struggled for words. 'How much, er, well, I, you see.' Boy, he was the shyest person I had ever seen. He just couldn't seem to get anything out. Finally the words 'one dozen' managed to escape from his frozen mouth.

Jenny started to wrap up the roses. She always goes to a lot of trouble to make them look good. She wraps the stems up in pretty paper and then she gets a long length of ribbon and ties a bow. Next she runs one of her long slender fingernails along the ends of the ribbon and they curl up like magic. I have tried to do this myself many times but it never works. Probably because I bite my fingernails.

'Are they for your girlfriend?' asked Jenny. She is a bit on the nosy side, is Jenny. The red-faced boy shook his head and looked at his shoes.

'They are for a girl though, aren't they?'

He nodded unhappily.

'Is this the first time you have given flowers to a girl?' she asked gently.

He nodded again and made a gurgling noise in his throat.

'What shall I write on the card?' I could see that Jenny felt sorry for this kid. She was trying to help him all she could. The poor thing couldn't seem to talk at all. 'What about your name?' she suggested. 'You will have to put who they are from.'

'Gerald,' he answered at last. 'My . . . my name's Gerald.'

Jenny smiled. 'And who are they for?' she asked kindly.

He didn't know which leg to stand on. He was really embarrassed. He looked at me as if he wished I wasn't there.

'Go away,' said Jenny. 'You are embarrassing a customer.'

She was the boss so I went up to the back of the shop and started stacking up some heavy concrete pots.

Jenny wrote something on the card and tied it on to the ribbon. I snuck along behind a row of daffodils so that I could hear what happened. I really hoped that things would work out well for this shy boy.

Jenny put the finishing touches to the bunch and passed over the flowers. 'Now,' she went on. 'They are two dollars each. That will be twenty-four dollars.'

Forget about Gerald being red in the face before.

That was nothing compared to what happened next. He went as red as the dozen bloomin' roses he had just bought. This great wave of redness swept down from his ears, down his neck, and for all I know, right down to his toes.

Jenny and I didn't know what was the matter. It was only later I found out that he thought flowers were about two dollars a bunch at the most. He had got Jenny to wrap up the flowers and now he couldn't ask her to take them back. He was too embarrassed. He pulled his grandmother's pension money out of his pocket, looked at it frantically, then thrust it into Jenny's hand. For a minute I thought he was going to say something to me. I tried to look as if I hadn't been listening. He took a few steps towards me, then changing his mind, grabbed his change and fled out of the shop.

'What a strange bloke,' I said. 'I bet we never see him again.'

2

I was wrong. Half an hour later he got into the same carriage as me on the train.

I groaned. Not because of Gerald and his flowers but because Scouse the skinhead was in my carriage. He was a great big hulk of a bloke and he was real mean into the bargain. He liked nothing better than picking on anyone weak and giving them a hard time. He always caught the same train as me but usually I managed to get into another carriage. He looked at Gerald, gave a twisted sneer and then spat on the floor.

Gerald was as red as ever and he stood with his back to the door, holding the flowers behind his back. He was trying to hide them from the other passengers. He didn't want to be seen carrying flowers in the train. Every now and then he looked over at me in an agitated fashion.

The train was one of those silver ones where the two doors slide automatically into the middle when they close. As the train lurched off they shut with a bang. Right on Gerald's roses. He just stood there shivering and twitching and holding onto the stems with his hands behind his back as if nothing had happened. The stems were on the inside of the train and the flowers were on the outside.

Everyone on the train started to grin. I bit my tongue like mad to stop myself from smiling but I have to admit that it really was funny. Gerald just looked at a spot on the roof and stood there with his hands behind his back, pretending that nothing had happened.

A few people started twittering and giggling. The poor kid just didn't know what to do so he just kept on pretending that everything was all right. Gerald looked around desperately. I'm sure that if the door had been open he would have jumped out of the moving train just to escape from the mirth.

The only person in the train who hadn't noticed the

flowers was Scouse. He was too busy scratching his shaved head and taking swigs out of a tinny. Every now and then he would give a loud burp.

The train plunged into a tunnel and everything went black. I stopped biting my tongue and allowed myself a big grin. I just couldn't help it. Anyway, Gerald couldn't see me smiling in the dark. Right at that moment the lights switched on and Gerald looked into my eyes.

He had seen me grinning. His bewildered eyes seemed to say, 'Not you too.' It was at this moment that I realised I had betrayed him. I forced the smile from my face and opened my mouth to speak but he looked away just as the train stopped at an underground station.

The doors slid apart and Gerald stared at what was left of his twenty-four-dollar bunch of flowers. They had gone. He stood there lamely holding twelve broken stems wrapped in pink paper. There was not one petal left. They had all been ripped off in the tunnel. Now he had lost his grandmother's money and his flowers. And even worse, he had made a fool of himself in front of a whole carriage full of people including me.

With a strangled cry he jumped off onto the platform. Scouse jumped after him. 'Look at the little fairy clutching his invisible flowers,' sneered Scouse.

I stepped off the train too and stood aside as it sped past me.

Scouse snatched the rose stems from Gerald's hand gleefully. 'Look at this,' he mocked as he read the card that Jenny had written:

TO SAMANTHA WITH LOVE FROM GERALD.

'I'll bet she likes getting these.' He shoved the prickly stems into Gerald's face.

Gerald grabbed the broken stalks and looked around like a hunted rabbit. He looked straight at me, red with shame. He wanted to escape but Scouse was blocking his way. Without a sound, Gerald jumped off the platform onto the tracks and ran up the tunnel.

'Come back!' I shouted. 'Trains come through the loop every five minutes.'

He made no reply and I heard his clattering feet disappear into the tunnel.

'Let the little fairy go,' said Scouse, showing his yellow teeth in a leer. Then he spat into my face and walked off laughing.

I ran screaming down the platform to find a porter. 'There's a boy in the tunnel!' I yelled. 'Stop the trains.'

The ground began to tremble gently and a rush of cold air came out of the tunnel. There was a low rumble and then a scream.

The train rushed out of the tunnel. As it slowed I noticed a bunch of broken flower stems wedged on one of the buffers.

3

There were not many people at ⟨...⟩ from the priest and the undertak⟨...⟩ and Gerald's grandmother. After ⟨...⟩ lowered into the ground we walk⟨...⟩ gate. I told the old lady about what happened in the flower shop. She already knew the rest from the police. She smiled sadly and explained about her pension money that he had spent. 'Not that I care about that,' she said. 'If only I had Gerald back I would give everything I have.'

I watched with tears in my eyes as the bent old lady slowly walked off. I had told her about that ratbag Scouse but I didn't mention that I had smiled in the train when the roses got caught in the door. I felt too ashamed.

That night I had terrible dreams about roses and thorns. I kept seeing a dark tunnel from which a lonely voice sadly called my name.

It was no better that day at work. I kept dropping things and breaking them. And the palm of my hand was itchy. I kept scratching it but nothing would stop the itch.

I was glad when it was time to knock off. I went out into the potting shed to get my parka. A terrible feeling of sadness suddenly swept over me. It seemed to flow out into my body from the palm of my left hand.

And then it happened. From the palm of my left

d a blood-red rose erupted from my flesh. Slowly it unfolded, budded and bloomed. A magnificent flower nodding gently on the end of a graceful stem. I tried to scream but nothing came out. I shook my head wildly and my rose fell to the ground.

I fell in a chair, dazed, and watched with horror. No, not horror: awe, as eleven more perfect blooms grew from the palm of my hand.

I knew after the third one that there would be a dozen. A dozen bloomin' roses. Blood-red and each with two dots on each perfect petal. And under the dots a downturned line.

I stared at the dots. They were eyes. Unhappy eyes. And underneath, a sad little suggestion of a mouth. Each petal of each rose held a portrait of the dead boy's face. I knew that Gerald had sent me a message from beyond the grave.

I collected the roses in a daze and took them into the shop. Then I wrapped them in pink paper and tied them up with a bow. I ran a chewed fingernail along the ends and curled them up. After that I wrote on a small card and attached it to the ribbon.

Then I set off for home.

Scouse was on the train.

He leered as soon as he saw me. I stood with my back to the sliding doors and as they slid closed I let the roses become trapped in the door. I stood there, saying nothing as the train lurched off.

There was no one in the carriage except Scouse. 'Another little person with flowers in the door,' he mocked. He stood up and poked me in the stomach. It hurt. 'Another sap. Another creep who buys flowers.'

I grabbed his wrist with my one free hand and tried to stop him jabbing me.

Just at that moment the train plunged into the tunnel and Scouse broke my hold in the blackness. I felt his powerful arms on my neck and I fought desperately for breath. I was choking. He was strangling me.

I felt my life ebbing away but I just couldn't bring myself to let go of those roses, and so I only had one free hand and couldn't stop him.

Without warning the doors burst apart as if opened by giant arms. A roaring and rushing filled the carriage. A sweet smell of roses engulfed us. The hands released my neck and Scouse screamed with terror. As the light flicked on I saw that the compartment was filled with rambling roses. They twisted and climbed at astonishing speed. They covered the luggage racks and the safety rails. They twisted along the seats and completely filled the compartment. I couldn't move. Then I saw that the long tendrils wound around Scouse's legs and arms. And neck.

Tighter and tighter they drew around the hapless man's throat until at last he lay still on the floor. I knew that he was dead.

And then, as quickly as they had come, the creeping

roses snaked out of the door and vanished into the black tunnel. There was not a sign that they had ever been there. Except the one dozen roses that I had started with. They were perfectly intact. Not damaged a bit by their exposure to the tunnel. I smoothed down my dress and then picked up the bunch of roses as the train stopped at the station.

I looked again at the label I had written. It said:

TO GERALD WITH LOVE FROM SAMANTHA.

When I got home Mum was amazed by the roses. 'Why Samantha,' she said. 'They are beautiful. And look, each petal has two little dots that look like eyes and a little line like a mouth. They are faces.'

I could feel tears forming in my eyes. 'Yes,' I said, examining them closely. 'And each little face is smiling.'

AGGHHHHH! NO!

Spooks Incorporated

The house was enclosed in darkness and Miss Pebble was alone. She had been alone for sixty years. She had no family and there was no one to care for her or help her. And now she was scared. But it was no good calling out. She was alone in the night.

She loved her old house. She had lived in it all her life. She loved the old verandah and the tin roof. She loved the old cellar under the ground. She loved everything about it. It was her home.

A few days earlier a shifty-looking character had offered her a lot of money for the old cottage. But Miss Pebble wouldn't sell. She wanted to live in the house until she died.

People said there was a ghost in the house. They said Ned Kelly had once lived there many years ago. Before he had been hanged for murder and robbery. Some people said that Ned's ghost walked at night. Moaning and groaning and wearing the steel armour and helmet that he had made to protect himself from the bullets of the police. Miss Pebble didn't believe it. She didn't believe the house was haunted. She had never heard any moaning in the night. Not until now.

She sat up in bed. There was someone in the house. She could hear movement. It sounded like someone crying.

The noise was coming from the kitchen. It was very soft. She told herself not to be silly, there was nothing there. It was just her nerves. But she could feel her hands shaking in the dark. She wanted to turn on the light and go and look. She knew she couldn't go to sleep until she had checked in the kitchen. But she was too scared. So she lay there all alone. In the dark.

The noise grew louder. It was coming closer, coming along the hall. Miss Pebble heard clinking. And clanking. It sounded like chains being dragged along. Something was coming towards her room. It was definitely moaning and groaning and clinking and clanking. Miss Pebble gave a little sob. She wanted to scream. She wanted to shout for help. But she didn't. She lay there saying nothing, hoping it would go away.

The noise came closer and closer.

Light appeared under the bedroom door. Soft flickering light, like light from a candle. Miss Pebble gasped. Her heart beat quickly and her head started to spin.

And then the door began to open. Slowly. Light flickered into the room. Slowly, slowly the door opened. And there in the dark hall he stood. The ghost of Ned Kelly. He had a steel helmet over his head with a slit cut out for the eyes. His chest was covered with steel plates. In one hand was a candle and in the other was a revolver. Green eyes glowed through his helmet.

Miss Pebble froze. Her heart almost stopped with fear.

Ned Kelly started to walk towards the bed. He moaned. His armour creaked. He stretched out a hand for Miss Pebble, a long, skinny hand. Then the candle went out. It was completely black.

Miss Pebble screamed. She put her hands to her mouth and screamed and screamed. Then she jumped out of bed. She stumbled through the darkness out into the hall. Out through the front door.

It was raining outside. It was freezing cold. But Miss Pebble didn't care. She ran out into the street screaming. She was soaking wet and her bare feet were cut and bleeding. She fled down the road and into the dark night.

Ned was alone in the bedroom. He walked over to the door and switched on the light. Then he looked at his watch. It was a digital watch. It said 12.45 a.m.

The figure pulled off his hood. He wasn't Ned Kelly at all. And he wasn't a ghost. He was a young man, a teenager. He laughed to himself. 'That will make the old bag sell the house,' he said. 'Or my name is not Mick Harris.'

2

The next night in another town an old man was locking up a church. His name was Mr Pickle. All the others had gone. Choir practice was over. It was dark outside and cold. He put his hat on his bald head and shivered. He wished he was home, having his supper of cheese and biscuits and a nice glass of port.

He thought of the warm fire at home and his favourite TV show – *A Country Practice*. He decided to hurry back.

He took the short cut home through the graveyard. The graves were old and the grass was long. But there was a little track that went past his mother's grave. Mr Pickle looked after her grave. He kept it tidy and he put flowers on it every Sunday after church.

But tonight it was windy and cold and dark. He took his hat off as he went past his mother's grave but he kept walking. Then he stopped. Something was different. The flower bowl had gone. He turned round and went back to the grave.

The moon went behind a cloud. The night grew even darker and it was hard to see. Mr Pickle bent down and looked at the grass on the grave. His heart almost stopped. He saw something terrible. The grass moved. He was sure the grass had moved.

He took a step back. The grass on the grave was moving up and down. He was filled with horror. There was a scraping noise, like digging. Something was digging its way out of the grave. Suddenly a small hole appeared. And out of it came the bones of a hand. The skeleton of a hand and an arm appeared.

And waved around. On one finger was a wedding ring.

Mr Pickle was filled with fear. He opened and closed his mouth. 'No, no,' he screamed. He took a step backwards. Then he felt a sharp pain in his chest and down his arm. He put his hand over his heart. The pain grew worse. It was killing him. He fell to the ground and lay still.

A man ran out from behind a tree. It was a fat man dressed in a suit. He bent over Mr Pickle. He put his head on Mr Pickle's chest and listened. Then he picked up Mr Pickle's arm and felt his wrist. There was no pulse.

The skeleton was still waving around in the hole. The man in the suit ran over to it. He pulled out the arm and threw it on the ground. A groan came out of the hole.

'Shut up, Mick, you fool,' said the man. 'Pickle is dead. He's croaked. We've gone too far this time.'

The man grabbed a shovel. He started to dig in the grave. He uncovered a long box. Then he opened the lid. A young man sat up, a teenager. 'What's up, Shifty?' he asked.

'You're a fool. That's what's up,' said Shifty. 'He's dead. Pickle is as dead as a doornail. And it's your fault.'

'It was your idea, not mine,' said the teenager.

'Listen, Mick,' said Shifty, 'I told you to get in the box. I told you to wave the skeleton hand. But I didn't tell you to put a ring on the finger. He thought it was his mother's ring. It was too much for him. It gave him a heart attack. Now he's dead.'

'Don't try to blame me,' said Mick. 'Or I'll flatten you.'

'Okay, don't get ants in your pants. Let's get out of here before someone comes.'

Shifty and Mick ran back to the road. They got into an old truck. On the side it said:

SPOOKS FOR HIRE

Mick and Shifty drove home quickly. They wanted to get away from Mr Pickle's body. They didn't want to get caught.

3

The two men ran a business called SPOOKS INCORPORATED.

They dressed up as ghosts to frighten people. They went to old houses that were supposed to be haunted and scared the owners so that they sold their homes. Mick and Shifty's friends bought the houses cheap, then paid the two crooks for what they had done.

'Will we get paid now that Mr Pickle is dead?' said Mick. 'We were only supposed to scare him. Not kill him.'

'Of course we'll get paid,' said Shifty. 'His house will have to be sold now. Dead men don't own houses. This has been a good week. Last night we scared the daylights out of old Miss Pebble, and tonight we knocked off Mr Pickle. We get a thousand dollars for each. Two thousand dollars for two nights' work. That's good money. Real good.'

'What's the next job?' asked Mick. 'Who do we scare next?'

'There's a pub in Melbourne called Young and Jackson's,' replied Shifty. 'It's supposed to be haunted. We are going to scare the owner into selling it for a cheap price.'

'Tell me the story about the ghost in the pub,' said Mick. 'Not that I believe in ghosts. Only fools believe in ghosts.'

'Well,' Shifty said. 'A long time ago a bloke called John Heart owned Young and Jackson's. He wanted to see if he could stop meat going bad. So he got a chicken and chopped off its head. Then he filled the chicken up with salt. He thought that filling the chicken up with salt would stop it going rotten.'

'Did it work?'

'No one knows,' said Shifty. 'He cut himself while he was chopping off the chook's head and the next day he died.'

'And now his ghost is supposed to haunt the pub,' said Mick.

'No,' yelled Shifty. 'The ghost of the headless chicken is supposed to haunt the pub.'

Mick and Shifty started to laugh. They both thought it was funny. Very funny indeed.

The next day Mick and Shifty made their plans. They were going to spook the owner of the pub so that he would get scared and sell it.

'How are we going to get the ghost of a headless chicken?' asked Mick. 'Dressing up as Ned Kelly was a good idea. That scared Pebble, but I can't dress up as a chicken. I'm too big.'

'We are going to make one,' said Shifty. 'We are going to make a headless chicken.'

Mick and Shifty spent ten days making a mechanical chicken. They used feathers, wheels and a small motor, and they put red paint around its neck to look like blood. At last it was finished. Shifty put it on the floor. 'Terrific,' he said. 'It looks just like the real thing. The owner of the pub will be scared out of his wits.'

'Let's see if it can walk,' said Mick. 'Press the remote control.' Shifty pressed a button and the headless chicken ran around in circles. It flapped its wings and shook its headless neck. 'Wonderful,' Mick went on. 'In the dark it will look just like the real thing. The ghost of the headless chook. Something is missing, though. It's good, but it needs something else.' He looked at the mechanical chicken for a while. Then he said, 'I know. It needs to make a noise. It needs to cluck.'

'Don't be a fool. How can it cluck?' Shifty replied. 'It has no head. A chook can't cluck without a head.'

'That's all the better,' Mick told him. 'Don't you see? A chicken with no head that makes a noise is more scary. It will be more ghostly if it clucks. All we have to do is put a tape recorder inside it. You can make some clucking noises and I will put them on tape. Then we put the tape inside the chicken.'

'Great,' yelled Shifty. 'A terrific idea. You go and get a blank tape. And I'll find a small tape recorder.'

A few minutes later Shifty came back holding a cassette tape. 'I can't find a blank tape,' he said. 'But this is an old tape with folk songs on it. We can tape the chicken noises over the top.'

Mick put the tape in the recorder and pressed the RECORD button. Shifty started to cluck like a chicken.

'Wonderful,' said Mick. 'You sound just like the real thing.' After a while he stopped the tape recorder. 'That will do the trick. That should be enough clucking to scare anyone to death.'

They put the mechanical chicken on the floor and started it up. Once again it ran around in circles and flapped its wings. But this time it clucked as well. 'Fantastic,' shouted Mick. 'That tape sounds just like a chicken.'

4

That night Mick and Shifty crept down to Young and Jackson's pub. They waited outside. At midnight the lights went out. The back door opened. The landlord came out carrying a rubbish bin. 'This is it,' said Mick. 'This is where we give the poor sucker the fright of his life.' He put the mechanical chicken on the footpath and hid behind a fence. The chicken ran out onto the road. It flapped its wings and clucked. Red paint dripped from its neck.

The landlord just stood there holding the bin. He couldn't believe his eyes. Then he groaned. 'It's true,' he said. 'The story is true. It's the ghost of the headless chicken.' His knees knocked together. His hands shook. He tried to run but he couldn't. He was glued to the spot. The chicken kept running in circles, clucking loudly.

Mick whispered to Shifty. 'Let it go for a while. Give him a good scare. Then we might not have to come back again.' The two crooks peeped around the fence. They laughed to themselves. They thought it was a great joke. The landlord was so scared he couldn't move.

After a while Mick stepped out onto the path. He pretended he was just walking along the street. The poor landlord saw him. 'Look,' the landlord managed to say. 'The ghost of the headless chicken.'

'Where?' said Mick. 'I can't see anything.' This was a trick he often used. He pretended not to see the chicken. Even though it was flapping and clucking right in front of him.

The landlord leaned against the wall. His face was white. He looked as if he was going to faint. But before he did, something happened. The chicken started to sing. It ran around flapping its wings. And singing. It sang:

'There was a wild colonial youth,
Jack Doolan was his name;

AGGHHHHH! NO!

Of poor but honest parents

He was born in Castlemaine.'

'You fool, Shifty,' yelled Mick. 'You didn't wipe all the folk songs off the tape.'

Shifty put his head around the corner. The chicken went quiet for a second but it kept running around. Then it started up again:

'"I'll fight but I won't surrender," said

The wild colonial boy.'

The landlord stared at the chicken. Then he stared at Mick and Shifty. 'A trick,' he yelled. 'A dirty, rotten trick.'

He ran over to the mechanical chicken and picked it up. He saw it had wheels. He threw it on the ground with an angry roar. Then he turned to Mick and Shifty. The landlord was a big man. Very big. 'I'll teach you ratbags a lesson,' he shouted. 'I'll get you for this.'

Mick and Shifty turned and ran. They ran for their lives. Down the street they went. Faster and faster. But the landlord followed them. And after him came the chicken.

The landlord started to slow down. He couldn't keep up. But the chicken could. It passed him and followed Shifty and Mick down the street. It was flapping its wings and clucking its head off.

The chase went on for quite a while but eventually the landlord gave up. He shook his fist at the two men and the chicken and turned round and went back towards Young and Jackson's pub.

Mick looked over his shoulder. 'It's all right,' he puffed. 'He's gone back.' Then Mick noticed the chicken. 'Well, look at that. The stupid mechanical chicken has come after us. I thought it was supposed to run around in circles.'

They both looked at the chicken. It was flapping its wings and moving up and down on its legs. 'Hey,' yelled Shifty. 'When did you put those legs on the chicken? I didn't know it had legs.'

The headless chicken sat down on the footpath. Then it stood up. There was something underneath it. 'An egg,' screamed Shifty. 'It's laid an egg.' His eyes almost popped out of his head. He couldn't believe what he was seeing. He bent down to pick up the egg. But his fingers couldn't grab it. He couldn't pick it up. He could see right through it. The egg was transparent.

'Ahgggg,' he screamed. 'It's a ghost egg.'

'Rubbish,' shouted Mick. 'I'm sick of this.' He ran at the chicken and kicked at it. His leg passed though the chicken and he fell flat on his back. The chicken sat there clucking. It wasn't hurt at all. They both stood there looking at it. The moon came out. This time it was Mick who screamed. 'Ahgggg, I can see through it. And there's no meshing inside it. It's salt. That's not our chicken. It's the ghost. It's the ghost of the real chicken.'

For a second they just stood there. They were too scared to move. Then the chicken flapped up onto Mick's shoulder. Little drops of blood fell from its headless neck. Both men screamed together. They turned and ran for their lives. Down the streets and through lanes they fled. And close behind followed the ghostly chicken.

At last they reached the river. Shifty was puffing. He was out of breath. 'Quick,' he grunted. 'Down here. Down these steps.' They ran down some steps that led to the Yarra River. There was a rowboat at the bottom. The chicken was right behind them. They jumped into the little boat and floated out onto the river. Shifty took one oar and Mick took the other. Soon they were well out in the deep water.

'It can't follow us here,' said Mick. 'We're safe now.' But he was wrong. Sitting on the back of the boat, still clucking, was the ghost of the headless chicken. Mick stood up and started to scream.

'Sit down, you fool,' yelled Shifty. 'You're rocking the boat.' The boat started to rock from side to side. Mick grabbed at the edge. And the little boat tipped over. Mick and Shifty disappeared under the cold, black water. Neither of them could swim.

The landlord of the pub arrived home. On the footpath he found the mechanical chicken. Its battery had run out and it lay still on the footpath. He went over to the chicken and jumped up and down on it. Then he threw the broken pieces of wheels and wire into the bin.

The next morning while he was walking by the river, the landlord found two dead men in the mud.

5

They say that if you go down to the Yarra River on a dark night, just near Young and Jackson's pub, you see two ghostly men in a boat. They are rowing as fast as they can. They are scared out of their wits. Because in the back of the boat sit the ghosts of two headless chickens.

One of the chickens is stuffed with salt and is clucking. The other chicken is singing 'The Wild Colonial Boy' at the top of its voice.

GGHHHHH! NO!

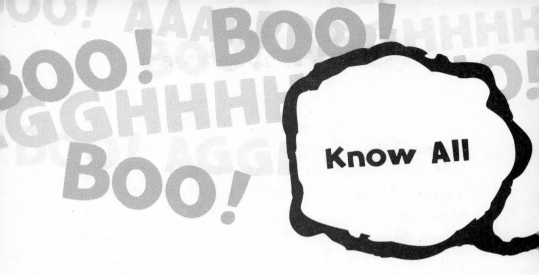

Know All

The old box lay half buried in the sand. I wish that I had never seen it. I wish the storm hadn't uncovered it. I wish we hadn't dug it up. But it's no good wishing. We did dig it up and we took the old chest home. And everything went wrong.

'I wonder what's in it?' said Dad. He was like a big kid. He loved bringing home junk from the beach. Every day he would climb down our cliff and walk along the sand looking for stuff that had washed up.

I looked at the box and shivered. I just had a feeling about it. I didn't like it. It wasn't like the other things Dad had brought from the beach. His other finds were all hanging off the walls and ceiling. We had empty cray pots, old buoys, fish nets, driftwood, bottles and other junk scattered about in every room. But this was different. This trunk had bad vibes.

'Don't open it,' I said. 'Let's take it back.'

'Whatever for, Kate? There could be something valuable inside.'

'Like treasure,' said my brother Matthew. 'It could be full of jewels.'

'No,' I said. 'Let's take it back to the beach and leave it. There is something awful inside. I just know it.'

Matthew looked at me. 'Sometimes you're a bit of a know-all, Kate. You couldn't possibly know what is in that box.'

'It's old,' said Dad, 'and it's waterproof. All the joins are covered in tar. Whatever is inside might still be in good nick.' He picked up his hacksaw and began cutting away at the old, rusty padlock.

I didn't want to watch. I went outside and stared out to sea. The salt mist hung heavily in the air. Off-shore I could see two whales spouting in the swell.

I heard a sudden call from the kitchen. 'Got it. I've got it.'

'Come and help,' yelled Matthew. 'Don't be a sad sack, Kate. Come and help.'

I went back into the kitchen and saw Dad and Matthew struggling away with a lever. The lock was off but the lid was stuck and they couldn't get it open. I stood back and shook my head. I didn't want to help.

Then, slowly, with a creak and a groan it yielded. The lid began to lift. They both stared inside in silence.

'Wow,' said Matthew after a bit. 'Look at that.'

It wasn't treasure. I could tell by the way he said 'wow' that it wasn't that good.

2

'Well I'll be blowed,' said Dad. 'It's clothes. It's full of clothes.' He reached in and started dumping them on the floor. Soon there was a big pile of them heaped up on the carpet.

They weren't just ordinary clothes. They were old. But there was something else as well. These were special outfits. One of them was covered in stars and moons. Another consisted of a frilly dress with tights. There was a top hat and a blade coat and heaps of other combinations.

Dad picked up a pair of baggy trousers. Folded up inside them was a pair of enormous shoes and a long false nose. 'Circus outfits,' said Dad. 'They are clothes from a circus.' He seemed a bit disappointed. I think that secretly he had been hoping for treasure too.

Matthew laid all of the clothes out in order on the floor. There was a knife-thrower's outfit – it had a leather belt with places for the knives. There was a juggler's costume and a clown's. There was also a fortune teller's outfit and two sets of tightrope walkers' clothes. Altogether there were about fifteen different sets.

I looked at the two tightrope walkers' outfits – one was blue and one was red. They both consisted of tights and tops covered in silver stars. Matthew held the red outfit up to himself. 'This would fit me,' he said with a grin.

A shiver went down my spine. 'Don't put it on,' I told him.

'Why not?' he asked.

'I just have a feeling,' I said. 'I think that it once belonged to someone mean. Someone awful. Someone cruel. Someone dead.'

Matthew laughed. 'Okay,' he said. 'I won't put it on. But what will we do with them all? And where did they come from?'

'From a shipwreck,' said Dad. 'I'll bet a ship with circus people in it was wrecked off the cliff. Years ago. This trunk has been buried in the sand ever since.' He gave me a big grin. 'It might not be treasure but it can still be useful. We'll put one of the outfits on the scarecrow.'

Dad pointed to the scarecrow at the bottom of our garden. Two crows and a starling were sitting on top of it. The birds actually seemed to like this old scarecrow. It had never worked. All it ever did was provide a handy seat for the crows.

'Which outfit?' said Matthew. 'Will we have a clown scarecrow or what?'

'The red tightrope walker,' answered Dad. 'Seeing Kate doesn't like that costume we will put it on the scarecrow.' Dad picked up the red tights and jacket and walked down the garden. He pulled off the old clothes and put the new ones on. It was the strangest scarecrow I had ever seen. It looked a bit like Superman. Matthew ran back inside and fetched the top hat. He banged it onto the scarecrow's head. We all laughed.

But the scarecrow didn't laugh.

'Its face seems different,' I said.

'It's still smiling like before,' said Matthew.

'I know,' I answered. 'But it isn't a nice smile any more. It seems to be leering. It seems to be leering at Dad. It doesn't like Dad. It's the clothes. The clothes don't like Dad because he's put them out here on the scarecrow.'

'Nonsense,' said Dad as we walked back to the house. 'Whoever heard of clothes not liking anything?' I turned and looked at the scarecrow. One of its hands was bunched up into a fist. It looked just as if it was threatening to punch someone. I had never noticed its hand bunched up like that before. I thought that it must have happened when Dad put the red tightrope walker's outfit on it.

Matthew fooled around with the other costumes all afternoon. He put on the clown's baggy pants and long nose. He really did look funny and Dad and I couldn't stop laughing. The pants kept falling down all the time and Matthew tripped over his own feet so many times that it's a wonder he didn't hurt himself. He made a terrific clown. Good enough to be in a circus. Which was a bit strange really because normally Matthew is serious and not very funny at all.

Next he put on the blue tightrope walker's set of clothes. He went down to the back fence and walked along the top edge. It was a high paling fence and it was a bit wobbly. Matthew held out his arms to the side like plane wings and started to walk. He was great. He walked the whole length of the fence without falling off.

'That was terrific,' I yelled. I gave him a big clap.

The scarecrow regarded us with its frozen grin.

It didn't clap.

That was when I noticed how quiet the garden was. There was no noise at all. Not a rustle. Not even a bird call. I looked around and saw the crows sitting far off in some trees. The birds were too frightened to even come into the garden.

'Those clothes have done wonders for the scarecrow,' said a voice behind us. 'The birds won't come anywhere near it.' It was Dad.

'I don't blame them,' I answered. 'I'm not going anywhere near it either.' The scarecrow seemed to have its gaze fixed on Dad. It hated him. I knew that it hated him. 'It's proud,' I said. 'And it's haughty. And it's mean.'

'And it's only a scarecrow,' added Dad. 'I don't care what it looks like as long as it keeps the birds off.'

The crows started to caw. Long, mournful cries like lost babies in the night.

3

Matthew went inside and put on the knife-thrower's outfit. The whole thing was made of leather covered in little scratch marks. When Dad wasn't looking, Matthew took a sharp knife out of the kitchen drawer and snuck off along the cliff. I knew that he was going to pretend to be a knife thrower in the circus.

I looked out of the window at the scarecrow. It seemed to be closer to the house than it was before. It was on the edge of the vegetable patch instead of the middle. It was grinning horribly. It was staring straight at me. I went into my bedroom and hid behind the curtain. I peeked at it through a chink so that it couldn't see my face. I felt a bit silly. Dad was right. It was only a scarecrow.

And then my heart almost stopped. The scarecrow now stood on the edge of the lawn. It had moved forward about a metre while I was changing rooms. There was no one around outside. Dad was in the lounge watching the football on television.

'It's coming,' I screamed. 'It's coming.'

Dad rushed into the room. 'What's coming?' he asked.

'The scarecrow,' I said. 'It's coming to get us. No. It's coming to get you, Dad. It hates you. Look. It's moved onto the lawn.'

Dad peered out of the window. The scarecrow was back in the middle of the vegetable patch.

'You've been watching too much television,' said Dad. 'I don't want to hear any more nonsense about that scarecrow.' A great roar erupted from the TV set. 'A goal,' said Dad. 'And I missed it because of a scarecrow.' He gave me a black look and rushed back into the lounge.

A little later, Matthew's face appeared at the window.

He was holding his finger up to his lips. 'Shh,' he whispered. 'Come and watch this.'

I followed Matthew along the cliff until we were out of sight of the house. He was still dressed in the knifethrower's costume. He stopped at a large fence-post on the edge of the cliff. Then he turned and walked backwards twenty steps until he was about seven metres from the post. He took out the silver kitchen knife and suddenly threw it at the post. It spun like a propeller flashing silver in the sunshine. With a dull 'thunk' it dug into the post. It quivered silently in the still sea air.

I didn't like what I was seeing. I started to understand what was happening but I had to be sure. Matthew was grinning. His grin was almost as big as the scarecrow's. 'Do it again,' I said. 'Let's see you do it again.'

'No worries,' said Matthew. 'I'm an expert. I have natural talent.' He fetched the knife and walked back another twenty paces. This time he turned his back to the post. 'Watch this,' he said. He held the knife by its blade and threw it over his shoulder. He threw the knife at the post without even looking. Once again the knife spun, glittering and humming in the air. Once again it thunked into the post, splintering the grey wood as its point found the target.

Matthew smiled. A happy, boastful smile. 'I'm a fantastic knife thrower,' he said. 'I never miss. Fancy that. I lived for fourteen years without knowing what a good knife thrower I am.'

'It's not you,' I whispered hoarsely. 'It's the clothes. You are getting strange powers from the clothes. That outfit belonged to a knife thrower in a circus. Now he is dead and you are getting his skill from the outfit.'

The smile fell from his face. 'What do you mean?' he said. I could tell that he didn't like what I was saying.

'When you had the blue tightrope walker's outfit on you could walk the fence without falling off,' I said. 'And when you wore the clown's clothes you kept acting the fool. You get the powers from the clothes.'

'Bull,' said Matthew angrily. 'You're jealous. You're a know-all. You think you know everything.' He turned around and stomped off.

'It's the same with the scarecrow,' I said. 'It's got powers from the red tightrope walker's outfit. Only it's got something else as well. Something worse. It's got the evil mind of whoever owned the clothes. And it's coming to get Dad. It's moving. I saw it.'

Matthew looked at me in a funny way. 'You really saw it move?' he asked.

I went red. 'Well, I didn't actually see it but it did move. It was in a different place.'

Matthew turned round and stormed off. He wouldn't let me say one more thing. He went so fast that I couldn't catch up with him.

4

By the time I got home Matthew had told Dad the

whole thing. Dad was cross with both of us. He told Matthew off for taking the kitchen knife but he was really mad at me. 'I don't know what's got into you,' he said. 'First you start raving on about the scarecrow coming to get us and now you're trying to make out that these clothes have strange powers. Don't be such a know-all, Kate.'

Then he said something that made my blood run cold. 'I'm taking Matthew into town. He's staying with Aunty Ruth for the night. You can make the tea while I'm away.'

'You can't leave me here alone,' I yelled. I pointed out the window at the scarecrow. 'Not with him.' Dad's face grew angry. I knew that I had better not say any more. 'Okay,' I said. 'Okay. I'll see you when you get back.'

I heard the car drone off into the distance as Matthew and Dad bumped down our track to the front gate. I was alone. The sea was strangely quiet. I gazed along the bleak and empty cliffs. There was no wind and mist was rolling in from the sea. I looked around the land-scape for comfort but there was not another house in sight. In the backyard the scarecrow grinned with a twisted smile. I stared at it like a mouse hypnotised by a snake. I couldn't take my eyes off it.

Its hat was cocked to one side. Its red tightrope outfit bulged over the straw stuffing. Its legs dangled, moving gently in the breeze.

What breeze?

There was no breeze.

I gave a stifled cry as it made another movement. The scarecrow's mouth opened. Its jaw just slowly fell open revealing a black hole. A horrible black hole. I screamed and ran into the loungeroom. I looked out of the loungeroom window. It had moved. It was dangling from its pole, which now erupted from the middle of the lawn. It was much closer to the house.

My mind went numb. I was only a kid. A kid alone in a house with a live scarecrow outside. A scarecrow which was coming towards the house. I panicked. I ran to the front door and bolted it. Then I ran to the back door and turned the key. I checked all of the windows. I told myself that I was safe – but I knew that I wasn't.

The scarecrow still stood in the same position. I watched it from the window. It didn't move. It didn't seem to want to move while I was watching it. My heart beat a little slower. My brain started to work. I would stand there and not take my eyes off it. Then it couldn't move.

We stood there, we two. We stood watching, staring, neither of us moving. I frowned at him and he grinned at me. An hour passed. My legs grew numb but I dared not stir. As long as I held the scarecrow in my gaze, he would not move. The afternoon sky darkened and the sea mist grew thicker.

How long could I stand there? Where was Dad? What if he didn't come back until after dark? Would the scarecrow stalk the darkness, knowing that he was safe from my gaze? Would his powers increase at night? Would he care if I saw him move in the blackness of midnight?

I looked around for a weapon. I had none. None that could fight this terrible spectre. I had to do something before darkness fell. And then my glance fell upon the pile of circus clothes. I tore my eyes from them and fixed the scarecrow with my gaze. I couldn't let my eyes wander but my mind was free to roam. An idea nibbled away at the back of my mind. There was help in those clothes – I was sure of it.

5

I backed towards the pile, still keeping my eyes firmly on the scarecrow. I bent down and picked up one of the outfits. I put on one piece after another until my normal clothes were completely covered. Then I sat and stared and stared and stared.

'Now, Mr Scarecrow,' I said after a long time. 'Now I know what to do.'

I tore off the outfit. I had a big job in front of me and it had to be done before dark. I gathered up all of the circus clothes and stuffed them into a plastic garbage bag. Then I rushed out to the garage and fetched a coil of rope, a short length of chain and Dad's wire strainers.

I also grabbed his longest fishing rod – a huge bamboo surf rod. My load was heavy, but fear gave me strength.

I headed off towards the cliff, pausing every now and then to look behind me. I came to a fork in the track. One track led down to a small bay and the other headed off to the edge of Dead Man's Drop – a deep chasm between two high cliffs. Dad would never let Matthew or me go near Dead Man's Drop. The cliffs fell straight down to the surging waves beneath. Anyone who fell would not return.

I struggled on until I reached the edge of Dead Man's Drop. A barbed-wire cattle fence ended at the edge of the cliff. Whoever had put the last post in had been brave. It was concreted into the ground at the very edge. I put down my load and picked up the surf rod. I took off the hooks and tied a heavy sinker to the end. Then, after checking the reel, I cast the sinker towards the cliff on the other side. It arced high into the air – too high. The sinker plunged down into the savage waves below. I wound the line in as fast as I could. I knew that my first cast wouldn't work.

I tried again.

This time I did it right. The sinker curved beautifully through the air and landed on top of the cliff on the other side. I put down the rod and cut off the line. Then I tied the fishing line to one end of the long coil of rope. I tied the other end of the rope to the fencepost.

I looked at the sky. It was growing dark. I looked down the empty track.

Nothing.

I took out one of the outfits and folded it up next to the post. All the other costumes I threw over the cliff into the sea. The greedy waves consumed them and the clothes soon vanished beneath the boiling water. I disconnected the fishing reel and laid the bamboo rod on top of the one remaining outfit.

Taking the short length of chain and the wire strainers with me, I ran along the edge of Dead Man's Drop. It was about a kilometre to the other side. As I ran I looked over my shoulder down the darkening track. Still nothing.

At last I reached the other side. I searched around in the stubble for my sinker. I finally saw it lying close to the edge of the cliff. I managed to retrieve it by lying on my stomach and stretching out my hand. I pulled the fishing line in and drew the rope gently after it, across the top of Dead Man's Drop. Next I tied the short chain to the end of the rope. Then I grabbed the wire strainers and stretched the rope tight against another fencepost. It had to be tight. Very tight.

The sky grew dark. The clouds were now scudding across the sky and the angry waves below crashed and reached up at me with foaming claws.

Across the other side, down the darkening track, I saw a stumbling figure. It was Dad. He was running and looking over his shoulder as he went. Behind

AGGHHHHH! NO!

him, with its straw arms stretched to the sky, came the scarecrow. It strode with sure and savage steps, its pole held in one crooked claw, its mouth agape, twisted into an angry snarl.

I could see that Dad was terrified. He stumbled to the fork in the track and took a few steps down towards the bay and then, changing his mind, headed towards Dead Man's Drop as I knew he would.

With amazing speed the scarecrow circled out from the track, trapping Dad against the edge of the cliff. It raised its quivering arms against the heavens and gave a terrible roar. I knew that Dad would be no match for its evil strength.

6

Dad first gazed down at the sucking sea and then he looked up. He saw me on the other side. 'Put on the clothes,' I yelled. 'Put on the blue outfit.'

I watched him examine the tightrope walker's outfit and shake his head. The snarling red scarecrow had tripped over. It let out a grizzly groan and then began crawling forward.

'Quick,' I screamed, 'put on the clothes. It's your only chance.' Dad pulled off his shoes and clothes, tearing at them like a madman. In a flash he was dressed in blue. He picked up the long bamboo fishing rod and, using it as a balancing pole, took a few steps out along the rope that I had stretched across the ravine. The sea called to him in a savage voice. The needle-sharp rocks thrust upwards from the smashing foam. Dad tottered and then, as if he had been doing it all his life, began walking across the rope. There has never been a feat like it. With firm, unfaltering steps Dad walked out to the middle of the rope. Not once did he look down. The skills of the long-dead tightrope walker passed on to Dad through the suit of clothes.

By now the scarecrow was on its feet at the edge of the cliff. Its face was twisted with hate and rage. It bent down and tried to shake the rope but I had strained it too tight. It wouldn't move. The scarecrow tried to untie the knot which held the rope to the post but its straw-filled fingers could not budge it.

With an angry scream the scarecrow picked up its pole and followed Dad out onto the stretched rope. Two acrobats, the blue and the red, held onto their balancing poles and stepped firmly but precariously into the misty evening air.

'Come on,' I yelled. 'Keep going. You can make it. I know you can.'

And he did. It seemed like a million years but at last Dad stepped onto firm ground. I threw my arms around him and gave him a big hug. 'No time for that,' he screamed. He was looking at the scarecrow, coming, coming, coming, across its road of rope.

'Quick,' yelled Dad. 'Untie the knot before it gets here.'

'No need,' I said. 'The birds will get it.'

Dad looked around at the empty sky. 'What are you talking about?' he yelled. 'I don't see any birds.'

'They will be here in a minute,' I said.

The scarecrow strode forward. I could see its horrible black hole of a mouth twisted with rage.

7

'Look,' I shouted. 'There they are.' Hundreds of birds swept low across the cliff. They flew high above the red figure of straw and then began to swoop. The scarecrow's hat was knocked from his head and it tumbled into the waiting sea. He raised his stick and began swiping at the birds like a man trying to swat flies. Faster and faster they swooped, pecking, fluttering, flapping.

And then, slowly but certainly, the creature of straw began to totter. He fell, twisting and turning in terrible loops until at last he plunged into the arms of the tearing tide beneath.

The birds vanished as quickly as they had arrived. Dad and I stood silently staring.

After a bit Dad took off the blue outfit and threw it into the sea. He stood there shivering in his underpants. 'How did you know those birds were coming?' he demanded.

'I knew,' I answered.

'And how did you know that I would take the track to the cliff and not the track to the beach?'

'I knew. I knew what would happen. I knew you

would get across safely.'

'How did you know?' he said urgently. 'How did you know?'

'Back at the house,' I said. 'I put on an outfit.'

'Which one? Which outfit did you wear?'

He laughed when I told him, 'It was the fortune teller's costume.'

Grandad's Gifts

'We can't open that cupboard,' said Dad. 'I promised my father. Grandad locked it up many years ago and it's never been opened.'

'What's in it?' I asked.

'No one knows,' said Mum.

'But it's in my bedroom,' I said. 'I need to know what's in it. It could be anything.'

'I lived in this bedroom for nineteen years,' said Dad. 'And I kept my promise. That cupboard has never been opened. Now I want you to promise me that you'll never open it.'

They both looked at me, waiting for my answer. Suddenly there was a knock on the door downstairs. 'It's the removal van,' said Mum. 'About time too.'

Mum and Dad rushed down to help move in our furniture. I wandered around my new room. It was small and dusty with a little dormer window overlooking the tangled garden.

No one had lived in the house for years. It was high in the mountains, far from the city. The garden was overgrown. Ivy had climbed the gum trees. Blackberry bushes choked the paths and strangled the shrubs.

I walked over to the forbidden cupboard and gave the handle a shake. It was locked firm. I put my eye to the keyhole but everything was black. I sniffed under the gap at the bottom of the door. It was musty and dusty. Something silent inside seemed to call me.

It was almost as if a gentle voice was stirring the shadows of years gone by. The stillness seemed to echo my name. 'Shane, Shane, Shane . . .'

2

'Shane,' Mum shouted up the stairs. 'Come and help bring these things in.'

They were lifting a large machine from the van. The removalist man had one corner and there was one left for me. 'Quick, grab it,' said Dad. 'It's heavy.'

I helped lower the machine onto the ground. 'What is it?' I asked.

'A mulcher,' Dad told me. 'You put in branches and leaves and twigs and it chews them up into mulch. We're going to use it to clear up this garden.'

I stared around at the tangled yard. That's when I saw the two lemon trees for the first time. A big one over near the gate. And a small, shrivelled up one near the back fence. The big tree was covered in lemons. But the small one had only two. It wasn't much of a tree.

Dad pointed to the big lemon tree. 'It's always grown

well,' he said. 'Grandad shot a fox. He buried its remains under that tree.'

I gave a shiver. I knew that I would never peel one of those lemons. Or eat one.

I carried a box back to my room and started to unpack. I turned my back on the secret cupboard and tried not to listen to the gentle voice lapping like waves in my head. 'Shane, Shane, Shane . . .'

Once again I peered through the keyhole. This time I thought I saw two points of light twinkle in the darkness. I shivered. This was creepy. I didn't really want to live in this room.

3

That night I couldn't sleep. Every time I opened my eyes I saw the cupboard door. After a long time I finally drifted off. I had a wonderful dream about trees. The branches reached out and stroked me. They lifted me high into the air and passed me along the roof of the forest. I was filled with a wonderful floating power. The soft branches took me wherever I wanted to go.

In the morning I woke feeling wonderful. Instead of getting dressed I decided to move the bed. I wanted to sleep so that I could see out of the window. The bed was old and heavy. It wouldn't move. I could see that it had been in that spot for years and years.

I ran outside and fetched a long plank. I used it to lever the bed. After a lot of creaking it started to move.

Inch by inch. Finally I had it up against the window. The place where the bed had been was covered in dust. I swept it up gently.

The floor creaked under my feet. I knelt down and looked. There was a loose board.

'Breakfast,' yelled out Mum.

'Coming,' I shouted back.

I tried to prise up the board but it wouldn't budge. Suddenly it gave way and sprang out. It was almost as if a hidden hand had heaved it up.

I stared inside. Something glinted dully. I reached down and pulled out a rusty key.

'Shane,' yelled Mum.

'Coming,' I called. I shoved the key in my pocket and raced downstairs. I bolted my breakfast down. I was sure that the key would fit the door of the cupboard. The cupboard I had been forbidden to open.

'You can help me today,' said Dad. 'I'm going to cut back the overgrown trees and put the branches through the mulcher.'

I groaned inside. I was dying to run up and try the key in the cupboard. Now I wouldn't get a chance until after tea. Dad was a slave driver. He'd give me a big lecture about laziness if I tried to nick off.

4

All day we worked, cutting down branches and feeding them into the mulcher. It roared and spat out a waterfall of woodchips. It was amazing how it could turn a whole tree into sawdust in no time at all.

'Are you going to cut down the lemon trees?' I asked.

'Yes,' said Dad. 'I'm putting in native plants. Go on, you can go now. Thanks for helping.'

I ran up to my room and shut the door. Then I took out the rusty key and walked over to the cupboard. I put it in the lock and tried to move it. Blast. It didn't seem to fit. I jiggled and wiggled it. Then, just like the floorboard, it moved without warning. As if hidden fingers had twisted it.

The doorknob turned easily. I swung open the door.

The fox didn't move. It had been dead a long time. It hung from a hook at the back of the cupboard. Its body was flat as if it had been run over by a steam roller. Its long, bushy tail hung almost to the floor. Its eyes stared ahead without movement. They were made of glass. I could see that they were sewn on like buttons.

Suddenly the fox moved. Its mouth opened a fraction. My brain froze. The world seemed to spin. I was filled with terror. I gave a scream and slammed the door shut. Then I ran downstairs.

Tea was on the table. I didn't know what to do. Had the fox's mouth really opened? It couldn't have. Maybe I had disturbed it with the breeze of the door opening.

I wanted to tell Dad and Mum. But they had ordered me not to open the cupboard. Dad had lived in that room for all those years and he had never opened it.

I could just hear him giving me a lecture. 'One night,' he would say. 'You couldn't even go one night without breaking your word.'

I hadn't given my word actually. But that wouldn't make any difference. An order is an order.

As I ate my tea I thought about the fox. I'd seen it somewhere before. Then suddenly I realised. On the kitchen wall was an old photo of Grandad. Behind him was a hall stand. There were hats and scarves and umbrellas hanging on it. And a fox skin.

'What's that thing?' I said to Dad. I jumped up and pointed to the fox skin.

'A fox fur. It's the one Grandad shot. He preserved the skin and made it into a fur wrap for Grandma. But she wouldn't wear it.'

'Why not?'

'She said that she wasn't going to wear a dead animal around her neck. She felt sorry for it. She said it looked as if it was alive. Grandad was disappointed that she didn't like his gift.'

'What happened to it?' I asked.

'No one knows,' said Dad. 'I couldn't find it after Grandad died.'

'It might be in that locked cupboard,' I said.

Dad looked at me in a funny way. I went red. 'If it is,' he said, 'it stays there. A promise is a promise.'

We all looked at the picture. 'Pity the photo's only brown,' said Dad. 'That coat of Grandad's was bright red.

And his eyes were the clearest blue.'

I wasn't really interested in the colours that weren't in the photo. I was in a real pickle and I didn't know what to do. I had to sleep in a room with a dead fox in the cupboard. Why had Grandad locked the door and made everyone promise not to open it? What was it about that fox?

5

That night I dreamed more dreams about trees. But this time it was lemon trees. Or should I say lemon tree. A voice seemed to call me. It wanted me to go to the large lemon tree. The voice inside my head told me to go out into the night. And pick a lemon.

I cried out and sat up in bed. The cupboard door had swung open. The fox's glass eyes glinted in the moonlight. I thought it moved. It seemed to sigh gently.

Suddenly I knew I had nothing to fear. The fox was my friend. It was sad. Lonely. Lost.

I walked over and gently reached out. I stroked the soft fur with my hand. Dust fell softly away. A great sadness swept over me. The fox was like a beautiful empty bag. Its bones and heart and life were long gone.

And I knew where they were.

'All right,' I said. 'I'll do it.'

The fox made no answer. It hung limply like the moon's cast-off coat. I crept down the stairs. Mum and Dad were asleep. I walked between the shadows until

I reached the large lemon tree. Where the carcass of the fox had been buried, many years before.

The ripe lemons drooped between the silvery leaves. I knew which one to pick. My hand seemed to have a life of its own. It reached up and plucked a lemon from high on the tree.

I tiptoed back inside the house and crept up the silent stairs. The cupboard was open like a waiting mouth. I wasn't sure what to do with the lemon. The fox skin hung silently on its peg. I gently opened its jaws and placed the lemon between its teeth. Then I shut the door and jumped into bed.

I pulled the pillow over my head. But even so, I could hear a gentle chewing, sucking, swallowing sound from behind the door.

The fox was feasting.

I finally fell asleep. Deep in carefree slumber.

6

In the morning I peered into the cupboard. At first I thought that nothing had changed. The fox fur still flopped from its peg. But the lemon had gone. I stroked the fox. I ran its tail between my thumb and finger. At the very tip of its tail I stopped. It was hard inside, as if a piece of a broken pencil had been inserted there. It was a small bone.

I gasped. That bone had not been there the day before.

The next night I visited the lemon tree again. Again I fed the fox. And again his tail grew firmer. Strengthened by another bone.

Each day I helped my father chop the trees and feed the mulcher. And each night I fed the fox from the lemon tree.

At the end of two weeks the fox was round and plump. Its fur had lost its dust. It glistened, strong and full. It was a fine fox. But it still hung from the peg. Its head flopping near the floor.

My work was nearly done. On the second-last night I placed my hand on its chest.

I can't describe the thrill that ran up my arm. The fox's heart was beating. It was alive but not alive. It still dangled from the peg. But its nose was wet and warm. A red tongue trembled between its teeth.

I had done my work. The lemons had given back what my grandfather had taken and buried beneath the tree. I opened the cupboard door wide. 'Go,' I said. 'This is your chance.'

The fox didn't answer. Didn't move. Something was wrong.

The glass eyes stared without life.

The eyes. It needed its real eyes.

7

I stared out of the window at the first signs of the day. The last two lemons glowed redly in the sunrise.

The tree stretched upwards from its roots. Its branches were like arms offering gifts from below.

'Tomorrow,' I said. 'Tomorrow I'll get your eyes.'

I closed the door and snuggled down into my bed. I fell asleep for many hours.

The sound of the mulcher drilled away at my slumber. There was something wrong. In my dreams I knew it. I sat upright and listened to Dad feeding branches into the hungry machine.

'No,' I yelled. 'No.' I ran over to the window. 'Stop,' I screamed. 'Stop.'

I was too late. The lemon tree was nothing but a pile of wood chips. I ran down the stairs in my pyjamas and bare feet. 'The lemons,' I shouted. 'Did you save the last two lemons?'

Dad looked up in surprise. 'No,' he said. 'They were green.'

Tears ran down my face. I thought of the blind fox, still hanging in the blackness of the cupboard that for so long had been its coffin. I stood there and sobbed.

'They're only lemons,' said Dad. 'For goodness' sake. What a fuss.'

I couldn't tell him. I couldn't say anything. I trudged back to my room. 'I'm sorry, fox,' I said. 'Now you'll never see.'

A voice floated in the window. It was Dad. 'This little lemon tree still has two lemons, Shane. If you want lemons, why don't you take these?'

I stared sadly down. That tree wasn't any good. It wasn't growing where the fox had been buried. Still and all, it was worth a try.

8

I waited all day. I waited until the sun had set and the moon filled the evening. I walked slowly. Not really hoping. But wanting so badly to give the fox my last gifts.

The lemons seemed to tremble. They dropped into my hands as I reached up. As though they had been waiting.

What was inside? For a moment I wondered what I would see if I peeled the lemons. Two eyes? Or just pith and pips and lemon pulp? I shuddered.

I placed the lemons between the white teeth of my friend the fox. And shut the door. I heard nothing. No sighs. No chomps. No swallows.

I had failed the fox.

Slowly I walked downstairs to supper. Dad and Mum tried to cheer me up. 'Are you ill?' said Mum.

'Yes,' I said. 'I think I am. But you can't fix it with medicine.'

Dad looked up. 'What was that?' he said. 'I thought I heard something upstairs. Someone's in the house.'

We all ran up to my room. The cupboard door was open. The window was open. Dad looked at the empty cupboard. And then at me. I nodded my head. I didn't care what he said or what he did. I was happy in a way that I had never been happy before. I picked up the two glass eyes that lay rejected on the floor.

'Look,' shouted Mum.

On the edge of the garden, under the little lemon tree, stood a magnificent fox. Its tail glistened in the silver light. Its shoulders shivered. Its ears pricked and pointed towards us. It took our scent and turned and gazed.

We all gasped. 'Look at its eyes,' whispered Mum.

The fox stared at us. Unafraid. Its large blue eyes drank us in. They looked deep into me. I knew what they were saying.

'Thank you. And farewell.'

My eyes were moist. I wiped away a tear.

When I looked up, the fox had gone. I never saw it again.

In the morning the little lemon tree was dead. Every leaf was curled and brown.

'It's never grown well,' said Dad. 'And it should have. Because we planted it on Grandad's grave.'

Listen Ear

Tell one lie to your parents and you are history. One little fib and they won't ever believe you again.

1

'Brad,' said Dad, 'never, ever, ever touch this.' In his hand he had the most fantastic compass you have ever seen. Not the type that shows you where to go. The sort you draw circles with.

It was silver and had little metal bolts and a point as sharp as a needle. Instead of a pencil it had a little piece of lead held in by a tiny screw. I whistled. 'Wow,' I said. 'I bet it's worth a fortune.'

'It is,' said Dad. 'And I need it for my work. SO DON'T TOUCH IT.' He put it in the top drawer of the dressing table in his bedroom and shut it before I could even get a good look.

Geez, I longed for that compass. Just to hold it, I mean. Not to steal it or use it or anything like that. Just hold it. That's all I wanted to do.

That compass called to me. 'Brad,' I could hear it

saying, 'come and get me. Aren't I great? Pick me up. Look at me. Try me out.'

It didn't really say that. But in my mind it did. All I wanted was a hold. One mingy little hold.

After tea, Mum and Dad and my little sister Sophie went into the lounge to watch TV. It was my turn to do the dishes. Rats. I hate doing the dishes. It is so boring.

'Come and hold me,' called the compass. 'Brad, Brad, Brad.'

I had to go. I just had to. All I wanted was a look. That's all. Just a look. With the teatowel still in my hand I crept up the stairs. Click – I turned on the bedroom light. Softly, softly I tiptoed across the room. Gently, gently I pulled open the drawer. There it was. Dad's compass in all its glory. It sparkled. It twinkled. It was great.

'Pick me up,' it called. 'Pick me up. Just once.' I rubbed my glasses with a dirty finger and stared down at the compass.

It was more than flesh and blood could stand. I put the tea-towel down on the floor and picked up the compass with trembling fingers. It was much heavier than I expected. I opened it up and pretended to draw a little circle in the air.

Just then I heard a sort of scuffling noise. It was almost as if someone was watching. Oh no. Dad would kill me if he caught me with the compass. I dropped the compass into the drawer. Then I turned and ran.

As it turned out no one was coming. Mum and Dad and Sophie were still watching TV. Maybe the noise was a rat or something.

I walked into the lounge and sat down with the others. 'Bedtime,' said Mum. 'I'll finish the dishes.'

I snuggled down into bed. Something was wrong. The compass was going to cause trouble. I just knew it was. I couldn't get to sleep no matter how hard I tried. I always seem to break things. I mean, it isn't my fault. Mostly it is bad luck.

But parents don't understand about accidents. They still think it's your fault. That's why Dad didn't want me to touch the compass. But what could go wrong? I mean, I didn't break the compass, did I? It was safely back in the drawer.

I tossed and turned for a couple of hours until something terrible made me jump up. A yell filled the air. It was Dad. I could hear every word even though he was upstairs. 'The compass,' he screamed. 'It's gone.' I could hear footsteps coming my way quickly. I closed my eyes and pretended to be asleep. Maybe they would leave me alone until morning.

Fat chance. Dad ripped the covers back off the bed. 'Don't try that one,' he said. 'I know you're awake.' Boy was he mad.

'Brad,' he said, 'this time you've really gone too far. Where's my compass?'

'I don't know,' I said truthfully. 'I haven't touched it. Sophie must have taken it.'

'Sophie would never take it,' said Mum.

'Neither would I,' I said.

Mum and Dad both looked at me in silence. I knew they were remembering all the bad things I had done. Like eating Sophie's chocolate Easter bunny one night. Well, she didn't want it. It was five months old and starting to turn white. You know what it's like. You just start by nibbling a tiny bit off the ear where it won't be noticed. Then, before you can blink, the whole ear has gone. So then you might as well scoff the lot because you are going to get caught anyway.

'Did you go in our bedroom?' said Mum.

'No,' I said.

'Did you open the drawer?' asked Dad.

'No,' I answered.

'The drawer was open when we went up to bed,' said Dad.

They both looked at me with cold eyes. I felt sick in my stomach. I must have forgotten to close the drawer.

'And you didn't go into our room?' Mum asked again.

'No,' I said. I know I shouldn't have lied but someone stole the compass and it wasn't me. I didn't want to get the blame for something I didn't do.

'Well,' said Mum, 'if you didn't go into the room how come this was there?' She held up the wet tea towel that I had been using to dry the dishes. I suddenly went cold all over. Now they would never believe that I hadn't taken the compass.

Well, talk about trouble. They went on and on and on. They wouldn't believe me. Just because I told one little lie. I was grounded until the compass was returned. They wouldn't even let me go to the movies with them the next night. Even though they had promised to take me. And the worst of it was that Sophie got to go. And it must have been her who took the compass.

That's how I happened to be home on my own. Late at night.

2

'The baby-sitter will be here in half an hour,' said Mum.

'I don't need a babysitter,' I said. 'I'm not scared. And anyway, she just sits on the phone talking to her boyfriend all night.'

'Where does he live?' said Dad. He was always worried about people making long-distance calls.

'Darwin,' I said.

'He does not,' said Mum. 'He lives right here in Melbourne.'

Dad looked at me with a bit of a smile but he soon lost it when Mum started up. 'Brad, I really thought you'd have learned not to tell lies by now,' she said.

'It was just a joke,' I said.

The three of them hurried out to the car and drove off.

I locked the front door and stared out of the window. It was growing dark. And it was raining. The clock ticked loudly in the hall. It felt as if I was the only person in the world. I started to feel sorry for myself. It wasn't fair. Okay, I did tell a couple of porkies but I didn't steal the compass. I really wanted to go to the movies and now I was being punished for something I didn't do.

I went over and looked at my face in the lounge-room mirror. My reflection stared back at me. My face looked mean. I just stared and stared into my own eyes. Suddenly I got the creeps. It was as if the reflection wasn't me. As if it was someone else. I gave a shiver and turned on the television.

Where was that babysitter? She should be here by now. Outside it was black and cold. I tried to watch the television but my mind just wasn't on it.

Boomp, scroffle, scraffle. What was that? A sound upstairs. Rats. The rats were in the roof again. Or were they? A little shiver ran down my neck.

Maybe the babysitter had crashed her car. I decided to ring up and see if she was okay. June, that was her name. But what was her other name? Dalton. That was it. June Dalton.

Suddenly something terrible happened. The picture on the television zapped itself into a tiny square and disappeared. At the same time the lights went out. Oh no. A power failure. The lines were down again.

I ran to the phone. Nothing. Just a low whistling noise coming down the line.

The house was silent. Where was the babysitter? I knew deep inside that she wasn't coming. It was going to be a long night.

Boomp, scroffle, scraffle. There was that noise again. This time from downstairs. Rats. Of course it was rats. No one would want to get in and get me. Would they? The hairs started to stand up on the back of my neck.

There was only one thing to do. Go to bed and fall asleep as quickly as possible. I couldn't spend all night in the dark scared out of my wits. I felt my way along the hall and into my bedroom.

I pulled off my shoes, took off my glasses and jumped into bed with my clothes on. Then I closed my eyes and tried to sleep. But sleep wouldn't come.

3

So here I am, surrounded by the sounds of the night.

Houses make a lot of noise when you are the only person in them. Squeak. Creak. Rustle. Rumble. What was that? Nothing. Don't be silly. You are alone. Aren't you?

Who would want to get you? Just a boy. Just an ordinary boy. Okay, so I told a couple of lies. But I'm not really mean. I don't deserve to die. I'm quite a nice person really.

What if there was someone under the bed? What if

a hand slowly started to pull the blankets down. Until I was uncovered? A horrible cold hand with grey fingers. Go away. Go away if you are there. Leave me alone. I won't tell any more lies, God. I promise. And I'll do the washing-up on my own. Every night.

Well, nearly every night.

Where did that shadow in the corner come from? It looks like a man with a hat. Standing. Staring. Who's that breathing so loudly?

Me, of course.

Only me. I am alone. I hope. I try to breathe softly. Just in case there is someone creeping around looking for me. They won't know where I am. Unless I make a noise.

The room starts to become lighter. It's funny that – how you can see better in the dark after a while. It is not a man in the corner. It is just my dressing-gown hanging on a hook.

But what is that lump on the wall? That wasn't there yesterday. A small bump in the plaster. It must be my imagination. I can't see a thing without my glasses. I reach out and put them on. Then I take another look. Yes, it is a lump on the wall. Where did that come from? It looks like a table-tennis ball half buried in the wall. I stare and stare at it.

It's weird how your mind plays tricks on you. I could swear that the lump is bigger than before. I could swear that it is growing.

Aaaaaaaaargh. It is growing. I can see it wobbling and moving. I can't take my eyes off it. I am hypnotised by it. A horrible, swelling growth on the wall.

'Mum,' I want to scream. But I am too frightened. The word is frozen in my throat.

I am trembling with fear. I am too scared to run. And too scared to stay. Help. Help. Someone. Anyone. Please. Make the lump go away. Come and save me.

I need help.

It is wiggling. The ear is wiggling.

The ear?

Yes. Oh horrible, horrible, horrible. The lump is in the shape of an ear. A wiggling, disgusting, plaster ear on the wall. It is listening. Listening. Listening.

It is the ear of the house. I bet it heard me tell Mum lies. It is the ear that hears all. Knows all. Understands all. Sneaky. Snaky. Snoopy. It is looking for liars.

Well, listen, ear. Just see what you think of this. I take a deep breath. I fill up my lungs. I am terrified but I must be brave. I yell as loud as I can.

'Nick off, ear.'

The sound echoes around the empty rooms. But the ear does not nick off. It just wiggles a little bit. Like a worm on the end of a hook.

4

All is silent again. Tick, tick, tick. Rustle, rustle. Breathe in. Breathe out. Silently. Quiet.

Wiggle, wiggle. There it goes again. Don't annoy it. Don't shout. Don't even look. Pretend it is not there.

The ghastly ear on the wall.

Oh, oh, oh. No. It isn't. Not another lump. It can't be. I sneak a look through half-closed eyelids. Another foul lump is swelling out of the plaster. Yes, oh yuck. Another ear. A pair of ears wiggling on the wall. Stop, stop, stop.

Be a dream. Be a nightmare. Don't be real. Please don't be real.

I look at the wall. But the ears are still there. This is not a dream. This is real. The ears are still there in the wall. One of them has an earring. Just like mine but made of plaster. The ears are living, wriggling plaster.

There is more movement. It is as if the plaster is growing a mole. Or bubbling like thick soup in a dark pot. Bits are boiling and growing.

Oh, what's this? A nose. And eyes. And a chin. A face grows like a flower opening on fast forward.

A face in the wall. The plaster eyes roll around. The nose twitches. The mouth opens and closes but it says nothing. It is like the television with the sound turned down. The eyes stare at me. They see me hiding there under the covers, trying not to look.

I have seen this face before. But where? Whose face is this?

What can I do? I can't stay here with the fiendish face. I will run for it. Down to the kitchen. I will wait in the kitchen until Mum and Dad come home.

The face is still boiling and bubbling. What? It has grown glasses. They are just like mine but made of plaster.

I stare at the face. It stares back at me. Blinking with plaster eyes.

I know where I have seen this face before. I have seen it in the mirror.

It is my face.

I scream. I jump out of bed. I race along to the kitchen and slam the door. I fall panting to the floor. I am never going in that bedroom again.

Oh Dad, Mum, Sophie, babysitter. Where are you? Come home, come home, come home.

I can't bear to look at the walls. Or go near them. So I sit on the floor with my back against the fridge. It is cold on the tile floor but I am going to stay there until someone comes home.

I lean my head back on the fridge door and close my eyes. The metal is cold and hard against my head. And it is moving. Like worms crawling in my hair. For a moment I just sit there, frozen. Then I scream and scramble across the floor.

The face has erupted in the door of the fridge. Only now it is a horrible, horrible steel face with shiny white skin and lips and eyes. Its glasses are also white steel.

The face, my face is trying to talk. Its lips are moving but nothing is coming out. What is it trying to say?

It is me. I know that it is me. It is my own conscience. Telling me not to tell lies.

'Leave me alone,' I scream. 'Leave me alone.' I bolt into the lounge and crouch behind the sofa.

But it has followed me.

There it is on the window. Now the face is made of glass. I can see right through its dreadful, moving lips. Is it calling me a liar? What is it trying to say? What is it doing? Why is it after me? Why? Why? Why?

I jump up and roar out of the room. I am running away from myself. No one can do that.

5

I bolt into Dad's study. The walls are all made of wood. The face can't get me here. I am safe.

Outside the rain has stopped. The moon is playing hide and seek behind the clouds. How I wish I was on the moon. I stare up but then look away. Even the moon has a face.

The moonlight shines on the dark wooden panels. The grain makes strange shapes like whirlpools in a rotting swamp. The lines begin to swirl and run like a crazy river.

My heart starts to beat faster and faster. I can feel the blood running beneath my skin. Sheer terror is washing within me.

The fearsome face has made itself in a panel. My awful reflection glares down at me through its wooden glasses.

Its mouth opens and shuts without a sound. It is trying to say something. But what?

It is no use running. The face can turn itself into plaster and steel and glass. And wood. There is no escape.

A saying that I once heard is stirring in the back of my mind. What is it? I know. 'The best form of defence is attack.'

Could I attack the face? It might grab me and pull me into the wall. Never to be seen again. But I can't keep running. If I go outside it might appear on a tree. Or the footpath. There is nowhere to run. Nowhere to go. No escape.

I must beat it at its own game. Think, think, think. What is its weakness? It is my face. How can I outsmart it?

I am breathing so heavily that my glasses start to fog up. I give them a wipe. I can't see a thing without my glasses. If I lose them I am gone.

The face still mouths silent words. And peers at me through its wooden glasses.

Okay. It is risky. It is a chance. But I have to take it. On hands and knees I crawl towards the grained face in the wood. Behind the sofa. Along. I must keep my head down. I must get close without it knowing what I am up to.

I crouch low behind the sofa like a cat waiting for a bird. I can't see the face and it can't see me. Unless it has moved.

Now. Go, go, go.

I fly at the face like an arrow from a bow.

Snatch. Got them. Got them. I can't believe it. I have grabbed the wooden glasses. The face is horrified. Its mouth opens in a silent scream. Its eyes are wide and staring. It rushes blindly around the walls. Like a rat running under a sheet it shoots across the floor.

Its features change as it rushes to and fro. Glass, wood, plastic. It bubbles across the floor. Searching, searching, searching. Its mouth snaps and snarls. Its eyes gape and glare but without the glasses it cannot see. Oh, what will it do if it catches me?

Flash. A blinding light fills the room. What? I blink in the glare. Oh yes, yes, yes. The power has come back on. I have light. Now maybe the fiendish face will go back where it came from.

But no. In the light it is more fearsome than ever. More real. I am so scared. My knees are shaking so much that I can hardly move.

Suddenly from the lounge room I hear voices. A woman's voice. And a child's. They are home. 'Mum,' I scream. 'Mum, Mum, Mum.' I race into the hall towards the lounge and the face follows my voice. But I don't care. They are here. Help has arrived. I am saved.

I rush into the lounge and then freeze. There are people there all right. But they won't be any use to me. They are on the television. The television has come back on with the power. It is my favourite show – *Round the Twist*.

6

I run out of the room and up the stairs. The face follows the sound of my thumping feet. Now it is made of carpet. A carpet face flowing up the stairs after my footsteps.

I run into Mum and Dad's room and slam the door.

Fool. Fool. What a mistake. The face heard the door slam. It bulges out onto the door. Staring. Searching. It knows I am in the room. I climb carefully onto the bed and try to breathe quietly. It can't find me. Not without the glasses. Not unless I make a noise. Don't move. Don't make the bed squeak.

The face starts to search. Up and down each wall. Across the ceiling. Under the bed. Its lips are pulled down in an unhappy pout. It circles the bed like a shark around a boat. It knows where I am.

'Listen,' I yell, 'I am sorry I told a lie. I'm sorry, sorry, sorry. Okay?'

This is weird. I am telling myself that I am sorry.

The face suddenly smiles. It is happy. Its mouth is making silent words. What is it trying to say? One word. It is saying the same word over and over again.

It is hard reading lips. But suddenly I know what the word is.

'Glasses,' I yell at the face.

The face nods. Up and down with a limp smile.

What is it about these glasses? I take my own glasses off and carefully put the wooden ones on my own face.

Straightaway everything changes. The whole house is different. I can see through the walls and the ceiling. The house is a ghost house and I can see right through it.

Wires and building materials. Nails. Rubbish. An old newspaper. A drink bottle left by the builders. A rat's nest underneath the dressing-table. A rat scurries away through a hole in the wall.

This is amazing. I can see into all the rooms from where I am standing. It is like X-ray vision.

My mind starts to turn over. Somewhere in all this is the answer to a puzzle. The rat's nest. I stare and stare at the rat's nest. All of this started with rats scuttling around in the wall. I stare into the nest. Then I smile.

So does the face. It is happy too.

I do not know if the face is my conscience. Perhaps it is the best and the worst of me. It has chased me around and made me feel guilty. And now it has helped me out.

I step down from the bed. I walk over to the grinning copy of myself and put the glasses on its cheeks. It blinks. 'Thank you,' I say. 'You can go now.'

Slowly, slowly, with just the hint of a smile, the face melts back into the wall. I know that it is happy.

Downstairs a door bangs. 'Mum,' I yell. 'Dad. Sophie.' I rush happily down the stairs.

'The babysitter rang the cinema,' says Mum. 'Her car broke down. And the phones weren't working. Are you okay?'

'Sit down,' I say. 'You are not going to believe this.'

They sit down and don't say a thing while I tell them the story. I tell them everything and don't leave out one little detail.

I am right about one thing though. They do not believe me.

'It was a dream,' says Mum.

'It was a lie,' says Dad.

They think I am still lying. They won't believe me. 'It's the truth,' I yell. 'It is, it is, it is.'

'There is one way to prove your story,' says Dad. 'We will move the dressing-table and see if there is a rat's nest underneath. Then we will know for sure.'

We all walk up to the bedroom and Dad tries to move the dressing-table. It is very heavy so all four of us join in and help. In the end we lift it into the middle of the room.

There against the wall is a rat's nest. There is no rat in it. It has run away because of all the noise. There is no rat. But there is a compass. Right there where the rat carried it.

'Now do you believe me?' I say.

I look at Mum and Dad and Sophie. Their mouths just open and shut but no sound comes out.

No sound at all.

Shadows

Think of the meanest thing you ever did.

Okay. So why did you do it?

You don't know, do you? No one knows why they suddenly do something mean.

Even your mum and your dad can be awful now and then. Or your lovely old grandma. Or the prime minister. Even the bishop in his church. Everyone is sneaky sometimes. Greedy sometimes. Rude sometimes. Selfish sometimes. No one is perfect. It is okay to be human.

Sometimes, when I am bad-tempered, my mum will say, 'Richard is not himself today.'

And this makes me wonder. If you are not yourself, who are you?

1

On the day I found out, I was walking around the fairground without a worry in the world. I had no money but there was plenty to look at for nothing. The animal nursery. The man on stilts. The busker playing the violin. The man throwing fire-sticks into the air. All the stalls selling jewellery and scented candles.

Little kids with their balloons. Mothers and fathers pushing prams.

Yes. The best things in life are free.

Except for show bags, the Ghost Train, the Sledgehammer, the Rocket to Mars, the Rotor, the Hall of Mirrors, and Bubbles Bo Bo.

All of them cost five dollars each to get in. And I had no dollars. And no cents. I was broke.

Actually, the Hall of Mirrors gave me the creeps. There was a little man sitting outside selling tickets. His name was Mr Image. He wore an old baseball cap and had a five o'clock shadow. And he had mean eyes. They seemed to see right into you. He made me shiver. But all the same, I wanted to go in. I wanted to have a look at myself in the Hall of Mirrors.

But not as much as I wanted to have a look at Bubbles Bo Bo. She was a beautiful lady sitting in a bath full of bubbles with nothing on.

Not a stitch on. That's what all the kids at school reckoned anyway.

I walked past her tent and pretended not to be gazing up at the painting outside. The one of Bubbles sitting in the bath with a bare leg held up in the air.

You couldn't see all the other bits. Bubbles was covered in bubbles, if you know what I mean.

Suddenly I had an idea. A way to get to see Bubbles Bo Bo for nothing.

I slowly walked up to the guy who was selling tickets.

He was a rough-looking bloke with a whole heap of earrings and tattoos.

'Excuse me,' I said. 'But would you like someone to sweep up inside? For nothing.'

He looked down at me with a big grin that grew bigger. And bigger. He threw back his head and started to laugh. He had long yellow teeth and he laughed so madly that I could see right inside his mouth. The dangling thing up the back was wobbling around like crazy. 'Hey, Harry,' he yelled. 'Get a load of this kid. He's trying to sneak a look at Bubbles by offering to sweep the floor.'

My face started to burn. I didn't know where to hide. Everyone in the world seemed to be grinning and looking at me.

A toothless, skinny man hurried out and started to cackle like a chook. He doubled up, clutching his side and gasping, 'Wants to sweep the floor – for nothing. Wants a free peek at Bubbles. Ha, ha ho, ho ha.'

Oh, if only I could have vanished. If only I could have gone up in smoke. All the passers-by seemed to be watching me. Knowing what was inside my head. What a sleaze. That's what they were all thinking.

I started to stumble away. Trying to find somewhere to hide. Looking for a rock to crawl under.

Suddenly I heard a voice.

'You can sweep my floor. And I'll pay you for it.'

It was Mr Image. The man of mirrors.

'Come back in the morning,' he said. 'At first light. I'll pay you ten dollars to sweep the Hall of Mirrors.'

A cold weight seemed to be sliding down my throat. Like an iceblock inside me it travelled down, down, down, until even my toes started to shiver.

He smiled. A cold smile. As if no one was home behind those mean eyes.

Everything inside me told me to run away. But I thought about the money. And Bubbles Bo Bo. And nodded my head.

2

The next morning I arrived at the fairground just as the sun was rising. All the show people were getting ready for the day. An old man was washing down his elephant. Two guys in a truck were unloading packets of hot dogs. A kid about my age was taking the covers off the dodgem cars.

I walked nervously over to the Hall of Mirrors. 'Ah, Richard,' said Mr Image, 'you've come to work.'

He handed me a bucket of water and a mop, and disappeared into the large gloomy tent. I followed him.

'How did you know my—' I started to say.

Mr Image interrupted me in a voice like a wet whisper. 'Use the mop,' he said. 'A broom raises dust and it gets on the mirrors.'

He poured some liquid soap into the bucket and

walked away. His feet made a rustling sound as if he was walking on dry leaves.

The tent was filled with corridors that were lined with mirrors. Like a maze with openings shooting off here and there. It was gloomy, which was strange for a place filled with reflections.

I started to clean up underneath a bent mirror. A fat, fat Richard copied my every move. I walked backwards and forwards, watching my image grow bigger and smaller.

All of the mirrors gave weird reflections. Fat. Thin. Ugly. Bent. Upside down. Crinkled.

I mopped and stared. Mopped and stared. It was lonely. It was quiet. It was creepy. Inside the Hall of Mirrors.

The silent morning moved on. I seemed a million miles away from the show and all its life outside. I was alone but surrounded by dozens of people. Bent and horrible copies of myself mopping the floors all around me. Repulsive reflections holding their warped mops in twisted fingers.

I shivered. Why had I taken this terrible job? I wanted to burst out of this tent and flee into the real world outside. But somewhere down there. In the gloom. Was Mr Image. Moving around like a rat in a cupboard. I was too scared to run out on him. He was the sort of person who would follow you. Not let go.

Minutes ticked by. Or was it hours? It was hard to tell.

My ugly companions mopped silently alongside me. They rested silently. Copied my every move without a sound.

I started to mop more quickly. I wanted to get it over with. Finish up. Take my money and run. Faster and faster I mopped. And faster and faster the freaky copies moved with me.

I turned a corner and faced a door.

On it was a sign which simply said: RICHARD'S ROOM.

3

A small building stood within the tent. Made of steel. About twice the size of a toilet.

Richard's Room? What did that mean? Had Mr Image put that sign there especially for me? Or was there another Richard? And what was inside?

I didn't know whether I was supposed to sweep in there or not. 'Hey,' I called out. 'Hey.' The silent army of terrible copies in the mirrors mouthed my words in silence. Jagged, torn mouths of every shape seemed to be laughing at me. Copies of myself.

It was like being left alone in bed in the dark of night. You hear a noise. You want to call out 'Mum'. But if there is a burglar, if there is an intruder, he will know where you are. And come for you like a shadow.

'Don't be silly,' I said to myself. 'Don't be stupid. It's just a room.'

I pushed open the door and stepped inside with my mop and bucket.

There was nothing in the room except one mirror, which filled up a whole wall. Not a trick mirror. It was straight and flat like the ones in your bathroom at home. The wall opposite the mirror was covered by a picture. A huge painting which reached from the floor to the ceiling. A scene with a flat plain that was edged with jungle growth.

The door clicked shut behind me. Just a soft sound. But I knew, I just knew that it was as final as the clang of a noisy lock on a jail cell.

There was no handle.

Just a keyhole.

No way of escape.

'Hey,' I screamed. 'Help. Let me out.' My words were soaked up by the thick walls. I knew that no one could hear me. I kicked and shouted and punched the door. It didn't move. Not even a rattle.

I was alone.

Or was I? The mirror glowed faintly as if it had a light of its own. I moved over and stared into it. The warmth from my body drained out through my feet and I shivered in horror. It was not an ordinary mirror. I could see the reflection of the wall behind me. The flat plain. The jungle. The vines and creepers and thorns. The towering trees. They were all there.

But I wasn't.

I couldn't see my own reflection. It was just as if I wasn't there.

I turned back to the door and began kicking and screaming and yelling. I kicked until my foot hurt. But no one came. I was locked away from the world in this silent room. I might as well have been in a coffin way under the ground. No one could hear me. No one except Mr Image knew where I was.

I stared into the softly glowing mirror. Something had changed. Something was different. There, across the plain. In a tree. On the edge of the jungle was something like a coconut on a tree. But it was moving. It ducked back out of sight.

A face. Someone or something was living inside the mirror.

I turned back to the door. 'Get me out of here,' I screamed.

No reply. I turned back to the mirror. The figure was no longer in the tree. It was moving closer. Dodging from one clump of grass to the other. It saw me and stopped. Almost as if frozen by my gaze.

Could this really be happening? I rubbed my eyes and then stared. Zip. It had moved closer.

Now I could see the figure more clearly. It was a person. Staring at me from the cover of a small bush. A person who I thought I knew.

My heart was pounding like a million mallets. My hands were clammy and cold.

I tried to stop panic taking control of me. I tried to force my brain to think. I didn't want this mirror man to come closer. I had to help myself. There was no one else.

I snatched a glance at the door. How could I get out?

Then I turned back to the mirror. He had snuck up. And he wasn't a mirror man. He was a mirror boy. Sneaking forward every time I looked away. There was something about him. What was it?

I stared and stared, trying not to blink. He stared back from a distance. Waiting for his chance to move forward.

Time passed. The seconds and minutes dragged by like a slug in the sunshine.

Who was he? I decided to find out. I closed my eyes and counted to five.

Oh, no. No, no, no. Now he was much, much closer. And I could see his face. I knew who he was.

Me. The boy was me. My nose, my ears, my hair. It was me but not me. Not a reflection. More like a living shadow.

He froze under my gaze. I was scared. More frightened than I have ever been in my life.

Think. Use your brain, Richard. That's what I told myself. He wouldn't or couldn't move forward while I was watching him.

I stared harder and harder. Not even blinking. He didn't like it. He didn't like me looking at him. Like a startled rabbit in the beam of a spotlight he blinked and shuffled. And started to move backwards.

'Go,' I said to myself in the mirror. 'Go, go, go.'

Slowly and then faster and faster, he moved away. Suddenly he turned and ran back into the jungle. He clambered up a tree. I could see him there. A tiny distant face. Like a coconut in among the branches.

But I knew he was waiting. Looking for his chance to creep up.

'Ah, Richard,' said a soft, wet voice, 'there you are.'

4

I hadn't heard the door open. But I heard it click shut. And I knew who it was. Mr Image.

'Look at me,' he said.

I snatched a glance. He was staring into the mirror himself.

I knew his game. He wanted me to look away from the mirror. So that my mirror shadow could sneak up again.

I wasn't falling for that. No way.

'Look at me when I speak to you,' he hissed.

I was his prey. Like a fly in a spider's web.

But I was in control. There was no way I was going to take my eyes off that shadow-boy in the mirror. No way. It wasn't going to sneak up on me.

I edged away from Mr Image. If he grabbed me and wrestled me to the floor it would give my shadow time to run up. Mr Image moved with me. I could feel his jacket brushing against me.

'Look at me,' he screeched. He didn't grab me. He was transfixed. He was staring into the mirror himself. Suddenly I realised why. There was another figure on the edge of the forest. Wearing a baseball cap. Unshaven and rough.

Mr Image had a shadow in the mirror himself.

Suddenly Mr Image lost his cool. He turned and grabbed me by the arm. 'Look here, look here,' he shouted.

But I didn't. I watched Mr Image's shadow sprint across the plain. Closer, closer. Jumping tussocks of grass. Dashing furiously towards us. The shadow was a copy of Mr Image. Another person like himself. Similar but not the same.

Mr Image grabbed my head. He twisted it towards himself. The pain in my neck was terrible. He was too strong for me. His own hatred and terror filled him with enormous strength.

I tried to speak but could only wheeze out the words, 'He's coming for you, Mr Image.'

He gave a strangled scream and let go. He peered into the mirror and saw his own shadow almost upon us. He stared and stared with wide-open eyes. The shadow halted. Frozen by his gaze.

Mr Image was terrified of the other version of himself. But I wasn't. The copy of Mr Image was not a copy. It was an opposite. It had a kind, loving face with warm eyes.

My own hateful shadow was now halfway across the plain. It had snuck up when Mr Image grabbed my head. It had been waiting for its chance.

There in the mirror our shadows were held frozen by our stares. Neither of us could look away.

Mr Image began to walk backwards in the small room. The door behind was locked. But he could get out. He would know how to open the door. He was feeling in his pocket for the key.

'I think you need a little more time on your own,' he said.

He was going to leave me in there by myself. In the end I would have to take my eyes off the mirror. In the end I would have to fall asleep.

And then. And then.

The shadow would come for me.

I had to do something. I had to stop Mr Image rushing out of that door. He took another step backwards.

Suddenly I tore my eyes away from the mirror. So did Mr Image. He was fumbling around with a key, trying to get it into the lock.

Out of the corner of my eye I saw the two shadows sprinting towards us. Mr Image's shadow was much closer. Almost up to us. My own was further back across the plain but running fast.

I looked around for a weapon. And found one.

'Cop this,' I shouted.

I threw the contents of the bucket into Mr Image's

face. He screamed as the soapy water stung his eyes. He rubbed and wiped and wept in anger. But he couldn't see.

I fixed my shadow with a stare. And held him there. Inside his glass prison.

Mr Image's shadow was closing the gap. Running furiously. Bigger and closer. He was upon us. He leapt at the mirror from the other side. Like a horse clearing a hurdle he passed through the mirror. He landed at the feet of Mr Image, who was still screaming and rubbing his eyes.

Without a word the shadow grabbed Mr Image, lifted him above his head and twirled him around. Then he threw him into the mirror.

Mr Image screamed. A drawn-out, horrible cry. It was pitched so high that it hurt my ears. Then, like a glass broken by the voice of an opera singer, the mirror shattered. It fell to the floor in a million pieces. Mr Image was gone. Trapped inside his own mirror.

I turned and faced Mr Image's shadow.

He smiled at me with a warm, kind face. Little crinkles ran out beside his friendly eyes. The shadow was nothing to fear.

'Thanks,' he said. 'It's nice to be back.'

The shadow unlocked the door and took me out into the sunshine. 'Here's your pay,' he said. 'Ten dollars as agreed.'

He was such a nice man. He really was.

I smiled back at him. 'What was all that about?' I asked as I took the money. 'Did it really happen?'

He nodded. 'Everyone has a shadow,' he said. 'We all have a mixture. Strong and weak. Kind and cruel. Generous and mean.'

I shivered. 'I'm scared of my own shadow,' I said.

He nodded. 'Don't be,' he said. 'Take a walk in the sun. Think about it.'

5

I did take a walk. Past the animal nursery. The man on stilts. The busker playing the violin. The man throwing fire-sticks into the air, and all the stalls selling jewellery and scented candles. Little kids with their balloons. Mothers and fathers pushing prams.

It was really busy. But I didn't feel part of it. I couldn't stop thinking about my shadow.

The thing about it was this. Your shadow couldn't get you if you kept an eye on it. You could learn to live with the other side of yourself. It really wasn't so bad. We all do selfish things now and then. But so what? Just don't let it get out of hand.

That's how I figured it anyway. I wandered back towards the Hall of Mirrors. I wanted to ask the man from the mirror if I was right.

But he was gone. The grass was all flattened where the tent had been. He had packed up and left.

The guy with the earrings and the tattoos was still

there with his tent though. I walked over to him. 'I've got a question,' I said.

He leered at me with a raised eyebrow. But he gave me the answer all the same.

'Five dollars,' he told me.

I pushed the five dollars into his hand and went in to have a peek at Bubbles Bo Bo.

Okay, so my mum wouldn't like it. And some people might even think I was a sleaze. But what the heck. There's two sides to all of us.

No one's perfect.

A Good Tip For Ghosts

Dad was scabbing around in the rubbish.

'How embarrassing,' said Pete. 'It's lucky there's no one else here to see us.'

I looked around the tip. He was right. No one was dumping rubbish except us. There was just Dad, me, and my twin brother Pete. The man driving the bulldozer didn't count. He was probably used to people coming to the tip with junk and then taking a whole pile of stuff back home.

It was a huge tip with a large, muddy pond in the middle. I noticed a steer's skull on a post in the water. There were flies everywhere, buzzing and crawling over the disgusting piles. Thousands of seagulls were following the bulldozer looking for rotten bits of food.

'These country tips are fantastic,' yelled Dad. 'Come and help me get this.' He was trying to dig out an old pram. I looked around and groaned. Another car had just pulled up. It was a real flash one. A Mercedes.

We had just arrived in Allansford the day before. It was a little country town where everybody would know what was going on. Pete and I had to start at a new school the next day. The last thing we wanted was someone to see us digging around in the tip.

A man and a boy got out of the Mercedes. They had a neat little bag of rubbish which the man dropped onto the ground. A cloud of flies rose into the air. 'Let's get out of here,' the man said to the boy. 'This place stinks.'

The boy was about my age but he was twice as big as me. He had red hair and he looked tough. I could see that he was grinning his head off and staring at our car. The back seat of our old bomb was full of Dad's findings. There was a mangled typewriter, a baseball bat, two broken chairs, a torn picture of a green lady lying on a tree branch and a bike with no wheels. I blushed. Dad just could not go to the tip without taking half of it back home with him.

I looked up at the kid with red hair again. He was pointing at Dad and laughing fit to bust. 'Oh no,' groaned Pete. 'Look what he has got now.'

Dad had run over to the bulldozer and held up his hand to stop the driver. He was digging around in front of its blade. He had found an arm sticking out of the junk. It looked like a human arm but it wasn't. It was the arm of one of those shop dummies they put dresses on. Dad pulled and yelled and jiggled until he got the whole thing out. Then he stood there holding it up for all the world to see. A female shop dummy with no clothes on.

It had a wig for hair but apart from that it was stark naked. Its left arm pointed up at the sky. It looked like Dad was standing there with a naked woman. The red-haired kid and his father were both laughing by now. The boy bent down and picked up something from the ground. Then they got into their Mercedes and disappeared through the gate. Pete and I hung our heads with shame. We couldn't bring ourselves to look as Dad dragged the dummy back to the car. I hoped like anything that the red-haired kid didn't go to Allansford School.

'Wonderful,' hooted Dad as he examined the shop dummy. 'Your mother will be pleased. She can use this for making dresses.'

'Don't give me that,' yelled Pete. 'You promised Mum that you wouldn't bring anything back from the tip.'

Dad looked a bit sheepish. 'This is different, boys. This isn't junk. This is valuable stuff. Now give me a hand to get this dummy into the car.'

'Not me,' I said.

'Nor me,' added Pete. 'I'm not touching her. She hasn't got any clothes on. It's rude.'

2

There was no room in the back of the car so Dad sat her up in the front. He put the seatbelt on her to stop her falling over. Her lifted-up arm poked through a rust hole in the roof.

'Where are we supposed to sit?' I asked. 'There's no room in the back.'

'One on each side of her,' said Dad. 'We'll all sit in the front. There's plenty of room.'

So that's how we went home. Shame. Oh terrible shame. Driving along the road with a naked dummy sitting between us. Every time we passed someone Pete and I ducked down so that they couldn't see us. Dad just laughed. It was all right for him. He wasn't starting at a new school in the morning.

Then it happened. A blue flashing light. A siren. A loud voice saying, 'Pull over driver.'

It was the police.

A policeman got off his motorbike and walked slowly to the car. He pulled off his gloves and adjusted his sunglasses. Then he leaned in the window. 'What's this naked lady . . . ?' he started off in a cross voice. But then he started laughing. He doubled up holding his side and pointing to the dummy. 'We had a report that there was a naked woman,' he managed to get out in between gasps. 'But it's only a shop dummy.'

I thought he was never going to stop laughing but finally he said, 'Where did you get all this stuff, sir?'

'The Allansford tip,' answered Dad.

'The locals call it Haunted Tip,' said the policeman with a grin. He seemed to want to stay and talk. He probably was trying to figure out if Dad was a nut case or not. Pete and I just sat there trying not to be seen.

'No one will go there after dark,' he told us. 'They say the ghost of Old Man Chompers walks that tip at night.'

'Old Man Chompers?' said Dad.

'Yes, he was the caretaker of the tip long ago. They say he was minding his two grandchildren there one day. The children disappeared and were never found. The ground collapsed and all the rubbish fell into a huge hole. People think the children were buried under piles of rubbish. Their bodies were never discovered because the hole filled up with water and formed a lake. Not long after that Old Man Chompers died. People say they have seen him walking the tip at night. He pokes at the rubbish, turning things over. He is looking for his lost grandchildren. He moans and calls out for his lost darlings.'

I shivered and looked at Pete. 'You won't catch me going to that tip again,' I said.

'Good,' said the policeman. 'It's a dangerous spot. No place for kids. Anyway – it is said that Old Man Chompers can't leave the tip until he finds his darlings. He has to stay there until he finds them. That's why he wanders the lonely tip at night. He might think that you two would do instead, if he caught you there.' Then he said something that made my knees wobble. 'His grand-children were twins. And Old Man Chompers had poor eyesight. He might mistake you boys for his lost grandchildren.' The policeman looked us straight in the eyes and then turned and walked off, chuckling as he went.

3

The next day Pete and I started at Allansford School. It was even worse than we thought it would be. The red-haired kid was waiting at the gate with his tough mates. 'Here they are,' he yelled with glee. 'The twins from the tip.' In a loud voice he started to tell everyone about Dad and the naked shop dummy. Pete and I looked at each other helplessly. We couldn't deny the story. It was true. I could feel tears starting to form behind my eyes. I had to stop them escaping so I blinked real hard. I noticed that Pete was doing the same thing.

It is bad enough starting a new school at the best of times. But when you have to live down something like this it is just terrible. Fortunately the bell went and we had to go inside.

At recess time, though, it was even worse. 'I'm the top dog here,' said the red-haired boy. His name was James Gribble. He pushed Pete in the chest. 'What's your name, kid?' he asked roughly.

'Pete.'

Gribble gave a twisted grin. 'This twin is Pete, so this one,' he said, pointing at me, 'must be Repeat. Pete and Repeat, the scabby twins from the tip.' All the kids started to laugh. Some of them weren't laughing too loudly though. I could see that they didn't like Gribble much but they were too scared of him to do anything.

After the laughter died down Gribble went and fetched a shoebox with a small hole in the end. 'I'm the boss here,' he said. 'Every new kid has to take my nerve test. If you pass the nerve test, you are okay. If you won't do it, I thump you every day until you do.' He held up a clenched fist. The kids all crowded around to see what would happen.

The shoebox had a lid which was tied on with string. Gribble pushed the box into my hand. 'Seeing you like the tip so much, Repeat,' he leered. 'I have brought something back from there for you. One of you two has to have enough nerve to put your hand in there and take out the mystery object that I found at the tip.'

Pete and I looked at the hole in the box. There was just room enough to put a hand inside.

'Go on,' said Gribble. 'Or you get your first thump now.'

I don't mind telling you that I was scared. There was something in the box from the tip. It could be anything. A dead rat. Or even worse: a live rat. Or maybe a loaded mouse trap. My mind thought of the most terrible things. I didn't want to do it but then I noticed one of the kids was nodding to me. A little kid with a kind face. He seemed to be telling me that it was okay.

I looked at Gribble. I have always heard that you should fight a bully when they first pick on you. Then if you fight hard and hurt them they will leave you alone. Even if you lose the fight everyone will respect you and it will be okay. I sighed. Gribble was twice as big as Pete and me put together. And he had tough mates. They would wipe the floor with both of us. Things like teaching the bully a lesson only happen on TV.

Slowly I pushed my hand into the box. At first I couldn't feel anything but then I touched something hard and slimy. It was sort of horseshoe shaped. I shivered. It was revolting. There were rows of little sharp pointed things. Then I felt another one the same. There were two of them. They reminded me of a broken rabbit trap. They felt like they were made of plastic covered in dry mould. I didn't have the faintest idea what I was holding, but all sorts of horrible things came into my mind.

Slowly I pulled out my hand and looked. It was a set of old, broken false teeth.

They were chipped and cracked and stained brown. They felt yucky but I smiled at the circle of kids around me. Pete was grinning too. I had passed the nerve test. Or so I thought.

'Okay, Repeat,' said Gribble with a horrible leer. 'You have passed the first bit of the test.' My heart sank. So did Pete's. I didn't realise that there was going to be something else.

Gribble pushed his face up against mine. He had bad breath. 'Now boys,' he growled, 'you have to take the false teeth back where they came from. Back to the tip.' He paused, and then he added, 'At night.'

Pete and I looked at each other. Goose bumps ran up and down our arms. Before we could say anything

Gribble told us the next bit. 'And just to make sure that you really go. That you don't just pretend to go. You have to bring something back with you. You have to bring back the steer's skull in the middle of the tip pond. By tomorrow morning. You have to prove that you went to the tip at night by bringing back the skull.'

Pete and I spent the rest of the day worrying. We couldn't concentrate on our school work. I got two out of twenty for my Maths. Pete got four out of twenty. The teacher must have thought that the new kids were real dumb.

That afternoon the boy who had nodded at me in the yard passed me a note. It said:

You had better get the skull. Gribble is real
mean. He punched me up every day for a month
until I passed his rotten nerve test.
Signed, your friend Troy

I passed the note on to Pete. He didn't say anything but he didn't look too good.

After school we walked sadly out of the gate. As we went Gribble yelled at us, 'Have a nice night, *my darlings*.'

Neither of us could eat any tea that night. Mum looked at us in a funny way but she didn't say anything. She thought we were just suffering from nerves about the new school. She was right. But only partly. We were also thinking about the ghost of Old Man Chompers and his lonely search for his lost darlings. I looked at Pete and he looked at me. It was like staring in a mirror. It reminded me that Old Man Chompers' lost grandchildren were twins too.

'We could pretend to be sick tomorrow,' I said to Pete after tea.

'It wouldn't work,' he answered. 'Mum never gets fooled by that one. Anyway, we would have to go back to school sooner or later.'

'We could tell Dad and . . .'

'Oh sure,' put in Pete before I could finish. 'And he will tell the teachers and everyone in the school will call us dobbers.'

'What about throwing the false teeth in the bin and getting a steer's skull from somewhere else?' I yelled. 'Gribble would never know that we hadn't really been to the tip.'

Pete looked at me as if I was a bit crazy. 'Great,' he answered in a cross voice. 'And where are you going to get a steer's skull at this time of night? It can't be any old steer's skull you know. It has to have white horns and horrible teeth. No – we will have to do it. We will take the false teeth back to the tip and bring the steer's skull back with us. There's nothing to be scared of really. Ghosts aren't true. There aren't any ghosts. People just think they see them when they are scared.'

I nodded my head without saying anything. I was scared already. And I didn't even want to *think* that I saw a ghost. But I knew Pete was right. We would have to go. It was the only way.

4

That night after Mum and Dad had gone to bed we snuck out of the window and headed off for the tip. We walked slowly along the dusty road which wound through the moonlit paddocks. Pete carried a rope with a hook on the end for getting the skull out of the middle of the pond. I carried a torch in one hand and the false teeth in the other. They felt all slimy and horrible. I sure was looking forward to getting rid of them.

There was not a soul to be seen. The crickets were chirping their heads off and now and then an owl would hoot. Cows sat silently in the dry grass on the other side of the barbed-wire fences. I was really scared but for some reason the cows made me feel a little better. I don't know why this was, because if anything happened the cows weren't going to help. A cow is just a cow.

The further we got from home the more my knees started to wobble. I kept thinking that every shadow hid something evil and terrible. The inside of my stomach wall felt like a frog was scribbling on it with four pencils.

Our first problem started when we reached the tip. It had a high wire fence around it with barbed wire on the top. And the gates were locked. A gentle wind was blowing and the papers stuck to the fence flapped and sighed.

'How are we going to get in?' I asked Pete. Secretly I was hoping we would have to go home.

'Climb over,' he said.

We threw over the rope with the hook on it and clambered up the high wire fence. The wire was saggy and it started to sway from side to side with our weight. We ended up perched on the top trying to get our legs over the barbed wire. Suddenly the whole fence lurched, sending us crashing onto the ground on the inside. The fence sprang back up again with the rope on the other side.

'Ouch, ow, ooh . . . that hurt,' I yelled. I rubbed my aching head.

'Quiet,' whispered Pete fiercely. 'You're making enough noise to wake the dead.'

His words sent a chill up my spine. 'I wish you hadn't said that,' I whispered back.

Pete looked up at the fence. We were trapped inside. 'We will never get back over that,' he said. I could tell that he was thinking the same thing as me. What fools we were. What were we doing in a lonely tip in the middle of the night? There was no one to help us. There was not another soul there. Or was there?

A little way off, behind some old rusting car bodies, I thought I heard a noise. Pete was looking in the same direction. I was too terrified to move. I wanted to run but my legs just wouldn't work. I opened my mouth to scream but nothing came out. Pete stood staring as if he was bolted to the ground.

It was a rustling, tapping noise. It sounded like someone digging around in the junk, turning things over. It was coming in our direction. I just stood there pretending to be a dead tree or a post. I wished the moon would go in and stop shining on my white face. The tapping grew louder. It was coming closer.

And then we saw it. Or him. Or whatever it was. An old man, with a battered hat. He was poking the ground with a bent stick. He was rustling in the rubbish. He came on slowly. He was limping. He was bent and seemed to be holding his old, dirty trousers up with one hand. He came towards us. With a terrible shuffle.

Pete and I both noticed it at the same time. His feet weren't touching the ground. He was moving across the rubbish about thirty centimetres above the surface.

It was the ghost of Old Man Chompers.

We both screeched the same word at exactly the same moment. 'Run.'

And did we run. We tore through the waist-high rubbish. Scrambling. Screaming. Scrabbling. Not noticing the waves of silent rats slithering out of our way. Not feeling the scratches of dumped junk. Not daring to turn and snatch a stare at the horrible spectre who hobbled behind us.

Finally, with bursting lungs, we crawled into the back of an old car. It had no doors or windows so we crouched low, not breathing, not looking, not even hoping.

Why had we come to this awful place? Fools, fools, fools. Suddenly the thought of Gribble and the steer's skull and the false teeth seemed stupid. I would have fought a thousand Gribbles rather than be here. Trapped in a tip with a ghost.

I could feel Pete trembling beside me. And I could hear the voice of someone else. A creaking, croaking cry. 'My darlings . . . my darlings . . . my darlings . . . my darlings.'

5

I knew it. I just knew it. The ghost of Old Man Chompers had seen us. He thought we were his lost darlings. His dead grandchildren. He was coming to get us. Then he would be able to leave this place. And take us with him. To that great ghost tip in the sky.

I thought of Mum and Dad. I thought of my nice warm bed. I would never see them again. Our parents would never know what had happened to us. Never know that we had come to our end in the bowels of the Allansford tip.

'At last, at last . . . my darlings . . . at last.' The wailing voice was nearby. He knew where we were. Without a word we bolted out of the car. We fled blindly across the festering tip until we reached the pond. The deep black pond, filled with floating foulness.

And behind, slowly hobbling above the bile, came the searching figure of Old Chompers. We were trapped against the edge of the pond.

In panic we looked around for escape. Mountains of junk loomed over us on either side. To the back was the pond and to the front . . . we dared not look.

'Quick,' yelled Pete. 'Help me with this.' He was pulling at an old rusty bath. Dragging it towards the water.

'It won't float,' I gasped. 'Look at the plughole. The water will get in. It'll sink.'

Pete bent down and scratched up a dollop of wet clay from the edge of the water. He jammed it into the plughole. 'Come on,' he panted. 'Hurry.'

The bath was heavy but terror made us strong. We launched it out into the murky water. Then we scrambled in. Just in time. The bath rocked dangerously from side to side but slowly it floated away from the approaching horror.

We paddled frantically with our hands until the bath reached the middle of the pond. Then we stopped and stared at Old Chompers. He hobbled to the edge of the water, he staggered towards us. He was walking on the water, his hands outstretched. 'My darlings,' he groaned. 'My long-lost darlings.' Pete and I clung to the sides of the bath with frozen fingers.

The moon went in and everything was black.

Suddenly there was a pop. The clay plug shot into the air followed by a spout of water. Brown wetness swirled in the bath. We were sinking. In a flash we found ourselves swimming in the filthy water. We both headed for the shore, splashing and shouting and struggling. Pete was a better swimmer than me. He disappeared into the gloom.

My jumper soaked up water and dragged me down. I went under. I came up again and spat out the lumpy brown liquid. I knew I would drown unless I could find something to grab onto. The bath was gone.

Then my hand touched something. It was a post with something on the end. I grabbed onto it and kicked towards the shore. As my feet touched the bottom I realised that the post had horns. Then I saw that it had a face. A staring dead face with sharp teeth. It was the horrible leering steer's skull.

I screamed and crawled over to where Pete lay on the shore.

We were both soaked to the skin. We were cold and exhausted. We were too tired to move.

The ghost of Old Man Chompers crept across the water with outstretched hands. His face was wrinkled like a bowl of hard, cold custard. His mouth was as a black hole, formed in the custard by a vanished golf ball. He chuckled as he looked at me.

In my left hand I still had the false teeth. All the time I had been running I had held onto them. I had no other weapon so I held them out in front of me. My fingers were shaking so much that it made them chatter.

As the ghost of Old Man Chompers jumped at me I screamed and screamed and tried to push him off with the teeth.

He grabbed the false teeth from my quivering fingers and shoved them into his mouth. 'At last,' he said. 'I've found them. My darlings. My darlings.' He opened and closed his mouth with joy, making sucking noises as he did it.

After a bit of this he pulled out a ghostly apple from his pocket and started to chomp on it. 'Wonderful,' he cackled. 'Wonderful. You don't know what it was like without my darlings . . . I owe you boys a big favour for bringing these back.'

We both lay there looking at the grinning ghost. Suddenly he didn't seem so scary. Pete found his voice first. 'You mean,' he said, 'that your darlings are your false teeth? Not your long-lost grandchildren?'

The ghost started to cackle even more. 'Them,' he said. 'Them brats. What would I want them for? I told 'em not to play around here. Told 'em it was dangerous. No, I was lookin' for these.' He smacked his lips again and showed the cracked brown teeth. 'Couldn't leave without these. Been lookin' for 'em for years. Now I can go. Now I can leave this rotten dump and join all the others.' As he said this he started to fade away. I knew that we would never see him again.

'Wait,' yelled Pete. 'Don't go. Come back.'

Chompers stopped fading and looked at Pete. 'What?' he said. 'What do yer want?' I could see that he was in a hurry. He didn't want to hang around the tip for any longer than he had to.

Pete looked the ghost straight in the eye. 'You said that you owe us a big favour for bringing your teeth back. Well we want to be paid back. We want one favour before you go.'

'Well,' said Old Chompers with a chipped smile, 'what is it?'

6

Old Chompers wasn't the only one who didn't want to hang around that tip. He showed us a hole in the fence and we ran back down that road as fast as we could go. When we got back to Allansford we climbed up a certain tree and looked in a certain window.

Gribble was fast asleep in bed. He had a big smile on his face. He had fallen asleep thinking about how smart he was making those dumb twins go to the tip in the middle of the night.

Suddenly he was awakened by a noise. It sounded like a person tapping with a stick. It was coming towards his window. Then he heard a croaky voice. 'My darling,' it said. 'At last I've found my darling.'

Gribble was terrified. He wanted to scream but nothing would come out.

A terrible figure floated through the wall. He had a face which was wrinkled like a bowl of hard, cold custard. His mouth was as a black hole, formed in the custard by a vanished golf ball. And in that black hole was a pair of cracked old false teeth.

The ghost chuckled as he held the horrible skull over Gribble's head. 'I think you wanted this,' he said as he dropped his load on Gribble's face.

'That was from Pete,' he screeched. 'And this,' he yelled picking it up again, 'is a Repeat.'

Gribble didn't feel the steer's skull the second time. Nor did he see the ghost fade away. He had fainted.

The next day at school, though, James Gribble was very nice to me and Pete. I had never met a more polite boy. And there is one thing I can tell you for a fact – he never mentioned anything about being the top dog ever again.

The Copy

I was rapt. It was the best day of my life. I had asked Fiona to go with me and she said yes. I couldn't believe it. I mean, it wasn't as if I was a great catch. I was skinny, weak, and not too smart at school. Mostly I got Cs and Ds for marks. And I couldn't play sport at all. I hated football, always went out on the first ball at cricket and didn't know which end to hold a tennis racquet. And Fiona had said she'd be my girlfriend.

Every boy in year eleven at Hamilton High would be jealous. Especially Mat Hodson. It was no secret that he fancied Fiona too. I grinned to myself. I wished I could see his face when he found out the news. He thought that he was so great and in a way he was. He was the exact opposite to me. He was smart (always got As for everything), captain of the footy team, the best batsman in the cricket team and he was tough. Real tough. He could flatten me with one punch if he wanted to. I just hoped he took it with good grace about Fiona and me. I didn't want him for an enemy.

I headed off to Crankshaft Alley to see my old friend Doctor Woolley. I always went to see him when something good happened. Or something bad. I felt sort of safe and happy inside his untidy old workshop and it was fun seeing what crazy thing he was inventing. Everything he had come up with so far had been a flop. His last invention was warm clothes-pegs to stop people getting cold fingers when they hung out the clothes. They worked all right but no one would buy them because they cost two hundred dollars each. All of his inventions had turned out like that. They worked and they were clever but they were too expensive for people to buy.

I walked on down past all the other little shop-front factories until I reached Dr Woolley's grubby door. I gave the secret knock (three slow, three fast) and his gnomish face appeared at the window. I say gnomish because he looked just like a gnome: he was short with a hooked nose and he had a white beard and a bald head surrounded with a ring of white hair. If you gave him a fishing rod and a red cap and sat him in the front yard you would think he was a little garden statue.

He opened the door. 'Come in, Rodney,' he said.

'Tim,' I corrected. He always called me the wrong name. He had a terrible memory.

'Where's that screwdriver?' he said. 'It's always getting lost.'

'In your hand,' I told him.

'Thanks, Peter, thanks.'

'Tim,' I sighed. I don't know why I bothered. He was

never going to call me by my right name. It wasn't that he didn't know who I was. He did. I was his only friend. Everyone else thought he was a dangerous crackpot because he chased them away from his front door with a broken mop. I was the only person allowed into his workshop.

'Are you still working on the Cloner?' I asked.

His face turned grim and he furtively looked over at the window. 'Shh . . . Not so loud. Someone might hear. I've almost perfected it. I'm nearly there. And this time it is going to pay off.' He led me across the room to a machine that looked something like a telephone box with a whole lot of wires hanging out of it. Down one side were a number of dials and switches. There were two red buttons. One was labelled COPY and the other REVERSE.

Dr Woolley placed a pine cone on the floor of the Cloner. Then he pressed the button that said COPY. There was a whirring sound and a puff of smoke and then, amazingly, the outline of another pine cone, exactly the same as the first, appeared. It lasted for about ten seconds and then the machine started to rock and shake and the whirring slowly died. The image of the second pine cone faded away.

'Fantastic,' I yelled.

'Blast,' said Dr Woolley. 'It's unstable. It won't hold the copy. But I'm nearly there. I think I know how to fix it.'

'What will you use it for?' I asked. 'What's the good of copying pine cones? There are plenty of pine cones already. We don't need more of those.'

He started to get excited. 'Listen, Robert.'

'Tim,' I said.

'Tim, then. It doesn't only work with pine cones. It will work with anything.' He looked up at the window as he said it. Then he dropped his voice. 'What if I made a copy of a bar of gold, eh? What then? And then another copy and another and another. We would be rich. Rich.'

I started to get excited too. I liked the way he said 'we'.

Dr Woolley started nodding his little head up and down. 'All I need is time,' he said. 'Time to get the adjustment right. Then we will show them whether I'm a crank or not.'

We had a cup of tea together and then I headed off home. That was two good things that had happened in one day. First, Fiona saying she would go with me and second, the Cloner was nearly working. I whistled all the way home.

2

I didn't see Dr Woolley for some time after that. I had a lot on my mind. I had to walk home with Fiona and every night I went to her place to study with her. Not that we got much study done. On weekends we went hiking or hung around listening to records. It was the best time of my life. There was only one blot on the horizon. Mat Hodson. One of his mates had told me he was out to get me. He left a message saying he was going to flatten me for taking his girl.

His girl! Fiona couldn't stand him. She told me she thought he was a show-off and a bully. But that wasn't going to help me. If he wanted to flatten me he would get me in the end. Fortunately he had caught the mumps and had to stay at home for three weeks. Someone had told me it was very painful.

I decided to go round to see Dr Woolley about a month later. I wondered if he had perfected his Cloner. When I reached the door I gave the secret knock but there was no answer. 'That's strange,' I said to myself. 'He never goes out for anything.'

I looked through the window and although the curtains were drawn I could see the light was on inside. I knocked again on the door but still no answer. Then I started to worry. What if he had had a heart attack or something? He could be lying unconscious on the floor. I ran around to the back, got the key from the hiding spot in an old kettle and let myself into the workshop. The place was in a mess. Tables and chairs were turned over and crockery was lying smashed on the floor. It looked as if there had been a fight in the workshop. There was no sign of Dr Woolley.

I started to clean the place up, turning the chairs up

the right way and putting the broken things into the bin. That's when I found an envelope with my name on it. Inside was a letter. It began, 'John', 'Peter', 'Robert', and 'Tim'. The first three names were crossed out. Dr Woolley had finally remembered my name was Tim after four tries. The letter said:

TIM

IF YOU FIND THIS LETTER SOMETHING TERRIBLE HAS

HAPPENED. YOU MUST DESTROY THE CLONER AT ONCE.

WOOLLEY

My eye caught something else on the floor. I went over and picked it up. It was another letter exactly the same as the first. It even had the three wrong names crossed out. The only difference was that this letter looked all back to front.

I looked at the Cloner with a feeling of dread. What had happened? Why did he want me to destroy it? And where was Dr Woolley? The Cloner was switched on. I could tell that because the red light next to REVERSE was shining. I walked over to it and switched it over to COPY. I don't know what made me do it. I guess I just wanted to know if the Cloner worked. I should have left it alone but I didn't. I took a Biro out of my top pocket and threw it inside the Cloner.

Immediately an image of another Biro formed. There were two of them where before there had only been one. I turned the Cloner off and picked up both pens. As far as I could tell they were identical. I couldn't tell which was the real one. They were both real.

I sat down on a chair feeling a bit dizzy. This was the most fantastic machine that had ever been invented. It could make me rich. Dr Woolley had said that it could even copy gold bars. All sorts of wonderful ideas came into my mind. I decided that nothing would make me destroy the Cloner.

I went over and switched the machine on to REVERSE. Then I threw both of the pens into the Cloner. I was shocked by what happened. Both of them disappeared. They were gone. For good. I turned it back to COPY but nothing happened. I tried REVERSE again but still nothing. It was then that I noticed a huge blowfly buzzing around the room. It flew crazily around my head and then headed straight into the Cloner. It vanished without a trace.

The Cloner was dangerous when it was switched on to REVERSE. It could make things vanish for good. I wondered if Dr Woolley had fallen into the machine. Or had he been pushed? There were certainly signs of a struggle.

I thought about going to the police. But what could they do? They couldn't help Dr Woolley if he had fallen into the Cloner. And they would take it away and I would never see it again. I didn't want that to happen. I had plans for that machine. It was mine now. I was the rightful owner. After all, Dr Woolley had said that 'we' would be rich. Unfortunately now it was just going to be me who was rich.

I went back to Fiona's house and spent the evening doing homework with her. I didn't tell her about the Cloner. I was going to give her the first copies I made from it. At ten o'clock I walked home through the darkened streets, keeping an eye out for Mat Hodson. I had heard he was over his mumps and was looking for me.

The next morning I borrowed Mum's gold cameo brooch without telling her. I decided not to go to school but instead I went to Dr Woolley's workshop. Once inside I turned the Cloner on to COPY and threw in the brooch. Immediately another one appeared. I turned the Cloner off and took out both brooches. One was a mirror image of the other. They both had the same gold setting and the same ivory face. But on one brooch the face looked to the left and on the other it looked to the right. Apart from that they were identical.

I whistled to myself. The copy was so good I couldn't remember which way Mum's brooch had faced. Still it didn't matter. I would put one of them back where I had got it and give the other to Fiona.

Next I decided to experiment with something that was alive. I went outside and hunted around in the long grass. After a while I found a small green frog with a black patch on its left side. I took it in and threw it straight into the Cloner. In a flash there were two frogs. They jumped out on to the workshop floor. I picked them up and looked at them. They were both alive and perfectly happy. They were both green but one had a black patch on the left and the other had it on the right. One was a mirror image of the other.

This Cloner was wonderful. I spent all day there making copies of everything I could think of. By four o'clock there was two of almost everything in the workshop. I decided it was time to go and give Fiona her cameo. She was going to be very happy to get it.

I never made it to Fiona's house. An unpleasant surprise was waiting outside for me. It was Mat Hodson.

'I've been waiting for you, you little fink,' he said. 'I heard you were hiding in here.' He had a pair of footy boots hanging around his neck. He was on his way to practice. He gave a nasty leer. 'I thought I told you to stay away from my girl.'

'She's not your girl,' I said hotly. 'She can't stand you. She's my . . .' I never finished the sentence. He hit me with a tremendous punch in the guts and I went down like an exploding balloon. The pain was terrible and I couldn't breathe. I fought for air but nothing happened. I was winded. And all I could do was lay there on the footpath wriggling like a dying worm.

'You get one of those every day,' he said. 'Until you break it off with Fiona.' Then he laughed and went off to footy practice.

After a while, my breath started to come back in great sobs and spasms. I staggered back into the workshop and sat down. I was mad. I was out of my mind. I had to think of some way to stop him. I couldn't go through this every day and I couldn't give up Fiona. I needed help. And badly. But I couldn't think of anyone. I didn't have a friend who would help me fight Hodson except Fiona and I couldn't ask her.

My mind was in a whirl and my stomach ached like crazy. I wasn't thinking straight. That's why I did the stupidest thing of my life. I decided to get inside the Cloner and turn it on. There would be two of me. Two Tims. I could get The Copy to help me fight Hodson. He would help me. After all, he would be the same as me. He would want to pay Hodson back as much as I did. The more I thought about it, the smarter it seemed.

I would make an exact copy of myself and together we would go off and flatten Hodson. I wondered what my first words to the new arrival should be. In the end I decided to say, 'Hello there, welcome to earth.' I know it sounds corny but at the time it was all I could think of.

I turned the Cloner to COPY and jumped in before I lost my nerve. In a twinkling there was another 'me' standing there. It was just like looking into a mirror. He had the same jeans, the same jumper and the same brown eyes. We both stood staring at each other for about thirty seconds without saying a thing. Then, both at the same time, we said, 'Hello there, welcome to earth.'

That gave me a heck of a shock. How did he know what I was going to say? I couldn't figure it out. It wasn't until much later I realised he knew all about me. He had an exact copy of my brain. He knew everything I had ever done. He knew what I had been thinking before I stepped into the Cloner. That's why he was able to say the same sentence. He knew everything about me. He even knew how many times I had kissed Fiona. The Copy wasn't just a copy. He was me.

We both stood there again for about thirty seconds with our brains ticking over. We were both trying to make sense of the situation. I drew a breath to say something, but he beat me to it. 'Well,' he said, 'what are we waiting for? Let's go get Hodson.'

The Copy and I jogged along the street towards the football ground without speaking. I wondered what he was thinking. He didn't know what I was thinking. We shared the same past but not the same future or present. From now on everything that happened would be experienced differently by both of us. I didn't have the faintest idea what was going on in his head. But I knew what was going on in mine. I was wondering how I was going to get rid of him when this was all over.

'Fiona will like that brooch,' said The Copy. I was shocked to think he knew about it. He was smiling to himself. I went red. He was probably thinking Fiona was going to give him a nice big kiss when she saw that brooch. It was me she was going to kiss, not The Copy.

At last we reached the football ground. Hodson was just coming out of the changing rooms. 'Well, look,' he said, 'It's little Tim and his twin brother. Brought him to help you, have you?' he said to The Copy. 'Well, I can handle both of you.' He screwed up his hand into a tight fist. Suddenly he looked very big. In fact, he looked big enough to wipe the floor with both of us.

I felt like running for it. So did The Copy. I could see he was just about to turn around and run off, leaving me on my own. We both turned and fled. Hodson chased after us for a bit and finally gave it away. 'See you tomorrow, boys,' he yelled. I could hear the other footballers laughing at us. It was humiliating. I knew the others would tell Fiona about what a coward I was.

I turned to The Copy. 'A fat lot of use you turned out to be,' I said.

'What are you talking about?' he replied. 'You're the one who turned and ran off first. You knew I couldn't handle him on my own.'

I realised The Copy was a liar. I decided to go home for tea. He walked along beside me. 'Where do you think you're going?' I asked.

'Home for tea.'

'We can't both turn up for tea. What's Mum going to say when she sees two of us? The shock will kill her,' I told him.

We both kept on walking towards home. The Copy knew the way. He knew everything I knew. Except what I was thinking. He only knew about what had happened before he came out of the Cloner. He didn't know what was going on in my mind after that. I stopped. He seemed determined to come home with me. 'Look,' I said, 'be reasonable. Think of Mum and Dad. We can't sit down for tea. You go somewhere else.'

'No,' he said. 'You go somewhere else.'

Finally we came to the front gate. 'All right,' I said to The Copy. 'You go and hide in the bedroom. I'll go down to tea and afterwards sneak you up some food.'

The Copy didn't like it. 'I've got a better idea,' he told me. 'You hide in the bedroom and I'll bring you up something.'

I could see he was only thinking of himself. This thing was turning into a nightmare. 'All right,' I said in the end. 'You go down to tea and I'll hide in the bed-room.' So that is what we did. I sneaked up and hid in my room while The Copy had tea with my parents. It was roast pork. My favourite. I could smell it from my room and it smelt delicious.

The sound of laughter and chattering floated up the stairs. No one knew The Copy wasn't me. They couldn't tell the difference. A bit later he came up the stairs. He poked his head around the corner and threw me a couple of dry biscuits. 'This is all I could find. I'll try and bring you up something later.'

Dry biscuits. I had to eat dry biscuits while The Copy finished off my tea. And I just remembered Mum had been cooking apple pie before we left. This was too much. Something had to be done.

Just then the doorbell rang. 'I'll get it,' shouted The Copy before I had a chance to open my mouth. He ran down the stairs and answered the door. I was trapped. I couldn't go down or Mum and Dad would see there were two of us.

I could hear a girl's voice. It was Fiona. A bit later the door closed and all was silent. The Copy had gone outside with her. I raced over to the window and looked out. It was dark but I could just see them under the wattle tree. The street light illuminated the scene. What I saw made my blood boil. The Copy was kissing Fiona. He was kissing my girlfriend. She thought he was me. She couldn't tell the difference and she was letting the creep kiss her. And what is worse, she seemed to be enjoying it. It was a very long kiss.

I sat down and thought about the situation. The Copy had to be sent back to where he came from. This whole thing had turned out to be a terrible mistake. I had to get The Copy back to the workshop and get rid of him.

After about two hours The Copy came up to the bedroom looking very pleased with himself. I bit my tongue and didn't say anything about him kissing Fiona. 'Look,' I said, 'we can't both stay here. Why don't we go back to the workshop and have a good talk. Then we can figure out what to do.'

He thought about it for a bit and then he said, 'Okay, you're right. We had better work something out.'

I snuck out of the window and met him outside. We walked all the way to the workshop in silence. I could tell he didn't like me any more than I liked him.

I took the key out of the kettle and let us in. I noticed the Cloner was still switched on to copy. I went over and turned it on to REVERSE without saying anything. It would all be over quickly. He wouldn't know what hit him. I would just push him straight into the Cloner and everything would be back to normal. He would be gone and there would be just me. It wouldn't be murder. I mean, he had only been alive for a few hours and he wasn't really a person. He was just a copy.

'Look,' I said, pointing to the floor of the Cloner. 'Look at this.' I got ready to push him straight in when he came over.

The Copy came over for a look. Suddenly he grabbed me and started to push me towards the machine. The Copy was trying to kill me. He was trying to push me into the Cloner and have Fiona for himself. We fell to the floor in a struggling heap. It was a terrible fight. We both had exactly the same strength and the same experience. As we fought I realised what had happened to Dr Woolley. He had made a copy of himself and they had both tried to push each other in. That's why there were two letters. Probably they had both fallen in and killed each other.

The Copy and I fought for about ten minutes. Neither of us could get the upper hand and we were both growing tired. We rolled over near the bench and I noticed an iron bar on the floor. But The Copy had noticed it too. We both tried to reach it at the same time. But I won. I grabbed it and wrenched my arm free. With a great whack I crashed it down over The Copy's head. He fell to the floor in a heap.

I dragged his lifeless body over to the Cloner and shoved him inside. He vanished without a trace. It was just as if he had never existed. A feeling of great relief spread over me but I was shaking at the narrow escape I had experienced. I turned and ran home without even locking up the workshop.

By the time I got home I felt a lot better. I walked into the lounge where Mum and Dad were sitting watching TV. Dad looked up at me. 'Ah, there you are, Tim. Would you fill out this application for the school camp? You put in the details and I'll sign the bottom.'

I took the form and started to fill it in. I was looking forward to the school camp. We were going skiing. After a while I looked up. Mum and Dad were both staring at me in a funny way.

'What's up?' I asked.

'You're writing with your left hand,' said Dad.

'So?'

'You've been a right-hander all your life.'

'And your hair is parted on the wrong side,' said Mum. 'And that little mole that used to be on your right cheek has moved to the left.'

My head started to swim. I ran over to the mirror on the wall. The face that stared back at me was not Tim's. It was the face of The Copy.

AGGHHHHH! NO!

The reporter looked at Tracy with a smile. 'I'd like to talk to you about your job,' he said. 'It would make a good story for the paper. Not many teenagers go into this line of work. Just how did you get started in it in the first place?'

'Well,' answered Tracy, 'it all began when Mum told me she was going to remarry.'

2

'I'm sorry,' said Mum, 'but I'm getting married whether you like it or not.'

'But Mum,' I started off.

'No buts,' she cut in. 'I'm lonely at night when you and Andy have gone to bed. And anyway, I love Ralph. He is a lovely man. I thought you liked him too.'

'I do,' I said. 'It's not him I don't like. It's his job. He buries people in the cemetery.'

'What's that got to do with it?' she asked hotly. 'I'm not going to stop loving Ralph just because he is an undertaker. You don't judge a person by their job.'

'It's embarrassing,' I said. 'Last night he took us down

the street to the fish-and-chip shop in his funeral wagon. Do you realise that our tea was brought home in a hearse? The same car that is used to cart dead bodies around. All the kids were laughing. One idiot lay down on the footpath with a flower in his mouth as we went by and pretended he was dead. Old Mr Manor takes his hat off as we go past. It's the absolute pits going around in a hearse. Why doesn't he get a normal car like other people?'

'Ralph can't afford another car at the moment,' said Mum sadly. 'Business has been bad lately.'

'I suppose he is waiting for an axe maniac to move into town, or perhaps things would pick up if we introduced the bubonic plague.'

'That's not funny, Tracy,' Mum yelled. She was starting to get angry so I decided to give in.

Anyway, I had to agree with her. Ralph was a nice bloke. It was just bad luck that he made his living by burying dead people. And animals. That's something else I should mention. He had a pet cemetery as well. He used to collect dead pets and bury them in a little plot just outside of town.

Well, Mum and Ralph got married and my little brother Andy and I had a new stepfather. We all went off to the snowfields together on the honeymoon. In the hearse, of course. I tried everything I could think of to talk Ralph out of taking the hearse but it was no use. 'It's just right for the snow,' he said. 'We can put the skis in the back and there's plenty of room for the luggage.'

It was terrible. A real shame job. Every day we arrived at the bottom of the ski slopes in the grey hearse with:

R HENDERSON BUDGET FUNERALS

AND

PET INTERMENTS

written on the door. People came rushing over to see who had been killed.

At lunchtime we would get out our portable barbecue and set it up behind the wagon. Ralph would cook chops and steak. A man came over and said that he knew that beef was expensive at the moment but wasn't this going a bit far? We were the laughing stock of the ski slopes. People called us 'The Skiing Cannibals'.

I was sure glad when that honeymoon was over. It was a nightmare. Not that things improved when we got home. They didn't. Ralph moved in with us and straightaway built a workshop at the bottom of the yard. 'What's it for?' I asked. 'And why hasn't it got any windows?'

He looked around furtively. 'Don't tell Andy,' he said. 'Your little brother is too young to understand. It's a workshop for making coffins.'

'What?' I screamed. 'What will my girlfriends think if they know we have coffins at the bottom of the garden?'

'Don't tell them,' said Ralph. 'What they don't know won't hurt them.'

'But I know,' I retorted. 'I'll never get to sleep knowing there are coffins in our home.'

'Don't be so sensitive,' said Ralph. 'They are just empty coffins. I wouldn't bring the corpses back here. They stay at the funeral parlour until the burial. You should try to get used to it. One day I am going to take you in as a partner in the business.'

'Over my dead body,' I said.

Ralph didn't even crack a smile. He had his heart set on me joining the business. He looked so upset that I even felt a bit sorry for him.

Just then Andy came into the room. 'What are those things that you are making?' he asked, pointing at three half-finished coffins.

Ralph didn't bat an eyelid. 'Boats,' he lied. 'I'm making some boats.'

Andy was only seven and he believed it. 'Wow,' he said. 'Fantastic.'

It was a stupid thing to say and I knew it would cause trouble. I wasn't wrong. Two days later, when I was at home on my own, the phone rang. It was the Portland Police. They asked me to come down to the main beach at once.

When I got there I saw the most humiliating thing of my life. The beach was lined with hundreds of people – all of them shrieking with laughter. Some of them were rolling around on the sand holding their sides. They were all laughing at the same thing. My brother Andy. He was paddling a coffin around in the water among the swimmers.

He had loaded a coffin up on my surfboard trailer and pulled it down to the beach behind his bike. Then he had launched it out onto the water. He really thought it was a boat. I couldn't believe it.

Of course, the whole thing was in the paper and on the TV. The whole family was disgraced. Everyone knew that my little brother had been sailing around in a coffin. I couldn't look the girls at school in the eye for months. And Ralph didn't even care. 'It was a good coffin,' was all he said. 'It didn't even leak one drop.'

3

After that, things just went from bad to worse. Mum decided that I would have to help Ralph on weekends as he couldn't afford to pay his helper overtime. 'I'm not going near corpses,' I said. 'No way.'

Ralph looked hurt. He really hoped that I would become an undertaker like him. 'That's all right,' he said. 'You can help with the pet side of the business. I don't expect you to go to the funerals of people just yet.'

This didn't sound too bad but in fact it turned out to be another disaster. Ralph used to pick up people's dead pets in the hearse and take them out to the pet cemetery.

It was amazing what some people would do. There

were little graves for dogs, cats, canaries, mice and rabbits. There were big graves too. You name it and it was buried there.

A lot of people think that their pets are human. You take old Mrs Trapp, for example. She wanted a special funeral for her cat, Fibble. 'Come round at four o'clock and fetch him,' she said on the phone. 'I want a proper burial with a priest, a hearse and flowers. Nothing is too good for my poor Fibble.' I could hear her sniffing on the other end of the phone. I shook my head. I just couldn't understand it. Fancy paying money to have a funeral for a cat.

'Good,' said Ralph. 'Four o'clock will be fine. I have to do a pick-up at the zoo at three. We can call at Mrs Trapp's house for Fibble on the way back.'

I groaned. 'What died at the zoo? I hope it wasn't the elephant.'

'No,' said Ralph. 'It's a baby giraffe.'

When we reached the zoo, Mr Proud, the director, was standing next to this poor dead giraffe. He was upset. 'I want you to do a good job,' he said. 'Dig a nice deep hole. I want this giraffe to rest in peace. Be careful with him. His last journey should be slow, dignified and gentle. I am going to drive to the pet cemetery and make sure you do it properly.'

His eyes were red and swollen. I could see he loved this giraffe a lot. He drove off to the cemetery and left us to load up the giraffe.

It was only a baby one but it was heavy. And it was

too big for the trailer. Its long neck and head hung over the back and touched the ground.

'We can't have that,' said Ralph. He tied a rope around its little horns and pulled. The giraffe's head lifted up off the ground. 'There's no way to tie it up and stop the head from drooping,' Ralph told me. 'You will have to stand in the trailer on top of the giraffe and pull on the rope to keep its head up in the air.'

'You're joking,' I exclaimed.

'No,' said Ralph. 'It's the only way. I'll drive slowly so you don't fall off.' Without another word he climbed into the hearse and started to drive away. I only just had time to scramble onto the dead giraffe and pull its head up.

We went out of the zoo and along the street. Did Ralph go around the back way so that no one would see us? No, he did not. He went straight through the middle of the town. You can imagine what we looked like. A hearse, followed by a trailer with a dead giraffe on it. And on top of the giraffe, a girl hanging onto a rope trying to keep its head from drooping onto the road.

It brought the traffic to a standstill. Everyone yelled and shouted. People rushed out of the shops to see the sight. It was worse than Andy and his coffin boat. We stopped at every traffic light, exposed for all to see. I have never been more ashamed in my life. But there was worse to come.

My arms started to get tired. A giraffe's neck is heavy.

The head drooped closer and closer to the road until at last it started to rub on the bitumen. I heaved it up but I couldn't hold it for long. 'Stop,' I screamed to Ralph. 'Stop. Its head is rubbing on the ground.' Ralph kept going. He was listening to the grand final on the radio and couldn't hear me. So we kept on in the same way all the way to the pet cemetery. The poor giraffe's head must have banged on the road a hundred times.

When we finally arrived, Mr Proud was waiting for us and dabbing at his red eyes with a handkerchief. He walked over to his dead giraffe to inspect it. Suddenly he stopped. His eyes nearly popped out of his head. 'What's this?' he screamed. 'My poor giraffe. Where is its nose? Its nose is gone. What have you done with its nose?'

'Sorry,' I said. 'It got rubbed off on the road. Its head was too heavy for me.'

'You stupid girl,' he yelled. 'You fiend.' He came towards me with his hands held out like claws. He had murder in his eyes.

I turned and ran. I fled down the road with the enraged Mr Proud behind me. He chased me for miles but in the end he gave up and went back.

I walked home with tears streaming down my face. I was sick to death of Ralph and his funerals – animal and human. My life was turning into a complete mess. I made up my mind never to have anything to do with Budget Funerals. There was no way I would ever get involved again. And as for becoming a partner in the business, well Ralph could just jump in the lake. I was sick of him.

4

I went up to my bedroom and shut the door. I made up a big speech about how I was never, never going to be a partner in Ralph's funeral business.

After about an hour there was a knock on the door. Ralph stuck his head in the room. He didn't say anything about the giraffe. He shook an old jar at me. I could see a coin rattling around in the bottom. 'Would you sell me one of the pennies from your coin collection?' he asked. 'I've only got one left.'

'What do you want it for?' I said suspiciously.

'They are hard to get. This jar used to be full but now I only have one left. Ever since they changed to decimal currency it has got harder and harder to get pennies.'

A nasty thought came into my mind. 'Has this got anything to do with the funeral business? Because if it has you are not getting any of my coins. I'm fed up with you and your dead bodies.'

'I have a man waiting for burial. Every corpse has to have two pennies. One for each eye. The spirits of the dead have no rest if they are buried without their coins.'

I picked up a pillow and threw it at him. 'Buzz off,'

I yelled. 'I don't ever want to hear anything about your rotten burials again. And get it into your skull, I am never going to work for you as an undertaker – never.' Ralph's sad face disappeared from the room.

A bit later I went downstairs. I could hear Ralph talking to Mum. I can't remember exact words but he said something like this: 'I'll leave the body in the workshop for tonight. I'm too tired to move it at the moment.'

My head started to spin. This was just too much. It was the last straw. Now he had gone and brought a corpse to our home. He was leaving a dead body in the workshop for some reason or another. And he had promised that he never would. I grabbed the key and charged down the backyard to the workshop, I opened the door and rushed inside, leaving the key in the lock.

I looked around and sure enough, just as I suspected, there on the table was a new coffin. The lid was firmly closed. Ralph didn't shut the coffin lids unless there was a body inside. Boy, was I mad. I turned around just in time to see the wind blow the door shut.

Immediately I found myself in the dark. It was pitch black. I stumbled over to the door and tried to open it. It wouldn't budge. Ralph had fitted a new deadlock after Andy had taken the coffin out for a sail. I was locked in. I couldn't even turn the light on because the switch was outside.

I yelled at the top of my voice and banged on the door as hard as I could. It was no use. No one heard me. After a while I slumped on the floor. I was exhausted. It was as quiet as a grave. I could hear my own heart thumping inside my chest. I was all alone in the darkness.

Or was I?

In the middle of the room was a coffin. With a corpse in it. I started to wonder who it was. Could it be the person who Ralph had wanted the extra penny for? Was there a body in there with one lonely penny on one of its eyes? What had Ralph said? The spirit would not rest without the pennies. And it was my fault. I wouldn't give him one of mine because I was mad about the giraffe.

I sat there in the silence and the blackness. My breath sounded as loud as a windstorm. I tried to breathe quietly. I didn't want to wake the dead.

I started to think about ghosts. I imagined a ghost with one eye leering at me. Coming to claim me. I told myself not to be silly. The dead didn't come back to life, I knew that. The trouble was, that sort of advice is fine when it is daytime and all your friends are about. But when you are locked in a dark, silent room with a corpse it is quite another thing.

The silence deepened. It grew cold and I started to shiver. I was too terrified to move in case the corpse heard me. I could imagine the eye without the penny. Was it swivelling? Was it seeking me?

Then something happened which froze my blood. I heard, quite distinctly, a soft sneeze.

There was no doubt about it. A sneeze had come from inside the coffin. The corpse was alive.

I almost shrieked with fear, but somehow I managed to keep control of myself. I shoved my fist into my mouth and crouched lower in the corner. Had it been my imagination? Had I really heard a sneeze? I knew I had. I strained my ears in the silence. What was that? A scratching noise. Coming from the coffin. It was trying to get out.

'Merciful heavens,' I mumbled. 'Don't let it get me.' The scratching grew louder.

What a fool I'd been. If only I'd given Ralph that penny when he wanted it. Then the body would have lain in peace.

'Please come, Ralph,' I whispered under my breath. 'Please come and save me.'

A wail came from the coffin.

'I'll do anything Ralph. I'll be your partner. I promise. I swear that if you come now I'll join you in the business. But just come and save me.'

At that very moment, as if he had heard my words, Ralph opened the door and came in. The room was filled with light. 'Hello,' he said. 'What are you doing here?'

I pointed at the coffin. 'It's alive,' I croaked. 'The body is alive. Save me and I'll be your partner.'

The smile vanished from his face. He walked over to the coffin and lifted up the lid. 'He is too,' he said. 'He's still breathing. Mrs Trapp will be pleased.'

'Mrs Trapp,' I managed to gasp. 'What's she got to do with it?'

'Well,' grinned Ralph as he lifted out the furry bundle, 'Ribble is her favourite cat.'

Batty

A stone with a hole in it. A sort of green-coloured jewel in a leather pouch. Just lying there in the beam of my torch.

Someone must have dropped it. But who? There was only Dad and me and our two little tents, alone in the bush. I picked the pouch up by the piece of leather thong which was threaded through it. Then I crawled into my tent.

I should have shown Dad the stone with the hole in it. But he was snoring away inside his tent and I didn't want to wake him. And there was something odd about it. The pouch was worn and the thong was twisted. As if it had hung around someone's neck for many years.

Who was the owner? Who had lost his way out here in the wilderness?

I snuggled down inside my sleeping bag and hoped that no one was snooping around. The noises of the bush seemed especially loud. Frogs chirped in a billabong. 'Well, they can't hurt you,' I said softly.

Something bounded through the scrub. 'Kangaroo,' I whispered to myself.

A growling grunt filled the night air. 'Koala,' I thought hopefully.

I closed my eyes and tried to make sleep come. I dared not listen to the rustlings and sighings outside. I told myself that Dad's tent was only a few metres away. But in that dark, dark night it could have been a million miles.

Scared? I was terrified. What if someone was out there? Creeping. Watching. Waiting. 'Get a hold of yourself, girl,' I said to myself. 'There is no one out there.'

A twig broke. Snapped clean in the night. I stopped breathing. I stopped moving. But I didn't stop thinking. 'Go away. Please go away,' begged my frozen brain. I wanted to call out to Dad but my mouth wouldn't work.

The flap of the tent lifted. I could see the stars and the black trees. Someone moved. A shadow rustling, searching. Hands took my bag and opened it. I wanted to cry out but something stopped me.

Two pinpoints of light moved in a dark head. Eyes. Desperate eyes.

Quietly I moved my fingers. Like a spider's legs they crept under the blankets towards my torch. Softly, don't disturb him. Don't make him angry. With shaking hands I pointed the torch into the gloom. I felt like a soldier with an empty gun. I flicked on the switch.

And there he was. A wild boy with tangled hair and greasy skin. He was covered in flapping rags.

The tent was filled with a terrible squeaking like a million mice.

The boy reared back. In one hand he held a piece of cake from my bag. And in the other was the pouch with the hollow stone. He sucked in air with a hiss, turned to flee and then stopped.

He looked at me with a silent plea. A desperate call for help. He held his hand in front of his face to stop the light of the torch. The moon escaped from a bank of clouds and softened the tent with light. I should have called for Dad. But my eyes were locked in silent conversation with the intruder.

I could see that the boy was as frightened as me. He was poised to run. Like a wild animal wanting food but unable to take it from a human hand. I had to be careful. A wrong movement and he . . .

'Hey,' yelled Dad.

It was just as if someone had turned out a light. The boy vanished in a twinkle. I didn't even see him go.

2

Dad and I sat up nearly all night talking about what had happened.

It seems that a hermit called Lonely Pearson had once lived out here in a hut with his wife and son. The wife was an expert on bats, like Dad. Nine years ago she died and Lonely became enraged with grief.

Lonely did some mean things. He burned everything

that belonged to her. Her books, her clothes, her photos of the bats. The lot. It was almost as if he was angry with her for dying and leaving him alone with his little five-year-old son – Philip.

The only thing that was left was a green stone with a hole in it. Philip's mother had always worn it around her neck. He used to play with it while she read him stories at bedtime.

After she died, Philip hid the stone. Lonely Pearson ranted and raved. He shouted and searched. He nearly tore their hut to pieces. But Philip wouldn't show him where it was. He closed his mouth and refused to speak. He kept his secret and Lonely never found the stone.

'So what happened to Philip?' I asked Dad.

'He ran off into the bush. Lonely couldn't find him. No one could find him. The police searched for weeks and weeks. Then they gave up. Everyone thought he was dead.'

I took a deep breath. 'What about Lonely?' I said.

'He spent every day searching for his son. He never gave up. Lonely died last year.'

I couldn't stop thinking about that sad, bewildered face staring at me in the moonlight.

'How can he live out here?' I asked. 'It gets really cold at night. And there's nothing to eat.'

Dad shook his head and turned down the kerosene lamp. 'That's enough for tonight,' he said. 'You go to sleep. We have two days of climbing before we reach the bat cave. You will need all the rest you can get.'

'But . . .' I began.

'Goodnight, Rachel.'

I heard him zip up his sleeping bag. I was in Dad's tent. It was a bit of a squash but Dad thought it was safer.

'Goodnight,' I mumbled. I was thinking about the next night. I was going back to my own tent. I had no doubts about that.

3

The next day was hot and our packs were heavy. Dad and I struggled through the dense bush. Down into wet gullies filled with tree ferns and leeches. Up dry, rocky slopes through sharp, scratching thorns. Along trails where kookaburras called and cicadas filled the air with chirping.

It was wonderful country but my pack was heavy. And so was my heart. There was a sadness in the air. At times I thought I glimpsed a hidden watcher. But I could never be quite sure. I would turn quickly. A branch moved slightly. Or did it?

We stopped for lunch in a mossy glen. Dad passed me a piece of cake. It was starting to go stale. I wrapped it up and put it in my pocket.

'Not hungry?' asked Dad.

'I'm keeping it for later,' I replied. I was too. But not for me. I had plans for that bit of cake.

We packed up and moved on. Sometimes we went up. And sometimes down. But we were getting higher and higher.

My Dad was a greenie. And of all living things, he loved bats best. He was mad about them.

We were heading for a bat cave in the mountain's highest tops, Bat Peaks. Dad was going to block off the entrance to the cave. The roof was beginning to fall in. If it collapsed the whole colony of bats would be destroyed.

'But they will all starve,' I had said when he first told me the plan.

'No,' he had replied. 'We block the cave entrance at night. When they are out feeding. They will be forced to find another cave. It's the only way to save the colony.'

So there we were. Trudging up the mountain. On our way to blow up a bat cave before it collapsed and killed the bats.

Dad had bats on his brain. But all I could think of was a boy called Philip.

4

That night we camped in a forest clearing. Our camp fire crackled between a circle of stones. Overhead the stars filled the cold night like a handful of sugar thrown at the sky. It didn't seem as if there could be anything wicked in the world.

The gums were ghostly and grey. The ground was home to pebbles, thorns and ants. I shuddered at the thought of someone living out there. Barefoot and alone.

Dad crawled into his tent. 'Go to sleep, Rachel,' he said.

'I'll just sit by the fire for a bit more,' I told him.

You couldn't put much over Dad. He knew what I was up to. 'He won't come,' he said. 'He's wild and frightened. We'll call out a search party when we get back.'

I sat there alone, but not alone, as the fire crackled and tossed sparks into the arms of the watching tree tops. The noises of the night kept me company.

I stared into the dark fringes of the forest. Watching for the watcher. Waiting for the waiter. Willing Philip to come.

At last the fire died and I shared the dark blanket of the night with the unseen creatures of the bush.

Quietly I walked to the edge of the trees and broke off a piece of cake. I placed it on a rock. A few metres away I did the same. I made a trail of cake leading to the edge of the dying fire.

Then I sat and waited.

Minutes passed. And hours. The moon slowly climbed behind the clouds. I struggled to keep my eyes open. But failed. You can only fight off sleep for so long. Then it wins and your head droops and your eyes close. That's what happened to me.

How long I dozed for I don't know. But something woke me. Not a noise. Nothing from the forest. More like a thought or a dream. Or the memory of a woman's voice. I woke with a start and stared around the clearing. Something was different. Something was missing.

The first piece of cake. It was gone.

At that moment I half saw two things. High in a tree off to one side was a shadowy figure, watching from a branch. And on the edge of the clearing was someone else. I was sure it was Philip.

It was.

He cautiously crept forward into the open. Shadows fell across his body. He was still dressed like a beggar. Hundreds of flapping rags hung from his body.

The boy's eyes darted from side to side. He looked first at the cake and then at me. He crept forward a few steps and bent and picked up the cake. The moon slid out from its hiding place.

And Philip stood there, revealed. For a moment I couldn't take it in. Couldn't make sense of what my eyes were telling me. His rags flapped in the breeze. But the night was still and there was no breeze.

They were alive. His rags seethed and crawled and squeaked.

The wild boy was covered in bats. They hung from his arms and hair and chest. He was dressed in live bats. I couldn't believe it. Only his eyes were clear. His beautiful, dark eyes. I gave a scream and staggered backwards.

5

The movement alarmed Philip and he threw his arms across his face. He was like a living book with its grey pages ruffling in a storm. Two bats flew up into the air and swooped under the trees.

Philip looked at me in fear and then up at the circling bats. Without a word he held his hands up to his mouth and started to whistle softly. The bats in the trees flew straight back and attached themselves to his hair. The others became calm.

'Sorry,' I said in a hoarse voice. 'I didn't mean to scare you.' There were lots of things I wanted to say. My stomach felt strange. I could feel myself blushing. I wanted to say something tender. Something caring. Something that would make us friends. Or more than friends. But all I could think of saying was, 'Have some cake.'

Philip stared at me. And then at the cake. I could see that he wasn't sure. I wondered if he had ever seen a girl before.

'I'm your friend,' I said. 'I won't hurt you, I promise.'

He was hungry. I guess that he hadn't tasted cake for a long, long time. Maybe he had been eating bat food. Fruit and moths and things.

He gave a sort of a smile. Only a small one. But it was enough to make my heart beat so fast that it hurt. Philip took a step towards the next piece of cake. He was starting to trust me. Maybe even to like me. As quick as a snake striking he pounced on the cake and began munching.

He ate like a five-year-old, shoving the cake in with both hands and smearing crumbs all over his face.

If only I could get him to trust me. I might then be able to talk to him. To make him stay. He swallowed the last crumb and then just stood there staring into my eyes.

Slowly I took a step forward. 'It's okay,' I whispered. 'It's okay.'

The bats murmured and fluttered. He was ready to run. But he let me approach. An invisible bond was holding us together.

'Aaagh . . .' There was a terrible scream from the treetops. A branch broke with a crack. The shadowy figure I'd seen plunged down, grabbing at branches and yelling. He landed with a thump and lay there groaning. It was Dad.

The bats scattered into the air like a swarm of huge bees. Philip's cloak was gone. He stood there, naked. He glared at me. He thought we had tried to trap him. He raised his fist and then, thinking better of it, fled into the forest.

'Come back,' I yelled. Tears flooded down my face. 'Please come back.'

But only the bats stayed, circling above me, squeaking in fright.

I ran over to Dad. 'Sorry,' he said. 'I couldn't let you

meet him alone. I had to keep an eye on you.'

'Are you okay?' I asked.

Dad tried to stand but he couldn't. 'Sprained ankle,' he groaned.

We both looked up at the circling cloud of bats. They didn't seem to know where to go. A sound drifted on the night air. 'Shh . . .' said Dad.

A soft, squeaking whistle pierced the night. It was the whistling noise Philip made through his fingers. The bats squeaked frantically, circled once and flew off after the sound. Dad and I were alone in the dark, silent clearing.

6

Frenzied thoughts filled my mind. Philip, Philip, we have betrayed you. Dad, how could you spy on me? Dad, are you hurt?

Dad was groaning and holding his ankle. 'That's the end of the expedition,' he said. 'I can't walk a step.'

'But what about the bats? The cave might fall on them. The whole colony will die unless we blow up the cave.'

'I'm sorry, Rachel,' said Dad. 'I can't move. And you can't go alone. We'll stay here. The Rangers know our route. They'll send a helicopter when we don't arrive back on time. We'll be safe if we stay here.'

I took a deep breath. 'But that's in three days. What if the cave collapses? I'm going on my own.'

'Don't be silly,' said Dad. 'You've never even seen a stick of dynamite. I wouldn't let you anywhere near it. You'd kill yourself.' He grabbed his pack and held it tight. The dynamite was inside.

'There's something you haven't thought of,' I said.

'Yes?'

'Philip. He is covered in bats. He wears them like clothes.'

'So?' said Dad.

'And he whistles through his fingers and calls them.'

'Yes?'

'Where do you think he lives? He is a bat boy. He must live in that cave with the bats. And the roof is about to fall in. We have to save him.'

Dad didn't say anything for quite a bit. He knew I was right.

'You're not going anywhere,' he said at last. 'You might get lost. You can't handle dynamite. The boy won't come out of the cave anyway. He's a wild thing. He hasn't spoken to anyone since he was five. No. We wait here until help arrives. And that's the end of it.'

When your father says, 'That's the end of it,' it usually means it is.

But not this time.

I don't know how to say it. But I couldn't get Philip's face out of my mind. My stomach was churning over. My face was hot. Just thinking about him gave me the shivers.

That cave might fall in at any minute. He could die alone, covered in bats. Far, far away from his people. In nine years he had never felt the touch of a woman's hand.

'I'm going,' I said. 'And you can't stop me.'

'No,' Dad said with an iron face. 'You're only fourteen. I forbid it.'

'You've got a sprained ankle and can't move,' I said. 'You can't forbid anything. Goodbye.' I just turned around and started walking out of the clearing into the night forest.

'All right. All right, Rachel,' he called. 'But come back. You have to prepare. Take food and a compass. Ropes. Everything. Otherwise there will be two dead teenagers.'

So that's what happened. I packed my knapsack with food and everything I might need. Except the dynamite. There was no way Dad would even take his hand off it.

By morning I was ready to leave. I headed off in the direction of Bat Peaks. The mountain loomed above us like a pair of giant wings. 'Remember,' yelled Dad, 'don't go inside the cave. Promise.'

'Yes,' I said as I pushed into the bush. 'I promise.'

7

It was tough going. The higher I went the more difficult it became. The trees gave way to giant boulders and scrub. My knees were raw and bleeding. My feet were sore.

But I didn't care. I had to get Philip and the bats out of that cave. But how?

I held my fingers up to my lips and blew. Nothing except a rush of hot air. Not so much as a squeak. If I could learn to whistle through my fingers I might be able to call him. And bring out the bats.

But I just couldn't get the hang of it. I always admired those kids at school who could whistle through their fingers.

The sun rose high above me and then began to lower itself towards the rim of the mountains. Before I knew it, the sky was growing dark.

I was perched high above the forest on a mountain ledge. The trees below looked like the surface of an ocean gently rippling in the last of the sunlight. Cockatoos circled, screeching above their roosts. I jiggled down into my sleeping bag and hoped that I wouldn't roll over the edge in my sleep.

Not that I did sleep. The ground was hard. And I couldn't stop thinking about Philip.

So I practised finger whistling. I blew until my lips were parched and dry. But not a sound could I get. It was hopeless.

The next day I scrambled up and on. Rocks tumbled and crashed under my feet. They bounded into the valley way below. I became reckless. I didn't stop to rest.

I knew that time was passing too quickly. I dreaded to think what I might find when I reached the bat cave.

I stopped for nothing. Not even to use the compass. After all, there was only one way to go. Up.

That's how I became lost. Found myself on a rocky outcrop. Tumbled into a crevasse. Lay dazed for hours. Lost my pack. Lost my compass. Lost my senses.

In the end I crawled out and sat and cried. I had no map. No way of knowing where I was. Or where the cave was. I was totally lost.

That's when I saw it. Just hanging there on a bramble. A leather pouch. I stumbled over and grabbed it. I fumbled with the catch and looked inside. The green coloured stone with a hole in it.

Philip must have dropped it again. Twice in three days?

I couldn't believe that he would keep dropping something so precious. It was the only thing he had to remind him of his mother.

I smiled. I told myself that he left it there on purpose. For me. To show me the way. That's what I thought anyway. That's what I hoped.

I grabbed the pouch and stumbled on. On to the very top. On to where the sheer rock cliffs fell down on every side.

A small bridge of rock spanned a drop into the valley miles below. It was so far down that my head swam.

And there, on the other side, hanging under an enormous shelf was what I had come for. The bat cave.

Normally I would not have crossed that rocky bridge. Not for anything.

But somehow I forced my trembling legs over. Until I stood there peering at the cave, staring into its black jaws.

All was silent except for the soft breath of the cold mountain breeze.

I looked at the roof of the cave. It seemed okay to me. How did Dad know that it was going to fall in?

I held my fingers to my mouth and blew. Nothing. I couldn't get a whistle. Not a squeak. It was hopeless.

'Philip,' I called. 'Philip, come out. The cave is going to collapse.'

Silence was the only reply.

I forgot my promise to Dad. Or I pushed it into the back of my mind. I'm not sure which.

With thumping heart I made my way into the gloom. Water pinged in the distance. A soft burbling noise surrounded me.

As my eyes became used to the dark I could make out a huge boulder in the roof. It seemed to move. It did move. It was covered in thousands of hanging bats. Their wings rippled like a blanket floating on a lake.

How long before that rock would fall? I trembled. 'Philip,' I called urgently. 'Philip.'

No answer. I raised my voice. 'Come out, you stupid boy,' I shouted. 'Come out.'

It was not Philip who was stupid. It was me. My voice echoed terribly around the walls. It bounced off the rocks. It shook the dry air.

Without a speck of warning the living boulder above plunged to the ground. It shook the mountain to its roots. It filled the cave with choking dust.

My voice had dislodged the boulder.

Thousands of bats mingled with the dust. Circling. Screaming. Screeching. I turned and fled into the glaring sunlight. Another boulder fell. The sound of its smash pummelled the walls. More rocks fell.

'Philip,' I screamed. 'Philip, come out.'

Dust, like smoke from a fallen chimney, billowed into the mountain air. And through it came Philip. Blood flowed from a deep wound in his head. He staggered out and fell at my feet. Unconscious.

I dragged him clear of the mouth of the cave. I pulled him towards the rocky bridge. And then stopped and stared, filled with terror at the sight.

The bridge had broken. Fallen into the valley below. We were trapped on the mountain top. There was no way back.

8

Naked. Not a stitch on.

Poor Philip. Lying there on the bare mountain. Exposed to the wind. Was he dead? I didn't know.

I should have put my jumper over him. Covered his

nakedness. But there wasn't time. Rocks were still falling. There was no way down. And the bats. The bats were doomed. 'Help. Someone help.'

No one answered. I was alone.

I held my fists up to my mouth and blew. I wanted so badly to save the bats. I tried to whistle loudly but nothing came.

The bats were still in there. They would die because of me. Because I raised my voice and disturbed the rocks. And Philip. Would he die too?

He opened his eyes. He looked at me. Was he accusing me? Did his eyes say that I had murdered his friends?

No, they did not. He smiled. He tried to speak but he couldn't. Instead he touched the pouch that hung around my neck. His mother's stone.

'This,' I said. He nodded and once more closed his eyes.

I took out the green stone and stared at it. I knew what to do.

I began to blow through the hole.

The air was filled with a whistle. A strong, clear squeaking. The most beautiful sound I had ever heard.

The cave echoed thunder. Not of falling rocks but of beating wings. Hundreds, thousands, millions of wings. The bats surged out of the cave. They darkened the sky. They filled the mountain top until nothing could be seen but a swirling swarm of grey. I had saved the colony.

Philip opened his eyes and smiled. He took the stone from my fingers and blew. He whistled his own message to the bats.

They dropped out of the sky like autumn leaves in a storm. I shrieked. They grabbed my hair. My feet. They pierced my jumper with tiny claws. The bats hung from me like rags.

I stared at Philip. He was no longer naked, but like me wore a living cloak. Bat boy. Bat girl. Stranded. Together on Bat Peaks.

The bats beat their wings in a terrible rhythm. They stirred up a storm of squealing fury.

My feet left the ground. I was flying. Carried up, up, up. Lifted into the sky by a flurry of flapping wings. Held by tiny feet.

The mountain lay far beneath. I saw an explosion of dust spurt out from the cave below. The roof had caved in.

I gasped in shock at the sight of the valleys below. Like the prey of a mountain eagle I was lifted between the mountain tops.

And above me, Philip, carried by his coat of friends, soared and swooped in the empty sky.

He waved and pointed.

Far, far beneath, in the tangled mat of trees was a wisp of smoke. Dad's camp fire.

The bats began to descend. Taking us down through the biting air.

BATTY

For the first time Philip spoke. He pointed down at
the camp fire and said just one word.

'Home.'

And that is where we went.

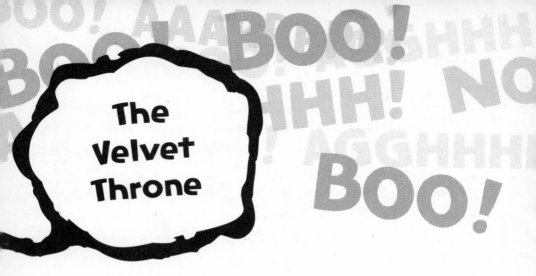

The Velvet Throne

Mr Simpkin decided to run away from home. But not for twelve hours. When it was dark he would sneak out of bed and tiptoe down the stairs. Gobble wouldn't know. He would be asleep by then. Snoring as usual.

The kettle began to whistle. Mr Simpkin hurried into the kitchen to make Gobble's coffee. Just the way he liked it. Four spoonfuls of sugar. Cream, not milk. Stirred five and a half times. No more, no less. The toaster suddenly popped. Mr Simpkin snatched the toast and buttered it. He had to hurry. Gobble hated cold toast. He was fussy about his food.

The boiled eggs were ready too. All nine of them. Each egg had a little woollen hat to keep it warm.

'Hurry up, idiot,' Gobble called from his bedroom. He was awake. He didn't like to wait for his breakfast.

Mr Simpkin's hands shook. He hurried into his brother's bedroom. 'Here it is,' he said nervously. 'Everything's just right.'

Gobble tried to sit up in bed. He was very, very fat. The bed sagged. It groaned and creaked. 'Help me up,' ordered Gobble. 'Don't just stand there like a fool.'

Mr Simpkin put the tray on the floor. He tried to heave Gobble up onto his pillows. But he couldn't. His arms were too thin. His muscles were too small. He went red in the face as he heaved and strained at the bulging body. Gobble pushed him away. 'Useless. Absolutely useless,' he grunted, pulling himself up.

With shaking hands Mr Simpkin put the tray on the bed. 'Twelve pieces of toast with jam,' he said. 'And four pieces with orange marmalade. Your favourite.' Mr Simpkin smiled at his fat brother. But the smile soon fell from his face.

'Idiot,' yelled Gobble. 'I ordered twelve pieces with orange marmalade and four with jam.' He picked up a slice of toast and threw it at the wall. For a moment it stuck there, glued to the wallpaper. Then it slid slowly down, leaving a jammy trail behind it.

'Clean that up,' shouted Gobble. 'And then bring me the newspaper. You always forget the paper.'

Mr Simpkin scurried off to fetch a sponge. 'Yes, Arnold,' he whispered.

Gobble's name wasn't really Gobble. It was Arnold. But Mr Simpkin always called him Gobble in his mind. He was too scared to say it out loud. But it made him feel better. He smiled to himself. Arnold would be furious if he knew.

2

Mr Simpkin opened the door of the flat and walked

down the stairs to fetch the paper. There were fifteen flights of stairs. He ran as quickly as he could to fetch the paper. He still had to make his own breakfast and then rush off to work. He didn't want to be late.

While Gobble read the paper in bed, Mr Simpkin prepared his own breakfast. He wasn't allowed to eat the eggs. Or the bread. Or the cereals. He took out a can of sheep's eyes and opened it. Last week, while shopping, he had bought a tin of sheep's eyes by mistake – he thought they were oysters. Gobble was furious. 'You bought them,' Gobble shouted. 'So you eat them.'

Mr Simpkin opened the can and shook the contents onto a plate. The horrible, wobbling eyes slid out with a slurp. They seemed to be staring up at him. The smell was terrible. Mr Simpkin was hungry. But not that hungry. He just couldn't eat them. He put the plate in the fridge and walked towards the door.

'Goodbye, Gobb . . . I mean Arnold,' he called.

'It's payday today,' yelled Gobble. 'Make sure you come straight home with the money. And don't open the packet. I don't want you wasting our wages on rubbish.'

'No, Arnold,' whispered Mr Simpkin. He crept off to work. Gobble had never had a job. He just lay in bed eating chocolates and watching television while poor little Mr Simpkin slaved away at the fertiliser factory all day.

At the end of every week Mr Simpkin handed his pay packet over to Gobble. If Gobble was in a good mood he would sometimes give Mr Simpkin a few dollars for himself.

Mr Simpkin just made it to work in time. He spent all day filling up fertiliser bags. It was hard work. He grew hungrier and hungrier. His stomach rumbled. At lunchtime he had nothing to eat. Gobble wouldn't let him have any money to buy food until he'd eaten the can of sheep's eyes. He was too scared to tip them down the drain in case Gobble caught him.

'Aren't you having any lunch?' asked Tom Richards, the foreman.

'I'm not hungry,' said Mr Simpkin. He wet his lips and watched sadly as Tom scoffed down his sandwiches.

After work Mr Simpkin collected his pay packet and walked slowly home. Gobble would stuff the money in his pocket. He would tell Mr Simpkin to eat the sheep's eyes for tea. He would fill his face with jellies and cakes while Mr Simpkin watched.

The rain drizzled down. Mr Simpkin walked more and more slowly. He thought about his plans to run away. Why wait until tonight? Why not run off now? Keep the money. It was his money. He could start a new life. Get another job where Gobble couldn't find him.

He could go to a motel for the night. Gobble had thousands of dollars in a tin under the bed. It was all money that Mr Simpkin had earned. He wished that he could get some of it but he knew that Gobble would never hand it over.

3

The streets were full of people rushing home. It was cold. But Mr Simpkin smiled to himself. He tore open his pay packet. The dollar bills were folded neatly. They were all his. Every one. It made him feel terrific to open his own pay packet.

He would do it. He decided straightaway. He would go to a motel and book in. He would order an enormous meal. Gobble could eat the sheep's eyes if he wanted. Just the thought of it made Mr Simpkin chuckle. A motel. That's where he would go. But first he needed to find a toilet. All of the excitement was making him nervous. He needed to go to the loo.

Nearby was a park. Mr Simpkin ran across the wet grass. Soon he was surrounded by trees. It was growing dark. Where was the toilet? There was one around here somewhere.

There it was. Under the trees. A bluestone building. Like a jail.

Mr Simpkin looked at his watch. Two minutes to five.

He found the MEN sign and hurried inside.

Someone had written on the wall. There was scribble everywhere. Mr Simpkin didn't read it. Graffiti usually said rude things. He tried not to look at the scrawled writing. But he couldn't help himself. Just above his head was scribbled:

1. THIS JOINT GETS LOCKED AT FIVE.

There was a loud clang and the sound of a key turning.

At first Mr Simpkin did nothing. Then he realised. Someone had shut the gate and locked it. He rushed over to the iron gate. It was fixed with a chain and padlock. 'Hey,' he called out softly. 'I'm in here.'

He was too embarrassed to shout. He heard footsteps disappearing. 'Excuse me,' he called softly. 'Er, excuse me.'

The footsteps disappeared. No one answered his call. He was alone. Locked in a public toilet. On a cold and wet night.

He plucked up his courage. 'Help,' he shouted. 'Help, help, help.'

The park was silent. The toilet was silent. He looked up at the roof where one lonely light globe glowed in the dark. There was no way out. He was trapped.

4

The night grew colder. Mr Simpkin shivered and drew his coat around himself. 'Help,' he yelled again. 'Help, help, help.'

The rain dripped silently. There was no answer. He knew no one would come until morning. He looked around for somewhere to sit. The floor was wet and cold. And he was hungry.

He started to look at the graffiti. There was another bit with a number. It said:

2. THE BEST SEAT IN THE HOUSE.

An arrow pointed to one of the cubicles. Mr Simpkin gave a weak grin. Someone had a sense of humour. He followed the arrow into the cubicle. And gasped. The toilet seat was covered in velvet. The pan shone like gold. The cistern button was a diamond. The toilet was more like a throne than a loo.

This was crazy. Why would anyone put such a wonderful seat there? Vandals could wreck it in no time at all.

He stared around the cubicle. There was another piece of numbered graffiti. It read:

3. NO STANDING.

Suddenly Mr Simpkin felt an urgent need to sit down. His legs seemed to make him walk. He shuffled forward and sat on the velvet-lined toilet seat. He tried to stop, but he couldn't. Well, he thought that he couldn't. Maybe he had been feeling a little tired. Yes, that was it.

Something scuffled in the gloom. He stared at the corner. A shadow moved. And scuttered. Mr Simpkin's heart froze. Little bumps spread across his flesh.

A rat. He hated rats. He lifted his feet off the ground. 'Shoo,' he said softly. 'Scat.'

The rat scurried into a hole.

The minutes ticked by. Mr Simpkin sat watching

for the rat but there was no sign of it. After a while he noticed more numbered graffiti. There was another piece of writing scrawled above the toilet-roll holder. It said:

4. ROCK'N'ROLL.

More jokes. He stared at the toilet-roll holder. It moved. He was sure that it moved. It gave a little jiggle.

Mr Simpkin shook with fear. Something strange was going on. He wanted to get out of this loo. Someone was playing jokes. And they weren't funny.

5

The toilet-roll holder began to jig. Back and forward. Up and down in a regular beat like a musician tapping his feet. It was jigging to silent music. It was beating out a tune. Mr Simpkin thought that he had heard it somewhere before. He was sure it was an old rock'n'roll number.

Without warning the jigging stopped.

Even though it was cold Mr Simpkin began to sweat. He was trapped like a rat in a crazy toilet.

He tried to figure it out. There was something strange about the writing on the wall. The first bit of numbered graffiti had said 'this joint closes at five'. And it had. On the dot. Nothing strange about that.

But the next one had pointed to 'the best seat in the house'. And it was the best seat. And the weirdest.

And then there was the 'no standing' sign. Forcing

him to sit down. And what about the 'rock'n'roll' paper holder? It had started to rock'n'roll. It really had. Or was it just the wind? Or the water pipes shaking it?

Mr Simpkin had the feeling that he was going out of his mind. But then – if you are mad, you are the only one who doesn't know, and he was wondering whether or not he was sane. So he couldn't be mad. Or could he?

'Get a grip of yourself, man,' he whispered. His voice echoed around the lonely lavatory.

There was only one explanation. He tried to push the thought from his mind. He tried to stop thinking it. But the unwanted thought winkled its way into his brain. The graffiti was coming true. Acting itself out. Everything written on the wall was happening.

Mr Simpkin's hands began to shake. He rushed over to the locked gate and shook the bars. 'Help,' he called. 'Get me out of here.'

Water dripped and pinged but there was no reply.

He shouted and yelled. Kicked and screamed. But the empty night gave no answer.

Slowly he walked back to the velvet seat and sat down. He closed his eyes tightly. He didn't want to read the walls. He was too terrified to think about it.

A sound disturbed the silence. A hinge creaked loudly. Mr Simpkin opened his eyes and stared. The cubicle door slowly swung outwards.

6

There was a big space underneath the door. Just above the gap was scrawled:

5. BEWARE OF LIMBO DANCERS.

Another joke. But Mr Simpkin didn't laugh. His lips were frozen in a bewildered grin. His tongue was stuck to the roof of his dry mouth. His eyes bulged.

Music began to play. It sounded as if a whole band was playing inside the toilet. An invisible orchestra. He knew the tune. 'The Limbo Rock'. Da da da da da da da da da. Da da da da da da da da. It surged and swelled. Rocking and rollicking.

Suddenly a dancing, swaying line of people filled the empty building. They seemed to appear from nowhere. They wore crazy hats and blew party squeakers. They clapped their hands and kicked their feet. The line swayed and swerved and approached the cubicle door.

One by one the partygoers leaned back on their heels and passed under the open door. They ignored Mr Simpkin. He was like an uninvited ghost at a banquet. He sat still, terrified on his velvet seat as the line came back for another limbo. Without warning a gust of wind slammed the door. It banged loudly. Mr Simpkin winced and closed his eyes. When he opened them, the line of dancers had disappeared. He was alone once more. Silence replaced the music.

What was going on? What? What? What? Was this a nightmare? Every bit of numbered graffiti was coming true. What else was written there? People wrote terrible things on toilet walls.

He looked above his head:

6. DROWNED IN THE DUNNY AT DAWN.

Mr Simpkin shrieked. He jumped off his velvet seat and stared down into the water. 'No,' he shrieked. 'Not that. No, no, no.'

He ran over to the corner. As far away from the pan as he could get. He squatted down on the floor, curling up into a tight ball. He closed his eyes and refused to read any more. He tried to sleep. So that he could wake up from this dreadful nightmare.

But sleep wouldn't come. He crouched there, not moving. The minutes and hours ticked by. His stomach rumbled. His legs were stiff. He thought his ordeal would never end. But at last the first rays of sunlight crept through the iron gate.

Dawn.

Mr Simpkin shook. He looked around for a weapon. There was nothing.

7

His eyes rested on a shape moving along the top of the wall of the empty cubicle. It was the rat. It crept forwards. Mr Simpkin crouched down. What if the rat leapt at him? Flew through the air with bared fangs?

It was better not to wait. He stood up and waved his arms. 'Shoo,' he yelled. 'Scat. Buzz off.'

The rat was startled. It reared up on its back legs. And slipped. It fell, tumbling into the velvet toilet. With the speed of a cobra, Mr Simpkin lunged across the floor and pressed the diamond button.

The rat disappeared in a gurgling flush.

Mr Simpkin slumped down. The writing had come true. The rat had drowned at dawn.

He wondered what else was written. It was no use putting it off any longer. He searched the walls for more numbered graffiti. And found one more piece. It simply said:

7. THERE'S NO PLACE LIKE HOME.

Without warning there was a clang. A key turned in a lock. The iron gate was thrown open.

Mr Simpkin took one last look around his prison. And fled. There was no sign of a gatekeeper. Who had opened the door? He didn't know. Or care. He was free. He fled across the park.

'There's no place like home. You can say that again,' he thought to himself. If he hurried he might get back before Gobble woke up. He could make Gobble's breakfast especially tasty. He would hand over his pay packet. Gobble might forgive him for taking a night off. If not, well, he would just have to take whatever punishment was dealt out.

Anything would be better than spending another night in that terrifying toilet. Running away had been a big mistake.

He was hungry. Starving. After he had fed Gobble he would make himself a nice meal of . . .

Sheep's eyes.

Mr Simpkin stopped running. He walked slowly with heavy steps. His shoulders were hunched as if he carried a great burden. Suddenly he stopped. And turned. He started to run back across the grass.

The gate of the toilet was still open. He hurried inside and looked at his watch. Two minutes to seven. He felt inside his pocket. And found what he was looking for – a blunt pencil.

He took it out and carefully wrote on the toilet wall:

8. GOBBLE DISAPPEARS FOREVER AT SEVEN O'CLOCK.

Mr Simpkin hurried home. He burst into the flat. 'Gobble,' he called. 'Are you there, Gobble?'

There was no reply.

His brother was nowhere to be seen.

I'll tell you one thing for sure. Fruitcake and Pancake were the best pets that Martin had ever had. Boy, he could train them to do just about anything.

Their best trick was to act as an alarm clock. Martin had rigged up the empty fish tank in his bedroom so that Fruitcake was on one side behind a piece of glass and Pancake was on the other. At exactly seven o'clock a little glass door would swing open and Fruitcake could hop through and stand on Pancake's back. By doing this he could reach up and catch a dead fly with his tongue. The fly hung on a piece of cotton which stretched across the bedroom and was tied to Martin's little toe. When Fruitcake grabbed the fly with his tongue the cotton would yank on Martin's toe and wake him up.

Martin sure was a brain.

And Fruitcake and Pancake were the smartest cane toads in the whole of Queensland. Martin had even taught them to row a little boat up and down the bath.

They were fantastic and Martin loved them just as if they were his children.

Now this might seem a bit strange to you or me because most people think cane toads are just ugly pests that look like frogs and live in the garden. But not Martin. He thought they were beautiful. I have even seen him kiss the two toads full on the mouth.

Don't laugh, because when I tell you how Martin saved the lives of those toads you will understand why he felt this way about them.

You see, there was this bloke called Frisbee who owned a shop near Martin. Frisbee was a great big bloke with a huge beer pot. His stomach hung out so much that his belt had to loop down underneath it. His shop was just out of town in the bush, near where Martin lived.

It was a tourist shop. It sold stuff like real plastic boomerangs and animals made out of shells from the Barrier Reef. He had genuine Aboriginal tapping sticks with elephants carved on them. He also sold a lot of wooden rulers and letter openers made from trees cut down in the rain forests.

His best-selling line was his toy koala bears. Once Martin peeked through a chink in the blinds at night and saw Frisbee cutting all the MADE IN JAPAN labels off the koalas. When he had finished he placed little Australian flags in the hands of the koalas.

Every night when he closed up the shop, Frisbee would pull down the blind and put up a stretcher. This was where he slept. He never washed and he never changed his clothes. He lived and slept in the same clothes for years and years.

But all these things are nothing next to what Frisbee used to do to cane toads. He hated cane toads as much as Martin loved them.

Frisbee was a cane-toad killer. He used to find a lamp post near a busy road. You know how the insects hang around the street lights and the cane toads hang around too, so that they can catch the insects? Well Frisbee used to catch himself a bucket full of cane toads underneath the street lamp. Then he would throw them out onto the road when a car was coming.

Some of the drivers were as mean as Frisbee and they would try to run over the toads. If they missed, Frisbee would yell out 'Fruitcake' at the driver as loud as he could. If the car hit the toad and squashed it flat, Frisbee would yell out 'Pancake' and jump up and down laughing his silly head off.

Sometimes Frisbee and his mean mates would go back a couple of days later. They used to prise the dried-out, flattened toads off the road and throw them to each other like flying saucers. This is how he got the name Frisbee.

Well, on the night I am talking about, Martin was walking down the street right when Frisbee was throwing his last two toads onto the road. Quick as a flash, and without thinking of his own safety, Martin nipped out and grabbed the two toads just as a truck was about to flatten them. Then he nicked off into the bush before Frisbee knew what had happened.

'Come back here, you squirt,' yelled out Frisbee. 'Give those toads back or I'll stuff them down your throat.' He ran off after Martin as fast as he could go. And that was very fast indeed. He was a good runner for a big bloke and he was as mad as a wombat.

Martin was scared as he ran through the dark scrub. He knew he would look like a squashed toad himself if Frisbee got hold of him so he did the only thing he could think of. He charged off into Tiger Snake Swamp which lay at the bottom of the hill.

Now there are only two things which live in Tiger Snake Swamp. There are cane toads and they wouldn't hurt a fly (so to speak), and tiger snakes, which are deadly poisonous. Also, it is possible to get lost in Tiger Snake Swamp because it covers hundreds of square kilometres with twisted trees and murky waterways.

Martin knew that it was dangerous, especially at night. He waded out through the weeds until he was up to his waist.

Frisbee was too chicken to go in the water so he just stood on the bank yelling and swearing at Martin. In the end he said, 'Don't think you are going to get away with this, toad lover. I am going to fix you up. For good. Your little toad-clearing business will soon be wiped out.' Then he turned around and stormed off into the night.

2

At this stage I should tell you about Martin's toad-clearing business. On weekends Martin used to go around to houses and offer to clear out all of the toads from people's backyards. Martin couldn't figure out why people didn't like to have thirty or so toads in their gardens. He didn't realise that some people were scared of them. Others didn't like standing on them in their bare feet at night. It was a bit yucky scraping the green and yellow stuff out from between their toes.

For three dollars Martin would collect all their toads and then let them go in Tiger Snake Swamp.

What he didn't know was that Frisbee was about to go into the toad business himself. In a big way.

As he waded out of the water Martin noticed that there were hundreds and hundreds of cane toads around him. Some of them looked familiar. Martin was the only person in the world who could remember the faces of toads. Most people think they all look the same. 'G'day, Dodger,' he said to one large toad. 'Aren't you the one I found in Mrs French's outside laundry?'

The toad gave a loud grunt as if to say yes.

Martin made his way home from the swamp with the two toads he had rescued from the road. 'I'll keep you two,' he said. 'I'll call you toads Fruitcake and Pancake. You might bring me luck.'

The two toads did bring Martin luck. Bad luck. As the months went by Martin found that his toad-clearing business went from bad to worse. Every house he went to had already been cleared out. No one wanted toads removed any more and he couldn't work out why.

Then one day he saw an ad in the local paper. It said:

TOAD STUFFERS PTY LTD

CANE TOADS REMOVED

FREE

PHONE 505 64 0111

No wonder he couldn't get any more toad-clearing jobs. Someone was doing it for nothing

Martin rang the phone number to see who it was but he already knew who was going to answer the phone. He wasn't wrong. It was Frisbee.

As soon as he heard Frisbee's voice, Martin sadly hung up the phone without saying anything.

That night Martin hid behind a tree and waited outside Frisbee's shop. At seven-thirty Frisbee left the house pulling a large box of wheels. He walked into town and went into the backyard of a flash-looking house. Martin looked over the fence. Frisbee was fishing around behind the plants with a torch looking for cane toads. Every time he caught one, he gave its neck a quick twist and threw the lifeless body into the box.

'Murderer,' gasped Martin under his breath. He wanted to rush over and stop Frisbee from killing the toads but he knew he wasn't strong enough. Frisbee was just too big for him.

When the box was full, Frisbee made his way back to his shop on the edge of town. He took the box inside and shut the door.

Martin peeked in through a crack in the blinds. What he saw made him shudder with horror. Frisbee put a hook thing into a toad's mouth and pulled out all the innards. Then he shoved some cotton wool in place of the gizzards and painted the toad with a clear liquid. Next he put a little skirt on the toad and placed a small tennis racquet in its hand. He sat it on a wire stand on a shelf next to another stuffed toad which also had a tennis racquet. A little net was stretched between the toads. It looked just as if they were playing tennis.

Frisbee wrote something on a piece of cardboard and placed it next to the stuffed toads. It said:

TENNIS TOADS $35.00

Frisbee gave a wicked chuckle as he looked at his work. Then he reached into the box and took out another dead toad.

Martin felt sick. The shelves of the hut were lined with stuffed toads. Hundreds and hundreds of them. Some were sitting inside little toy cars. Others held tiny fishing rods. One pair was kissing. There was even a toad sitting on a tiny toilet. And all of them had price tags.

At first Martin didn't know what was going on. Then he realised that Frisbee was killing all the toads he caught and stufffing them. Then he was selling the stuffed toads to tourists from down south. Martin noticed eighteen toads all dressed in little red-and-white football jumpers. The Sydney Swans. On another shelf the whole Collingwood team of toads was lined up.

This was the cruellest, meanest, most horrible thing that he had ever heard of. Martin knew that he had to stop this fiendish business but he didn't know what to do. He was only a pipsqueak next to Frisbee.

Then he had an idea. He walked home with a spring in his step. He would come back one night when Frisbee wasn't there. He would stop him stuffing toads once and for all.

3

Two weeks later, Martin crept up to Frisbee's shop. It was late in the night and very dark. Frisbee had gone off catching cane toads. Or that's what Martin thought anyway. He looked around into the blackness but saw nothing. Something rustled in the bushes. He hoped it was a toad or a rat.

Shivers ran down his spine. If something went wrong, there was nothing to help him. He took his father's pair of bolt cutters and cut through the padlock on the shop door. Then he went inside and turned on the light. Light filled the room for a second and then vanished. The globe had blown.

Martin switched on his torch and looked around.

STUFFED

The stuffed toads looked eerie in the torchlight. 'I hope toads don't have ghosts,' he said to himself. 'Because if they do, I'm a goner.' He looked at the tennis toads. They stood there as if frozen in the middle of an imaginary game.

He picked up the tennis toads. They were hard and lifeless. 'I'm going to give you a proper burial,' said Martin. He put them down and reached into a small sack.

In the silent night a twig snapped. He had to hurry. There was a sound of footsteps approaching. Someone was coming. He quickly finished, switched off his torch and slipped out of the door into the blackness.

And there stood Frisbee. Even in the dark Martin could see that his face was twisted up in rage. He let out a bellow and charged at Martin with outstretched hands. Martin turned and fled. He ran and crashed through the undergrowth. Branches scratched his legs and face but he didn't feel them. All he felt were his bursting lungs and the deep fear of what Frisbee would do to him if he caught him. He ran blindly, not even realising that he had come once again to Tiger Snake Swamp. He plunged into the water as before.

But this time Frisbee followed. Martin felt himself grabbed by strong hands and pushed under the water. He couldn't breathe. He tried to struggle free but Frisbee was too strong. Martin held his breath but the seconds seemed like hours. He knew he would have to

255

open his mouth and breathe in lungfuls of water. His chest hurt.

And then, suddenly, he was released. Frisbee let go.

Martin burst upwards and gulped in air. Then he looked at Frisbee. He saw an unbelievable sight. Frisbee was completely covered in a swarming sea of cane toads. They crawled over his shoulders and face and hair. He looked like a moving green beehive.

He screamed and yelled. 'Get them off. Get them off.' He scraped at them with both hands but for every one that he threw away another ten clambered on to the pile.

Frisbee struggled to the shore under the seething skin of toads. He grabbed a branch and started scraping them from his body. Then he staggered back towards his shop.

Martin followed at a safe distance. As he went he passed dead and dying toads. He could see that Frisbee was winning the battle and the covering of toads was thinning out. By the time Frisbee reached the shop there was only one toad left. Frisbee plucked it from his hair and threw it on the ground. Then he stamped on it viciously, and went into the shop, slamming the door behind him.

Martin smiled and quickly hooked the broken padlock through the latch.

'You're locked in,' he yelled to Frisbee. 'I'm not letting you out until you promise not to kill any more toads.'

There was a furious rattling as Frisbee shook the door. 'Let me out or I'll skin you alive,' he shouted. 'That's the only promise you'll get out of me.'

'Okay,' said Martin. 'See you later then.'

Frisbee heard footsteps disappear into the night.

Inside the shop it was dark. There was only a little moonlight filtering through the cracks in the blinds. The stuffed toads were silvery. They looked ghostly, sitting all around him on the shelves. Frisbee shivered. Then he went over and shook the door again. It was firmly locked. He could easily get out by smashing the window but he wasn't going to do that. A customer could let him out in the morning.

He set up his stretcher on the floor and sat on it. Then he opened a stubby and started swigging his beer.

The dead toads stared at him silently. The night was still. He heard a small shuffle. 'What was that?' he gasped aloud. There was no anawer.

He looked at the toad captain of the Collingwood football team. Its eyes seemed to stare back. Frisbee blinked his eyes and looked again. A cold shiver ran up his spine. Had that football toad blinked? Surely not. It couldn't. It was dead.

From the shelves, hundreds and hundreds of dead toads peered down at him. Their eyes seemed to say 'murderer'.

'Nonsense,' whispered Frisbee to himself. 'Dead toads don't know anything. Neither do live ones for that matter.' He felt foolish for whispering.

He heard another scuffle in the silence and jumped. He looked at the toad with the fishing rod. Had that line moved? Surely not.

For the first time in his life Frisbee was scared. He was terrified. The stuffed toads seemed to stare at him as if any moment they might jump down and attack him. He remembered that the Rambo toad had a sharp little hunting knife in its hand.

He heard another soft movement behind him. He looked around suddenly and nearly fainted with fear. One of the tennis toads was moving. He was sure of it. He could see its throat pulsing as if it was breathing. Suddenly the toad lifted up its tiny tennis racquet and threw its little ball into the air. It hit the ball over the net.

Frisbee rubbed his eyes and screamed out loud. The toad on the other side of the net returned the serve. The stuffed toads were playing tennis.

Frisbee charged at the locked door. His terror gave him super strength and he burst the door from its hinges and ran screaming into the night.

Martin laughed gently from his hiding place behind a tree. Then he walked into the shed and picked up the two tennis toads. 'Well, Pancake and Fruitcake,' he said. 'It was hard work teaching you to play tennis. But it sure was worth it.'

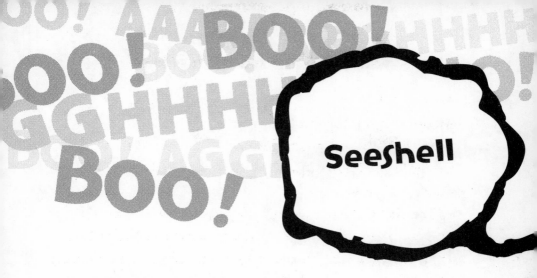

Seeshell

'The way I see it,' says Jacko.

'You're pretty small,' says Johnno.

'For a boy of fifteen,' says Tommo.

I look up at the three brothers. They are all wearing the same checked shirts. They all have the same tattoo on the backs of their hands. They are all real big guys. And they are right – I am small for my age.

'Geez,' I think to myself. 'I can hardly tell them apart. They even look like each other.'

I am very nervous. This is my first job ever and I want to do well. All my life I have dreamed about working on a fishing boat like this one. All my life I have wanted to get away and sail out on the open sea. It is only a holiday job but it is my big chance. If I do well the brothers might keep me on for good.

'Come aboard the *Oracle*,' says Jacko.

'And see if you like it,' says Johnno.

'Living on a cray boat,' says Tommo.

I follow the brothers up the gangplank and onto the deck. I breathe in deep. I take in the smell of the salt air and the coiled ropes and the scrubbed decks.

'Ah,' I say out loud. 'Excellent.'

The brothers grin.

'That is a very good sign, Alan,' says Jacko.

'That you are going to do much better . . .' says Johnno.

'Than the last boy,' says Tommo.

I stare up at them. 'What happened to him?' I say.

The three brothers look down into the dark, still water. The smiles fall from their faces. They all speak together. 'He is feeding the fishes,' they say with one angry voice.

I suddenly feel cold all over. A picture comes into my mind. A picture of a silent body lying still on the bottom of the ocean. Fishes nibbling at its toes.

I want to ask, 'What happened? Did he fall overboard?' But I look into the brothers' brooding eyes and decide not to.

2

The brothers give me jobs straight away. Scrubbing the deck. Stacking the empty craypots. Scraping rust from steel railings and painting them with red undercoat. I am so happy to be going to sea. And so are the brothers. They sing together as they work.

They seem to love one particular song. They sing it over and over. It's about some old guy who lives on a mountain with his daughter. And no one is allowed to go near her. Lots of guys want to because she has lips that are sweeter than honey. But everyone is too scared to risk it because the old guy is handy with a gun and a knife.

The way the brothers lift their voices makes it seem as if they know the person in the song. Sometimes tears come to their eyes as they sing about her tender lips.

Finally I just have to ask. I point to their tattoos and the word that is etched on each hand. 'Who is Shelley?' I ask. 'Is she your mother?'

The brothers stop work.

'She is our sun,' says Jacko.

'She is the stars,' says Johnno.

'She is our little sister,' says Tommo.

'And here she is,' says a soft voice.

I look up and see a girl. She is about my age and very pretty. She wears denim shorts all frayed at the edges. And a tight top. She has deep brown eyes and dark hair. And her feet are bare.

She smiles with a soft, kind mouth. A very nice thought about her tender lips comes into my mind. I try to push it away and stare at the distant cliffs. For a second the rocks at the end of the cliffs seem like two faces kissing. I rub my eyes and turn back to the brothers.

'This is Shelley,' says Jacko.

'If anyone ever touches her,' says Johnno.

'They will end up feeding the fishes like the last kid,' says Tommo.

Shelley gives me a warm smile and holds out her

hand. 'Hello,' she says. 'Don't take any notice of them. They don't really mean it.'

I look at the three brothers and can tell that they do really mean it. But I hold out my hand and try very hard not to think about how I would like to kiss Shelley. I try very hard indeed. I do not want to get the sack before I have even started. And I do not want to end up feeding the fishes either.

3

So the cray boat puts out to sea. With me and the brothers and Shelley. I love the work. I learn to put the chopped fish-heads and bones into the craypots for bait. I learn how to lower them down to the bottom of the ocean. How to attach them to buoys so that we can come back and recover the pots. I learn to empty the live crayfish into the holding tank down below. I learn to cook. And scrub. And to keep away from Shelley.

She is on my mind all the time. But every time I get anywhere near her one of the brothers pops up from nowhere and sends me to the other side of the boat.

Not that I would have a chance with someone like her. Beautiful and clever. Not like me. Nah, she wouldn't be interested in me. And even if she was I couldn't risk it. Those brothers mean it. They really would toss me overboard if I so much as touched her.

So I put all my thoughts into my work. I come to love that boat. It is much more than a place of work.

It is a home that goes everywhere with us. The sound of the engine turning is like a heart beating. It is almost as if the boat is alive. A friend that will never let me down.

'You are doing well,' says Jacko. 'But—'

'Don't love a boat too much,' says Johnno.

'It is only a boat,' says Tommo. 'It can't love you back.'

But I am not too sure. Sometimes at night when the moonlight is on the water and the sea is still, the boat seems to talk to me. I think I was born to go to sea.

4

One morning, early, I watch Johnno pulling in a craypot. It is deep in the green sea, somewhere out of sight. I watch the dark shape gradually take form as it nears the surface. Closer and closer. There is something in it but it is not a crayfish.

Johnno dumps the craypot on the deck. Then he gives a terrible scream. 'Aaagh. Seeshell,' he yells. 'Seeshell.'

Jacko and Tommo scramble over to the pot as fast as they can go.

I look at the shell. It is a creamy colour, rippled and shaped like a beautiful clam. It is tightly shut. The brothers are staring at the Seeshell as if it is a hand grenade that is about to go off.

Tommo races into the cabin and comes out with a pair of barbecue tongs. 'Shut your eyes,' he screams. 'Shut your eyes.' He lifts out the Seeshell very gently. His hands are shaking and I can see that he is scared.

Johnno has his eyes tightly shut. 'Careful,' he whispers.

Jacko has his hands over his eyes. 'Don't drop it,' he says. 'It might open.'

Tommo holds the Seeshell out over the water and lets go. *Plink*, it splashes into the ocean and swirls down into the depths.

The brothers start to race around like crazy. 'Lift the anchor,' yells Johnno. 'This is a bad spot for fishing.'

'Pull in the other craypot, Alan,' shouts Jacko.

Tommo disappears into the wheelhouse and starts the engine. The brothers sure are in a terrible hurry to get out of here. Shelley is down below. She doesn't know anything about what's been going on.

I start to pull up the rope on the other craypot. Faster and faster. Here it comes. There is something in it. A crayfish? A crab? What is it?

The brothers are all getting the boat ready to leave. Shelley is pulling in the anchor with the electric winch. Nobody is taking any notice of me.

I grab the craypot and haul it onto the deck. Then I look inside.

5

It is a Seeshell. Much smaller than the other one. It is also creamy and rippled. But one thing is different. The shell is starting to open and strange red tentacles wave like slippery eyelashes. I give a shudder and open my mouth to yell out to the brothers.

But then it happens. Oh, weird. Disgusting. Oh, yuck.

The shell opens right up and there inside is something looking out. An eye. Right in the middle is a bulging eye. Not a fish-type eye, cold and still. But a human type eye with a pupil.

The eye stares at me.

And I stare back.

I start to think. All my life I have been poor. I have never had expensive Christmas presents. I have never even owned a bike.

And now I am staring at a fortune. A shell with an eye? No one has ever seen such a thing. I could sell it. The story would be worth millions. Newspapers, magazines, television, the Internet. Everyone would want to see it. But for some reason the brothers do not want to keep the Seeshell. They are scared of it. Maybe they are superstitious.

If I show the Seeshell to the brothers, I already know what they will do. They will throw it back. But at the moment they are too busy getting the boat ready to leave. They are not paying any attention to me.

I see an old bait jar nearby. As quick as lightning I tip the contents into the sea. Then I grab the tongs that Tommo had thrown on the deck. With shaking fingers I drop the Seeshell into the jar and screw on the lid. The Seeshell closes up as tight as a clam. For the moment the eye is gone from sight.

I carefully hide the jar under some ropes and get on

with my jobs. After a couple of hours the brothers stop the boat.

'This is a much better spot,' says Jacko. 'We'll put down the pots.'

So that is what we do.

Dropping pots is slow work and it takes half a day to lower them down into the water. We attach a rope to each craypot and leave a buoy so that we can find it again. All the time I am working I can only think of two things. The eye in the Seeshell, and Shelley, the brothers' beautiful sister.

Shelley seems to want to talk to me but I am scared to go near her. Once my hand accidentally touched hers when we were cleaning fish. It sent a tingle right up my arm.

But I can't think about it. It is too dangerous. I get stuck into my jobs and try to forget about her. Finally I am finished. I grab the bait jar and then go to my favourite spot at the back of the boat. This part of the boat is low and I can touch the sea with my hand. I take the lid off the jar and fill it up with salt water. I don't want the Seeshell to die. It won't be worth as much if it dies.

I screw the lid back on the jar and watch. The Seeshell slowly opens. There it is. There is the eye. It stares at me without blinking.

Suddenly I see something weird. Not in the jar. Not on the boat. Not out to sea. Not even in the sky.

What I see is inside my head. A picture inside my mind. Just as clear as day. It's as if I am watching a movie. I see a little scene that is not really happening. I see Johnno coming up from below. He hauls himself up onto the deck, leans over the side and spits into the water. Then he wipes his forehead with his arm. Even when I close my eyes I can still see him doing it.

I open my eyes and see that the Seeshell has closed. There is no one else on the deck. My brain seems to freeze over. What is going on? Am I seeing things? Am I going crazy? Having visions about things that are not really there.

Suddenly I hear something from below. Someone is coming. I quickly shove the Seeshell jar under some ropes. I hear footsteps. Johnno hauls himself up onto the deck, leans over the side and spits into the water. Then he wipes his forehead with his arm.

Just like he did in my vision.

I saw him do that. I saw him spit into the water before he even did it. Something is terribly wrong with me. I need help.

But who can I ask? Johnno and Tommo and Jacko will be mad at me for keeping the Seeshell. I might end up feeding the fishes like the last kid. Is that what he did wrong? Kept a Seeshell when he wasn't supposed to?

What will I do?

6

'Okay,' says Johnno. 'Let's get going.'

'Let's find a place to anchor,' says Tommo.

'For the night,' says Jacko.

Tommo starts the engine and we head for shore.

There is nothing for me to do so I sit up the back of the boat and think.

I go over and over what happened. And it all comes down to this. When I looked into the eye of the Seeshell I saw something before it happened. I saw Johnno spit into the water before he did it.

Yes. There is no doubt about it. The Seeshell can see into the future. It knows what is going to happen. And it can send out thoughts. It can make me see what is going to happen too.

The sun sinks into the ocean and soft moonlight floats on the gently swelling sea. The jar with the Seeshell inside is out of sight under the ropes. I know what I should do. I should grab the jar and throw it into the ocean. Johnno and Tommo and Jacko don't like it. Seeshells are dangerous. I should never look at it again.

But then I think about it. It would be great to see into the future. You could win bets. You could tell someone's fortune. You would know what lotto numbers were coming up. You could win first prize every time.

I look into the jar. The Seeshell seems to be calling to me. It wants me to pick it up. 'Come here,' it seems to say. 'Fall under my spell.'

Is it the Seeshell speaking? Or are these my own thoughts?

Slowly, slowly, slowly, I reach under the ropes and pull out the jar. The Seeshell is tightly closed. It is keeping all of its secrets to itself.

Then suddenly it starts to open. It reminds me of a mouth yawning. And there it is. The terrible eye. Staring at me.

I shudder and shut my own eyes. Straight away I see another vision. I see a picture in my head. As clear as day. Only it is not day. It is night, and soft moonlight is floating gently on the swelling sea.

In my vision the *Oracle* is cutting through the water at high speed. It is heading straight for a reef of jagged rocks just above the surface of the water. In the moonlight I can plainly see the edges of a cruel reef. *Crunch*. The *Oracle* runs straight into the rocks. A terrible hole is torn into the bow just above the waterline.

I open my eyes in horror. The Seeshell has shown me what is going to happen. We are going to smash into a reef and damage the boat. And I am the only one who knows it.

Think, think, think. Yes, I know what to do. Yes, I know. I will make Johnno change course. Then we won't crash into the waiting rocks that lie out there in the night. We will go a different way. We will be saved.

But how can I make Johnno change course?

Simple.

'Rocks,' I yell. 'Rocks dead ahead.'

Johnno puts his head out of the wheelhouse. 'I can't see them,' he yells.

'Straight ahead,' I yell. 'Change course.'

Johnno shouts back in a hoarse voice. 'We're on course. We're in the channel. I've been here a thousand times. There are no rocks in the channel.'

He is not going to change course. And the Seeshell has shown me what lies ahead. I have to do something.

'I see them,' I yell. 'I see rocks.'

Johnno pulls fiercely on the wheel. The boat changes direction.

I have done it. I have put us on a different course. Now the Seeshell's prophecy will not come true. Oh, it is so good to be able to see into the future.

The *Oracle* is cutting through the water at high speed. The empty sea is . . .

Not empty.

The boat is heading straight for a reef of jagged rocks just above the surface of the water. In the moonlight I can plainly see the edges of a cruel reef.

Crunch.

The *Oracle* runs straight into the rocks. A terrible hole is torn into the bow just above the waterline.

7

The brothers run to the front and stare at the hole. We are not in danger but the boat has been badly damaged.

Johnno is furious. 'You mongrel. You led us onto the rocks,' he screamed. 'Look what you have done.'

He grabs my head and shoves it over the side. He wants me to look but I can't. The hole in the boat is like a gash in living flesh. A wound inflicted on a friend. I can't believe what has happened. The Seeshell showed me the boat crashing onto rocks. I tried to stop it. But my actions made it happen. There is no way to stop the future. Once the Seeshell shows you something you can't stop it happening.

Now I know why the brothers are scared of the Seeshell. Now I know why they moved to another fishing ground when they caught one. Seeshells are bad news.

There is only one thing left to do. I have to get rid of the Seeshell. And quick.

The brothers are pulling a cover over the hole in the bow. They ignore me. I am in disgrace. I make my way to the back of the boat and carefully take out the jar. It is dark and I can't see the Seeshell. Good. I am safe from it.

Oh, no, no, no. The moon comes out. And there in its silvery light I can see the eye of the Seeshell glaring up at me.

And I see something else. A vision. Inside my head. As clear as day I see the faces of the brothers. Watching something. Scowling. Angry. Creeping forward. And then I see what they are looking at. They are looking at me. And what I am doing.

Shelley and I are kissing.

Suddenly the Seeshell closes its eye and the vision is gone. The moon is still shining.

A sentence comes into my mind. A single sentence. A death sentence. The words ring in my head. *Feeding the fishes*. The brothers will catch me and throw me over the side. I will end up like the last boy on the *Oracle*.

But then I stop and think. I don't have to kiss her. It is up to me. The Seeshell can't make you do things. It can only show you what is going to happen.

Okay, so Shelley is beautiful. I can't stop thinking about her. But I don't have to kiss her, do I? It is up to me. I am in charge of what I do. I am not so love-crazed that I can't stop myself from kissing her.

But just to be on the safe side I will keep the Seeshell a little longer. Just in case. After all, the brothers are still mad at me. It could be useful to know what is going to happen.

Morning comes.

'Get below,' growls Johnno. 'And help Shelley cook breakfast. We are going to repair the damage to the bow.'

He is in a really bad mood, I can see that. So I hotfoot it down to the galley as quick as I can.

Shelley gives me a warm smile. 'You make the toast,' she says. 'While I fry the eggs.'

Oh, she is a beautiful girl. And kind. She is everything

a guy could want. Would I like to kiss her? Oh, would I? There is nothing in the world that I would like better.

But I am not going to. No way. Nothing can make me kiss her.

Firstly because I would never kiss a girl unless she wanted me to. And secondly because the brothers will kill me if I do.

So I am safe.

But I am also not concentrating on what I am doing.

'Look out,' yells Shelley.

Black smoke is pouring out of the toaster. The bread is burning. Shelley and I both run for it at the same time. *Crash.* We bump into each other and Shelley starts to fall. I grab her and just stop her from slipping.

Her eyes look into mine and we both laugh.

If ever I was going to kiss her it would be now. But I am not going to. No way. I am not going to end up feeding the fishes. There is nothing in the world that can make me kiss that girl.

So I don't.

But something does happen. Something I cannot stop. Something that is not my fault.

Shelley speaks to me in a trembling voice. 'I have been wanting to do this since the first time I saw you, Alan,' she says.

She pulls my head towards her and before I know what is happening she kisses me full on the lips.

She kisses *me.* No, no, no, no, no. I can't believe it.

And worse. So much worse. Through the swirling smoke I see the brothers. Coming towards me with fists bunched.

8

This is serious. I have to get away. And fast. I clamber up the emergency ladder and escape through a hatch.

I hear loud angry voices coming from below.

'Grab the little devil,' yells Jacko.

'After him quick,' yells Johnno.

'He kissed our sister,' yells Tommo.

I stare around the deck. Where can I run? Where can I go? What is going to happen?

There is one way to find out. I grab the jar and stare inside but the Seeshell is closed. Its shell is tightly shut. There is no eye in sight. I give the jar a shake. 'Wake up,' I yell. 'Wake up.'

The shell slowly opens and there it is. The terrible eye. Staring at me. Silent, unblinking. Staring into the future.

Straight away I see a vision. I see myself lying on the deck. I see my hands tied behind my back. My feet are lashed together. I am shouting something but I don't know what. I see the brothers lift up my struggling body. I see Shelley, locked in the cabin nearby, crying. The tears are running down her face. I see the brothers throw my struggling body over the side. I see myself sink beneath the waves. Gone to feed the fishes.

I am history. All of this is going to happen and there is nothing I can do about it.

'Get him,' says a voice. It is Johnno.

The brothers have found me.

'Grab him,' says Jacko.

'Quick,' says Johnno.

'Stop him,' says Tommo.

But they cannot stop me. I am already climbing up the mast. Up, up, up.

The deck is far below. The ship is swaying from side to side in a strong swell. It is a long way down. I am scared. And I feel sick. I hate heights. In my trembling hands I hold the jar. And in the jar is the terrible Seeshell. I cannot hold on to the mast and the jar at the same time. I need both hands. Suddenly the jar slips from my fingers. Over and over it spins and then – *smash.*

The jar breaks into a billion pieces on the deck.

For a second the brothers stare. Then they start to scream and yell. 'Aaagh. A Seeshell. Get rid of it. Quick. Don't look. It's opening. Don't look. Don't look.' The brothers hold their hands over their eyes. They turn their backs on the Seeshell. They are terrified of it.

Johnno falls down on his hands and knees. He has his eyes tightly closed. He starts to crawl forward, feeling his way like a blind dog. He feels around with his hands.

Touching this. Touching that. But not touching the thing he is after. The awesome, the all-knowing Seeshell. It is starting to open.

Closer and closer. He dabs at the deck with his fingers. Each time just missing the shell. Finally he finds it. Without opening his eyes he forces the Seeshell closed and throws it into the air. It cuts a wide arc above the boat. Plink. It is gone. Back where it came from. Into the ocean.

The brothers open their eyes and look up at me.

'So,' says Johnno.

'You looked at a Seeshell,' says Tommo.

'And now you know what you don't want to know,' says Jacko.

'I know what you are going to do,' I yell.

'You kissed our little sister,' yells Tommo angrily.

'No one gets away with that,' says Johnno.

'No one at all,' says Jacko.

Suddenly there is another voice speaking. A kind voice. But an angry voice. It is Shelley.

'He did not kiss me,' she says.

'We saw him,' the three brothers say in one voice.

'You did not see him kiss me,' she says. 'You saw *me* kiss him.'

The brothers look at each other. For once they do not know what to say.

'Come down, boy,' says Johnno at last.

I shake my head. He still sounds furious. He is still mad at me. 'No way,' I say. 'The Seeshell showed me what you are going to do. I know you are going to throw me over the side.'

'Then you also know . . .' says Jacko.

'That nothing can stop us doing it,' says Johnno.

'So you might as well come down and get it over with,' says Tommo.

9

So here I am. Lying on the deck. My hands tied behind my back. My feet lashed together. I am shouting something. 'Head first,' I yell. 'Head first.' I see the brothers lift up my struggling body. I see Shelley, locked in the cabin nearby, crying. The tears are running down her face. 'More,' I yell. 'More tears.'

I see the brothers throw my struggling body over the side. I sink beneath the waves.

Gone to feed the fishes?

No. I undo the quick-release knots on my hands and ankles. I float quickly up to the surface. Johnno is waiting there with an outstretched hand. So is Shelley. She is laughing and happy.

Johnno pulls me into the boat and gives me a towel. 'It worked,' he says. 'We acted your vision out perfectly. You can't stop the Seeshell's prophecy from coming true. But you can make it come true in your own way.'

I grin at the three brothers. It was a good plan. We acted out what the Seeshell saw. But we added our own little bit at the end. I undid the knots and escaped.

And Shelley cried really convincing fake tears.

The brothers helped me. They are not murderers

after all. Or are they? I frown and start to worry.

'What's up?' says Johnno. 'What's wrong now?'

'You are still killers,' I say slowly. 'What about the first boy? What about him?'

'We sacked him. He got another job,' says Jacko.

'But they are not going to sack you,' says Shelley firmly.

'How could he get another job?' I yell. 'You said he's feeding the fishes.'

'He is,' says Jacko.

'Definitely feeding the fishes,' says Johnno.

'He works in an aquarium,' says Tommo.

Mobile

Are you alone at the moment?

How do you know for sure?

There could be unseen people all around. Looking over your shoulder. Listening to what you say. In the room with you now. Maybe the picture on the wall is really staring down at you.

Okay, I can't prove it. But that doesn't mean it's not true.

I know from what happened to me that there is more to life than what you see.

1

Mum was too busy telling me off to notice how creepy the Bed and Breakfast place was.

'What was your father thinking of, Jeremy?' she said angrily. 'Giving a thirteen-year-old boy a mobile phone.'

'Lots of kids have got them,' I said.

'Yes,' said Mum, 'but their fathers haven't gone off and left them. Who's going to pay for the calls? That's what I want to know.'

'You get these little cards,' I said. 'They only cost . . .'

'Don't give me that,' said Mum. 'I'm sending it back.'

If your father wants to talk to you he can come and visit.

Hand it over.'

'No way,' I yelled. I pushed the phone deeper into my pocket. Normally I did what Mum told me. But not this time. She was mad because Dad had moved in with another woman. Mum didn't want me ringing them up.

She was about to freak out. But instead she froze with her mouth open. She had suddenly realised where we were.

Standing next to a ramshackle stone cottage on the edge of a foul swamp. She slowly walked to the front door and shivered as she stared at the decaying roof.

'It's not like I thought it was going to be,' she said slowly.

I touched one of the walls. It was damp. The windows were dirty and blocked by bars.

'Listen,' said Mum.

'I can't hear anything,' I said.

'That's just it,' she said. 'Not a sound. Not a cricket chirping. Not a bird singing. It's almost as if every piece of joy has been chased away.' She sniffed scornfully. A black-and-white cow was sleepily grazing in the swamp nearby.

'It's not much of a lake,' I said.

'It's not a lake at all,' said Mum. 'It's a disgusting bog.' Several green bubbles erupted on the surface and burst with a dull plop. It sounded like the rumblings from a rude giant's guts.

Mum stared at it sadly. She looked confused.

'I'll ring Dad,' I said, 'and ask him what to do.'

'Over my dead body,' said Mum. 'We don't need *his* help.'

Mum turned the door handle. As she did so, I noticed something weird. The door had a sliding bolt. On the outside. Mum slid it open.

We both stepped in and looked around.

'What a nerve,' said Mum. 'Fancy hiring this place out as a Bed and Breakfast. It's filthy. Dust and cobwebs everywhere.'

She was right.

'There's not even any bedrooms,' I said.

There was only one room. It held a fridge, a Laminex table, a microwave oven, two chairs and a dirty open fireplace.

Against the far wall was a pair of steel bunks. On the wall was a dark painting in a frame.

The furniture was modern but chipped and uncared for. I plonked our two backpacks on the stone floor.

'Look at that,' I said, pointing to a box on the table.

We both peered at the small metal box. There seemed to be a muffled noise coming out of it. I placed my ear against the lid. Yes, a fluttering noise. Unpleasant.

'There's something alive in there,' I whispered.

'Don't touch it,' said Mum. She flicked on the light switch. One dim bulb glowed feebly from the ceiling.

I rattled the bars on the windows. 'At least no robbers

can get in,' I said. 'It's like a fortress.' That's what I said. But what I was thinking was: It's like a jail.

'I'm going to ring up and complain,' said Mum. 'Maybe it's a mistake. It must be the wrong place.'

I took out my bright-red mobile and held it out. Mum glared at it as if it was a hot coal. 'No way,' she said. 'I'm not using anything *he* gave you. I'll go back to the car and get my own.'

'Don't be silly, Mum,' I said. 'It's a long walk.'

She shook her head. 'I need to be on my own for a bit,' she said. 'And I'm not going to drag those packs back for nothing. We might have to stay here. You mind our stuff while I'm gone.'

She marched off down the narrow track and disappeared over a scrubby hill.

I was alone.

2

I stepped outside and walked around the building. It was musty and dank. It had a smell of . . . I tried to think . . . Long ago. The odour of a dark and dangerous age. I hoped that Mum would hurry. It would be dark soon.

I went back to the door of the house and peered in. It reminded me of a foul mouth with rotten teeth and stinking breath. A black hole that would chew me up and swallow me down into a disgusting, heaving stomach.

'Don't be stupid,' I said to myself. I stepped inside.

A cold tide of fear began to wash over my body. Was

someone watching? Or *something*? I sat on one of the chairs in the middle of the room. Invisible eyes seemed to be staring at the back of my head. I kept turning around to grab a glance but the room was always empty.

It was as if a presence had disappeared just before I moved.

I picked up the chair and moved it so that I was sitting with my back against the wall. Now nothing could come close without me seeing it.

Or could it?

There *was* a presence in that room. I could feel it seeping down from above.

I jumped off the chair and examined the painting hanging there.

It was horrible. A vision from the far-off past when people drew pictures of hell and what awaited the wicked.

It was a painting of a skeleton holding a huge toad over an iron pot. Flames blazed in the fireplace nearby.

The room in which the painted skeleton stood was bare except for a chipped wooden table, two beds with straw mattresses, two stools, and two long sticks with cloth bundles tied to each of the ends. There was also a painting on the wall but it was too small to see what was in it.

I closed my eyes to shut out the terrible image. 'Don't be silly,' I told myself. 'It's only a painting.' My words had no effect. I shivered.

It was time to go.

I wanted Mum.

I bent over to pick up our packs. And as I did so a cold gust of wind came from nowhere and slammed the door closed.

I knew before I rushed over and shook the door handle that it would be locked from the outside.

It was.

I was trapped. There was no way out.

3

But. Oh, yes, yes, yes. There was something I could do.

Thank heavens for Dad. And his Christmas present. I could get help. I took out my mobile phone and feverishly pushed at the buttons. What was Mum's mobile number? 0419 5562 . . .? No, 0417 5561 . . .? Come on, come on. I knew it well but my mind wouldn't work properly. I was panicking. Quick, quick, quick. Think.

The fluttering from the box on the table grew louder. I backed away from it.

Click. The lid sprang open. Something zipped out.

A high-pitched buzzing sound filled the air. Oh, shoot.

A bright-red dragonfly circled angrily above my head. Down, down, down it came in ever smaller circles.

Do dragonflies bite? Or sting? I wasn't sure. I waved the mobile blindly above my head, trying to swat the dragonfly away. The thought of the huge insect's legs settling on my hair freaked me out.

Zap. What was that?

The mobile felt different in my hand. I stopped waving and gasped. I was holding a small wooden block with patterns dug into it. Some sort of ancient carving. My mobile phone had vanished.

Bzz, bzz . . .

The dragonfly was on the move again.

I threw the carving onto the floor and ran to the window. I grabbed the iron bars and put my feet up against the wall. I strained and struggled until the sweat poured down my face.

Bzz . . .

I pulled at the bars even more wildly. In that position I was totally at the dragonfly's mercy, not able to use my hands and feet.

'Move, move,' I grunted at the bars.

Zap.

What was that? I dropped to the floor and crouched down with my head between my knees. A soft crackling noise spluttered across the room. I sneaked a look.

Everything was just the same. No, it wasn't. A fire had burst to life in the fireplace. It had been empty before with not a stick of wood to be seen. Now it was blazing away. What was going on? Who had lit the flames?

Bzz. The dreadful dragonfly was still circling. It landed on the top bunk.

Zap. The bunk disappeared.

Now the buzzing red insect was heading down to the lower steel bunk.

Zap. The other bunk vanished.

The air shimmered. Something was growing where the bunks had been. I gasped in horror. It was like watching a tree sprout in fast forward.

Two rickety beds with straw mattresses appeared from nowhere.

The room began to take on an eerie air. The walls seemed to sob with the cries of long-lost souls. A chill arose through my shoes. The stones on the floor seemed as if they had been washed with a million tears.

I had to get out of there.

But how? I was trapped.

4

The dragonfly circled mercilessly. Once again I crouched in the corner with my arms over my head for protection.

Everything the dragonfly sat on had disappeared and been replaced by something else.

Above me was the picture. I couldn't see it from my crouched position but a sudden thought hit me like a bullet. The room in the picture was this room. The same fireplace. The same walls. And barred windows. It was a painting of the same room done long, long ago.

The dragonfly still circled.

Zap.

The dim globe dangling from the ceiling flickered and was gone. In its place a candle spluttered in a steel saucer attached to three chains.

Think, think, think, Jeremy.

What was going on? All of the new objects had come from the picture. I wanted to look at it but I was too scared to move.

Where was Mum? Gasbagging on her mobile, probably.

'Mum, I need you,' I whispered.

From somewhere deep inside I found the courage to move. I sprang to my feet and fixed my eyes on the painting. Oh, no, no, no. There it was. My mobile. And the Laminex table. The bunks were there too. And our backpacks. And the dangling light globe. Everything that the dragonfly landed on had swapped with something in the picture.

I stared with wide open eyes at the wicked skeleton holding the poor toad above his cauldron. What if he should come into my prison? The soulless bone-man who should be in his grave – not prancing around like a person.

I shrank back in terror from the red dragonfly. Was it about to bring this dead horror into the room?

Zap. Zap. Our backpacks vanished. And in their place were two long sticks with cloth bundles tied to the ends. I gazed at the picture again. It was modern and old at the same time. As if it had been painted by some ancient artist who could see into the future. I could see our modern hiking packs together with my mobile phone and the steel bunks.

Zap. A bubbling cauldron appeared at my side. It was filled with green gurgling liquid that burped and threw out a stench even worse than the bog.

By now, everything in the skeleton's painted room was modern. Except him and the toad.

The dragonfly began to circle above me. 'No, no,' I shouted. 'Get away.'

Down, down, down, it came. Like a dive-bomber about to attack.

Zap.

The world as I knew it began to fade. My blood was ice. My bones were sticks. My brain was filled with fog. And then, as the mist cleared, I saw a crazy world.

Upside down.

The skeleton danced a silent jig, holding me by one of my ankles. My head shook as he swung me around.

The toad was gone. I had taken its place. Inside the picture.

I was dead.

That was the thought that filled my head.

5

For some reason the thought gave me strength. Mum was in another world. I had nothing to lose. I kicked out at the skeleton with my free leg and caught him by surprise. His leg bones and skull scattered across the floor. I fell down onto the flagstones with a loud thump.

Quickly I sprang to my feet.

But the skeleton was not finished. No, not by a long shot. He reached out with spidery fingers, even though he was headless and legless. He began to place the bones into their correct positions one at a time.

Hurry, hurry. Use your brain, Jeremy.

The answer must be in the picture on the skeleton's wall. It was a drawing of the Bed and Breakfast room. A room that now had a crackling fire, a cauldron, and a toad. Yes, the toad had gone into the painting and replaced me. There was not one modern object there. And on the table. What was that? A metal box with an open lid. And a dragonfly hovering above it.

The skeleton and I were in a modern world. A world with a microwave. A light-glove, bunks, backpacks and a mobile phone.

I ran to the picture and squinted at the room I had just been in. I could see a woman outside the cottage. A modern woman walking past the window.

Mum.

In my world, the skeleton was still assembling himself. He was nearly done. His bone fingers reached out for his skull.

Would the dragonfly bite my mother and bring her here too? What would swap with her? I stared around.

There was only one thing left.

I had to warn Mum.

I pounced on my mobile and started jabbing at the buttons. Could you make a phone call from another world? Another time? It was worth a try.

I had to stop her swapping with the skeleton.

The skeleton seemed to sense what was happening. His feet were still scattered but he was putting himself together quickly. He crawled painfully across the stones, collecting the last few bones.

I jabbed at the buttons. *Ring, ring.*

'Please be the right number,' I groaned. 'Please.'

'Jeremy,' came Mum's voice over the phone, 'I told you not to use that mobile. Your father can . . .'

'Mum,' I said, 'shut up. If you love me, if you trust me, don't go into the cottage. There's a dragonfly. It bit me and took me away. Run, run for your life or it will get you too.'

'Where are you, Jeremy?' Mum shrieked.

'I'm in another . . .'

The phone was snatched from my hands. The skeleton held it above his head and threw it onto the bed. Two bony hands grasped my throat. They had enormous strength.

I knew that this time nothing would release me from the skeleton's grasp. He was wringing my neck. Wring, wring. Tighter and tighter.

His grip was so strong that I couldn't speak.

AGGHHHHH! NO!

Zap.

'Ha, ha, ha, ha . . .'

A terrible wicked laugh. An evil shriek. From the fading skull.

The skeleton began to shimmer. And was gone. He had got what he wanted.

Mum's shape appeared as if from a mist.

She looked at me with terrified eyes. 'Jeremy,' she said, 'what . . .? Surely I'm dreaming.'

'No,' I said. 'It's real. We are in another world. Inside the picture. Why didn't you listen to me?'

'Don't be silly,' said Mum. 'Everything's normal.'

She was staring around the room. She was right. The Laminex table was the same. The steel bunks were the same. And our packs. And the microwave. The fridge. And the empty fireplace.

I grabbed her hand and dragged her to the picture on the wall. The ugly skeleton was there, holding a toad over a cauldron. The candles were there. And the steel bunks.

Everything had swapped over.

The skeleton was now in his world and we were in ours. We were saved.

No. No. My hopes vanished like a glass of water tipped onto the desert sand. It was only the contents of the room that had changed.

Behind the skeleton, outside the window in the picture, was a black-and-white cow, grazing sleepily.

I rushed across our room and stared through the glass. The bog was still bubbling. But there were bent and gnarled trees that had not been there before. And just outside, playing in the dust, was a circle of ragged children, holding hands and singing in screeching voices.

Ring, a ring of roses,
A pocket full of posies,
A'tishoo, a'tishoo,
We all fall down.

They dropped down onto the ground laughing madly. Their hopeless, unhappy voices made my skin grow cold and sweaty.

A horse and cart rumbled along a bumpy road. Walking next to it were two stooped men. They wore long, grey cloaks. One was ringing a brass bell and calling out in a wavering voice, 'Bring out your dead. Bring out your dead.'

Mum gasped. 'Don't go out there,' she yelled. 'It's the Black Death.'

'What?'

'A terrible disease,' said Mum. 'From the Middle Ages. Long ago. We have to get out of here.'

I ran back to the picture. The hated skeleton was still there, living in our world, inside the picture. And we were trapped inside his.

Think, think, think. There must be something I could do. I hated that picture. I hated it. And this foul, fetid world from long ago.

'Mum,' I yelled, 'have you got any matches?'

She pulled a packet from her pocket. 'I brought them to start a barbecue,' she said.

I snatched the matches and then pulled the picture from the wall. I jumped up and down on it, smashing the frame to bits. My legs began to grow heavy. My hands and feet felt fat and useless. Some strange force seemed to know what I was doing. But I managed to kick the buckled picture into the fireplace.

With fumbling fingers I scratched a match along the matchbox. It broke. I scrabbled at another one but I couldn't pick it out. I tipped the matches onto the fireplace and managed to grab one.

Swshtch. The match flared.

My hand shook as I held it under the painting. Blue and red flames suddenly flared and ran across the canvas surface. In no time at all, the whole thing was alight.

A terrible screech filled the room. Everything began to float around in the air like the contents of a space capsule. Mum and I drifted eerily above the table. We were moving. We were mobile.

We began to swirl and tumble as if we were in a giant clothes dryer. We were mixed up with tables and backpacks and chairs and . . .

. . . a skeleton and a toad and a candle.

And a dragonfly.

Bits of both worlds were mixed together in a gigantic whirlwind. The skeleton began to shriek. His bony arms and legs jigged in a terrible dance of death. Faster and faster and faster we tumbled and turned. The world grew black.

Suddenly everything froze. We both fell heavily to the floor. The contents of the room were strewn about.

'Where are we?' I yelled.

I rushed over to the window. The trees had gone. The black-and-white cow grazed sleepily outside. We were back in our own world.

But what about the skeleton?

The painting in this world was still intact. Not burnt. I picked it up from where it lay upside down on the floor. Everything painted there was as it had been before. No it wasn't. The skeleton was there with his toad and cauldron. But . . . But . . . There was no painting on his wall. Just a dragonfly sitting on a faded patch where the picture had been.

'Let's get out of here,' said Mum.

She didn't have to say it twice. I was already halfway out of the door.

6

Mum drove fast. She was putting as many kilometres between us and that cottage as quickly as she could. She had only seen a bit of what happened. She had walked into the cottage and found it changed. She had seen the table and beds and objects from another time.

'I couldn't let you go on your own,' she said. 'So I let the dragonfly bite me too. Where you go, I go. That's what mothers are for.'

'And fathers,' I said.

Mum didn't say anything to that.

After a while I said, 'Do you think anyone will believe what happened?'

'I don't know,' said Mum. 'Why don't you tell your dad?'

'How?' I said.

'You've got a mobile phone, haven't you?' she said with a grin. 'Why don't you use that?'

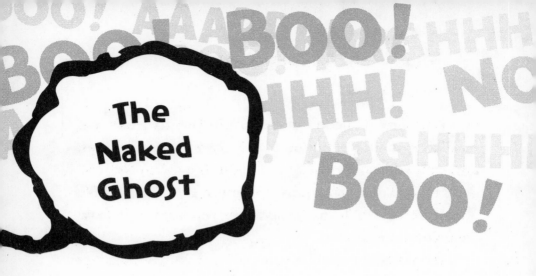

The Naked Ghost

I look like a boy of fifteen but I am really sixty-five years old. My brain is old but my body is young. I have smooth skin and thick fair hair. I have fine hair on my top lip but have not yet started to shave. Inside I am old and wise. Outside I am only a teenager.

If I look in the mirror I see a young reflection. I know, however, that I was born a long time ago.

I am not showing off when I tell you that I am wise. I have read a lot of books. Thousands and thousands of books. I have spent fifty years doing nothing but reading books. When people look at me they do not know why I am so smart. They see a fifteen-year-old boy. They do not see a man who has spent fifty years reading. I had to read. There was nothing else to do. Those books stopped me from going mad.

I had better tell you the story from the start. You probably won't believe it. I don't blame you if you think my story is a lie. It is not a lie, it is true. You might think a fifteen-year-old boy couldn't write this story. You are right. I am not fifteen, I am sixty-five.

When I was fifteen I lived near the sea. The place was called Port Fairy. Outside Port Fairy was an old fort. It was called Fort Nelson after an Admiral called Nelson.

No one was allowed to go near Fort Nelson. No one lived there. It was deserted. It was supposed to be dangerous.

The walls of the old fort were crumbling. Sometimes bricks or lumps of stone would fall down and crash to the ground. You would be killed if one hit you.

There were platforms on top of the walls. These platforms once had guns on them which pointed out to sea. The guns had gone. They had been put in a museum where you had to pay to get in to see them.

The buildings had gone too. They had been pushed over and wrecked. They were just ruins. All that was left were the walls and a deep well – and the story. There was a story about Fort Nelson called 'The Legend of John Black'.

John Black was also fifteen years old. He was alive when Fort Nelson was not a ruin and the buildings still stood. He used to go to the fort and watch the soldiers. He liked to watch them fire the guns at practice time, and he would go to the well to get the soldiers water to drink. He would lower a big bucket on a rope and wind the handle to bring up the bucket of water. Then he would climb the stairs and give the soldiers the water. They were not allowed to leave the gun platforms while they were on duty. They liked John Black because he was helpful. They told him jokes which made him laugh.

John Black's father did not like the soldiers. He said they were rough. He said their jokes were crude. He told John never to go to the fort. 'You are forbidden to go there', he said. 'If I ever catch you there I will thrash you. You are not to talk to those soldiers.'

John Black didn't take any notice. He disobeyed his father. He didn't like his father who was a cruel man. Once he had hit John across the face with a horsewhip. The whip left a scar on John's face which stretched from his mouth to his ear.

One day John Black was swimming in the sea near Fort Nelson. He was swimming with some soldiers who were off duty. All their clothes were on the beach. They were swimming in the nude. John and the soldiers were all as naked as the day they were born.

Suddenly John Black saw his father coming. He was frightened. He was terrified. He didn't want to be whipped again so he ran away to hide. He ran into the fort with no clothes on. The soldiers laughed. They thought it was funny to see a naked boy running away from his father.

John Black didn't think it was funny. He didn't want to be whipped. He ran to the well and started to climb down the rope which was used to bring up the water bucket. The rope was wet and slippery. The well was deep and the bottom was filled with cold, black water.

Now the soldiers didn't think what was happening

was funny either. They called out to John to climb up the rope.

A scream was heard. And a splash. Then silence. The water was still and quiet and terribly dark.

A soldier jumped into the well to look for John. He dived and dived but couldn't find him.

The next day all the water was pumped out of the well, but nothing was found. John Black's body was never discovered. He was never seen again.

Some people say that if you go to the ruins of Fort Nelson at night you will hear a strange echo in the well. It sounds like a boy calling for help. It is said that the ghost of John Black calls from the well, 'Let me out, let me out'.

That is 'The Legend of John Black'. I didn't believe it, not the bit about the ghost, anyway.

2

John Black was fifteen when he fell down the well. He had been dead for fifty years when I was fifteen.

I used to play in the ruins and think about John Black. I would climb up to the empty gun platforms and think of how he used to talk to the soldiers. I would look at the empty places where once there were buildings. I tried to imagine what Fort Nelson must have been like in the old days.

I was not supposed to be there. Outside the main entrance was a sign which said, 'Keep Out – Trespassers

Prosecuted'. I didn't take any notice of the sign. I went to the old fort every day. I was foolish. Something terrible happened to me there. It was the day that I decided to go down the well.

There was no water in the well any more. It was just a deep, dark, dry, empty hole. I couldn't see the bottom, but when I dropped a stone down I heard it clatter on something hard.

I had brought a rope from home because the rope to which the bucket had been tied had rotted years ago. I tied the rope to the wooden frame outside the well and threw the other end down the well.

Nobody knew I was there. I climbed down carefully. I didn't want to fall as John Black had so many years ago. The further down I went, the more scared I became. It was very dark. My knees began to knock.

Finally I reached the bottom. It was hard and stony. When I looked up I could see clouds far above. It was like looking up a round chimney. The sides of the well were smooth. I would never be able to climb up without the rope.

While I was examining the sides of the well I noticed something unusual. It was a door. A small, metal door with rusty hinges. It had a large, round brass knob.

For some reason the door made me frightened. It seemed to glow in the dark. I wanted to go back home, but I also wanted to know what was behind that door.

I turned the knob. It turned easily and the door swung open. Inside I was amazed to see a vast room lit with candles. I went in. I didn't really want to go in but something was making me. Something seemed to be forcing me to enter.

As soon as I was in the room, the door closed behind me. There was no knob on the inside. There were no windows and no other door. I was in a room at the bottom of a well and no one knew I was there.

Now I was really frightened. I tried to get out. I kicked at the door. I pulled at it with my fingers until my fingernails broke. It was no use. I could not escape.

I started to explore the room. It had a very high ceiling. I could see because candles were burning. I didn't know then, but later I discovered that the candles never went out. They burned on and on without getting smaller.

The walls were lined with books. More books than I had ever seen before. There were more books than in the Port Fairy Library. There were ladders on wheels which moved along the shelves. The ladders were there so that you could get to the books that were up high.

In the middle of the room was a bed. A large four-poster bed, big enough for four people. Above the pillows on the bed was a sign written in old-fashioned writing. This is what it said:

One child shall dwell within this room
For him to be a living tomb.

A lonely boy of fifteen years
Will cry and shed a thousand tears.
The sturdy door will only crack
For one with clothes upon his back.
It will open at the hour of three.
When the captive will be freed.

What did it mean? I read it again and again. It seemed to say that a boy of fifteen was trapped. I was fifteen. Was it me?

It said that the door would only open if the boy was wearing clothes. I was wearing clothes. What did the last bit mean about the hour of three? I thought it meant that the door would open at three o'clock. I looked at my watch. It was one-thirty.

I sat down on the bed and thought about it. I thought long and hard. The way I worked it out, the message said that the door would open in one and a half hours. It would open for a fifteen-year-old boy who was wearing clothes. It would not open for anybody who was not wearing clothes.

It was very strange. It was creepy. My head was spinning. This couldn't be true. Where was I? Was I dead? I didn't know. I wished I were home, away from this awful place.

The room was quiet. It was so still that I could almost hear myself thinking.

A feeling came over me that I was not alone. I thought

I heard whispers and soft footsteps. Bare feet on the cold stones.

My mind went back to 'The Legend of John Black'. He had fallen down the well fifty years ago. He was naked. Did this have something to do with him? Whose presence could I feel in the room? Was someone under the bed? I was too scared to look.

I took a marble out of my pocket and rolled it under the bed. It came out the other side. There was no one under the bed and there was nowhere else for anyone to hide.

I decided that I would have to wait and see what would happen at three o'clock. I sat on the bed and undid my shoes. I put them on the floor because they were muddy. I took off my socks and pushed one into each shoe.

I felt as if someone was close by. Something was happening. The hair on the back of my neck was standing up. I was cold all over. Then I noticed my socks. I couldn't believe it. They were walking around. They were walking with no one in them. I could see lumps where toes were pushing out but there were no legs and no body.

I looked at my own feet.

They were gone! I could feel them with my hand but couldn't see them. My feet were invisible and someone else's feet were walking around in my socks!

The socks walked over to my shoes and put themselves

into them. Invisible hands started to do up the laces.

I was frozen with fear. You can imagine what it felt like to see a pair of shoes and socks walking around on their own. Even worse, my feet had become invisible. The shoes walked off and parked themselves in a corner. I sat on the bed and looked at them.

An hour went by. It was two-thirty. The door was supposed to open at three o'clock. That's what the rhyme said.

It will open at the hour of three
When the captive will be freed.

A nasty thought was hanging around somewhere in the back of my mind. It would not quite come out. I kept thinking about another bit of the rhyme.

The sturdy door will only crack
For one with clothes upon his back.

No one was going to get out of that door without their clothes. I had already lost my shoes and my socks.

The shoes came walking towards the bed. The hair stood up on the back of my neck. I wanted to run but my legs wouldn't move. I tried to scream but nothing came out of my mouth. Unseen hands snatched the cap off my head. It floated through the air and landed in the corner of the room.

The buttons on my shirt began to undo. I wanted to fight but I couldn't. I was terrified. Frozen with fear. I felt cold fingers undoing the buttons. Someone or something ripped the shirt off my back and threw it on top of the cap. I thought my heart was going to freeze.

Next came my singlet. Damp hands pulled up my arms and peeled it off my body like a banana skin. I looked down at myself. The top part of my body was invisible. All I could see of myself was my trousers. I had almost vanished from sight.

My cap, singlet and shirt were all piled in the corner. The parts of my body they had covered were gone.

I was shaking like a leaf. I think I must have fainted for a minute or two. The next thing I can remember is noticing that my trousers had gone too. Now all that I could see of myself was a pair of underpants. The rest of me was invisible.

Suddenly my fear went. I was mad. Really mad. Whatever was doing this to me was not going to get those underpants. No way. I decided to fight my invisible enemy.

Chilly fingers began to tickle me under the armpits. I grabbed something. It was a hand. I bent its fingers back. A scream filled the room. It was a young voice. Like my own.

Then something poked into my eye. It felt like a finger and it hurt like mad. I held both hands up to my eyes. That was a mistake. My underpants were ripped off.

Now I was naked. I didn't have a stitch on. And I was invisible. The only sign that I existed was my watch. It looked as if it was floating in the air on its own.

Over in the corner my clothes were starting to dress themselves. First my underpants went on, then my singlet, shirt, cap and trousers. A person appeared. It was a boy about my age. He had black hair, black eyes and a large scar stretching from his mouth to his ear.

I decided to fight him. I wanted my clothes back. But before I could move he spoke to me.

'I am sorry,' he said, 'but I will be back to rescue you.' At that moment the door swung open and he jumped out through it. I rushed to the door but it slammed in my face. I kicked the door with my bare feet. I hammered against it with my hands. It was no use. I looked at my watch. It was three o'clock.

3

It is not going to take me long to tell you about the next fifty years of my life. They were all spent in that room. I tried everything I could to get out.

I tried to dig under the door with a stick. I dug a small hole but then it started filling itself in. Soon it was completely filled in. It was just as it was before I had started. The floor was smooth again. I tried to dig my way out time after time, but the same thing always happened. It was like trying to dig a hole in a pool of water.

The room seemed to be alive. No matter what I did it always stayed the same. Finally I gave up. I stopped digging. I had come to a dead end.

Next I tried to make some clothes out of the bedcovers. I thought the door might open for me if I did this. I made a needle out of a splinter of wood and pulled a thread out of a sheet. I used these to make a pillowcase into a shirt. It was a good shirt. But as soon as I put it on it fell to pieces. The pieces all joined themselves back into a pillowcase. I tried this over and over again, but the same thing always happened.

I did a lot of shouting. I banged on the door and yelled, 'Let me out, let me out!'

No one ever came. The room never got untidy. The sheets never became dirty or crumpled. The candles never burned out, and no one ever came. No one ever came.

I was never hungry, and I didn't eat or drink. I guess ghosts don't eat or drink. I was a living ghost.

There was only one thing to do – read. I read books for fifty years. There were books about anything that you could think of. I read them all. That is why I know so much now.

On one wall was a mirror. I looked in the mirror a lot. I couldn't see myself. Ghosts do not have reflections. I did a lot of thinking in those fifty years. I thought about that boy with the scar who stole my clothes. I knew he was John Black. The legend of John Black was true. He said he would come back, but he never did.

Sometimes I would get so lonely that I would cry. I would sit by the door and cry. I would call out for help.

I talked to myself a lot but mostly I read books. I read about far-away places. I read about clouds and flowers and waterfalls. I read about the ocean and the mountains. In my mind I could see all those places but I couldn't go to them. I was trapped underground in a room full of books.

I did many strange things and thought many strange thoughts. I'm not going to tell you about them, but I am going to tell you what happened after my fifty years in that prison.

4

In fifty years I never saw a face. Or heard a voice. When I finally saw another person it was a great shock. I wasn't ready for it. It happened out of the blue.

The door suddenly burst open and light poured into the room. A teenage boy came carefully into my cell. He pointed a lantern around. I had never seen a lantern like it before. It shone a very bright light wherever he pointed it.

He had pink cheeks and looked strong and healthy. He had red hair and brown eyes. He looked as if he had spent a lot of time in the sunshine.

The door banged shut behind him. He did just what I had done. He kicked the door and tried to open it. It wouldn't open, so after a while he sat on the bed.

He couldn't see me because I was invisible. I had been invisible for most of my life.

I wondered what the time was. My watch had stopped working many years ago. I had taken it off. I hoped that it was close to three o'clock. I am ashamed of what I did next. What I did was wrong. I know that it was wrong. I hope that you will understand. I had to get out of there. I had to see the rivers and fields again. I had to take this chance. It might have been my only opportunity to leave that room.

The boy was sitting on the bed. I could see that he was frightened. He was scared stiff. I crept up to him and grabbed his shoes. I pulled them off his feet. Then I ripped off his socks.

He fainted just as I had fainted all those years ago. He stayed unconscious for about five minutes. In that time I took off all his clothes. As I took off his clothes he began to disappear. Finally he was invisible.

Now there were two invisible people in the room. Neither could see the other. In the corner was a pile of his clothes. They were strange clothes made out of strange materials. But they were clothes. They would do the job.

I quickly put them on. I was a person again. I could see myself. I could see my hands and feet. They were young hands. They were the hands of a boy. I had thought that I would have grown old. I rushed to the mirror. I could see my face. I had a reflection. A young reflection. I should have been an old man. But I was still a teenager. I still looked just as I did fifty years ago.

A nasty thought struck me. When the boy became conscious he would be able to see me. He would be able to see me but already I couldn't see him.

I stood by the door, waiting for it to open. A long time passed. I could feel someone creeping around. It was the boy. He must have read the rhyme over the bed by now. He might have worked it out.

Something started pulling at my shoes, trying to get them off. It was him, trying to get his clothes back. Once again I was struggling with an invisible boy. I kicked out at where I thought he was. There was a sharp scream and then the sound of heavy breathing. I think I must have kicked him in the face.

At that moment the door swung open. I jumped out quickly. As the door began to close behind me, I called out, 'I'm sorry. I will be back. I will be back to rescue you.'

I was at the bottom of the well. There was a blue rope hanging down from the top. I had never seen a blue rope before. But I climbed up it quickly.

5

I have been back to that well many times since then. I have been down to the bottom with picks and shovels. I have dug and dug but there is no door there. It has vanished.

The world outside seems very strange to me. It has changed a lot in fifty years. The cars are very fast with fat tyres. They have strong lights that blind your eyes. They are dangerous. Many people get killed by them.

And the women! The women wear trousers. They think they are men. I cannot get used to it.

The aeroplanes have no propellors. How do they stay up without propellors? It is hard to understand.

Every home has a box which shows moving pictures which talk. The people on them are like ghosts. They are frightening. But not as frightening as the ghost of John Black.

No one believes my story about John Black. No one believes there is a room at the bottom of the well. I tell them there is a boy still trapped there. A naked ghost. They laugh. They think I am mad. They say I am insane.

They have locked me up with mad people. Once again I am a prisoner. This time I am not alone. I have a madman who shares my room. He thinks he is a chicken. The man in the next room thinks he is a tree.

I have been told that long ago there was another boy here like me. He thought he had been a ghost. He was never let out. They think I have the same madness.

I must get out of here. I must rescue the boy in the well at Fort Nelson. Someone must know that my story is true.

You believe me, don't you?

About the author

The Paul Jennings phenomenon began with the publication of *Unreal!* in 1985. Since then over eight million books have been sold to readers all over the world.

Paul has written over one hundred stories and has been voted 'favourite author' by children in Australia over forty times, winning every children's choice award. The top rating TV series *Round the Twist* and *Driven Crazy* are based on a selection of his enormously popular short-story collections such as *Unseen!*, which was awarded the 1999 Queensland Premier's Literary Award for Best Children's Book.

In 1995, Paul was made a Member of the Order of Australia for services to children's literature, and in 2001 he was awarded the prestigious Dromkeen Medal.

His most recent titles include *Paul Jennings' Funniest Stories*, and *Paul Jennings' Weirdest Stories*, *The Reading Bug . . . and how you can help your child to catch it* (2003), his *Rascal* storybooks for early readers and his first full-length novel, *How Hedley Hopkins Did a Dare . . .* (shortlisted for the 2006 Children's Book Council of Australia Book of the Year Award: Younger Readers).

This collection of twenty stories has been hand-picked by Paul from his extensive collection and contains some of his spookiest and fun-filled tales.

ALSO FROM PAUL JENNINGS

This collection of twenty-five hilarious stories has been hand-picked by Paul from the *UnCollected* series and is sure to have readers laughing out loud.

Also from the hugely popular *UnCollected* series, this special selection of tales showcases Paul's storytelling talents at their very best . . . and weirdest!